abstract passion

artist duet two

PERSEPHONE AUTUMN

Between Words Publishing LLC

Abstract Passion

www.persephoneautumn.com

ISBN: 978-1-951477-30-1 (Ebook)

ISBN: 978-1-951477-31-8 (Paperback)

ISBN: 978-1-951477-52-3 (Hardcover)

Editor: Ellie McLove | My Brother's Editor

Proofreader: Rosa Sharon | My Brother's Editor

Cover Design: Persephone Autumn | Between Words Publishing LLC

books by persephone autumn

Bay Area Duet Series

Click Duet

Through the Lens

Time Exposure

Inked Duet

Fine Line

Love Buzz

Insomniac Duet

Restless Night

A Love So Bright

Artist Duet

Blank Canvas

Abstract Passion

Devotion Series

Distorted Devotion

Undying Devotion

Beloved Devotion

Darkest Devotion

Standalone Romance Novels

Depths Awakened

Sweet Tooth

Transcendental

Poetry Collections

Ink Veins

Broken Metronome

Slipping From Existence

PUBLISHED UNDER P. AUTUMN

Standalone Horror Novels

By Dawn

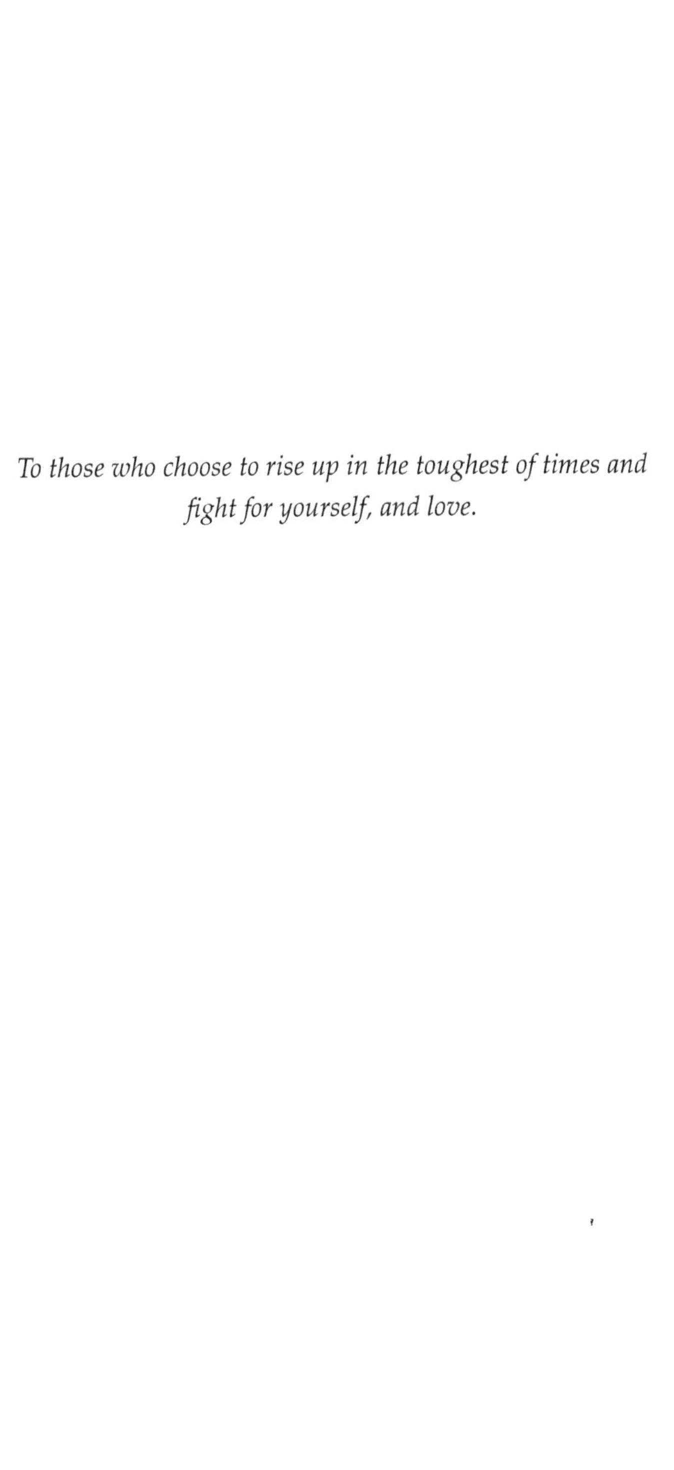

To those who choose to rise up in the toughest of times and fight for yourself, and love.

one

. . .

Shelly

A block from Devlyn's house, I pull over and throw the car in park. Tears spill from my eyes in a violent torrent of pain and confusion. Every muscle in me aches with agony.

I'm pregnant. No. No, no, no. What the hell am I going to do? What the hell am *I doing?*

I stare out the windshield with blurred vision and try to collect myself. Try to slow the tears and quiet my irrational mind. Try to stop the convulsive sobs crawling up my throat and spilling from my lips. I close my eyes and shut out the chaos whirling in my head. Eviscerate the words like *ruin* and *over.*

Swiping at my eyes, I wipe away the tears and look in the rearview mirror. Stare down the street behind me as a new version of panic squeezes my heart. As new found alarm constricts my airway.

Devlyn.

"What have I done?" I whisper in the cab of my car.

Understandably, he went into shock with the news.

So did I. Where he went completely still and utterly speechless, I went into full-on hysteria. My brain short-circuited and I made irrational decisions in the heat of the moment, undoubtedly hurting him.

What have I done?

I steer the Beetle into the next driveway, back out then drive back to Devlyn's house. The small neighborhood block feels miles long as I roll closer and closer. Two houses away, I swipe my cheeks dry and take a deep breath. When I pull into the driveway, I am definitely not prepared for what I see next. Devlyn curled into a tight ball, knees crushed to his chest, and head tucked as he rocks back and forth.

I press the heel of my palm to my chest as the pain beneath my breastbone kicks up to level ten.

Cutting the engine, I bolt from the car and run to his side. Drop down in front of him and gingerly lay a hand on his head. Lightly comb my fingers through his hair and hover over his bundled frame. "Devlyn," I whisper. His tempo and erratic rocking don't pause, so I try again and with more volume. "Devlyn."

He startles on the second call of his name. The constant shaking of his body stops. His head lifts and I am stabbed in the heart by the pain in his puffy, red eyes. The way he regards me, rakes his eyes over the lines of my face, it's as if he is unsure I am real or a figment of his imagination.

I add more weight to my touch on his head and in his hair. Slide my hand slowly down the side of his face. Wiggle my fingers in his hair and scratch them along his scalp. When my palm cups his cheek, he leans his weight into my hand. Closes his eyes. Inhales deeply and holds the breath in his lungs for three of my breaths.

When his eyes reopen, he scrambles forward and wraps me in his arms. "You can't go," he mumbles in my ear, voice strained and raw. "I need you." He hugs me tighter to his chest and kisses my neck. Takes another deep breath and sighs heavily. "Please stay."

My arms squeeze him impossibly tighter as my fingers roam his hair and my lips kiss his shoulder. "Let's go back inside." I lean back and frame his face in my hands. Hold his turbulent gaze as tears blur my vision. "I'm sorry. I wasn't thinking rationally." My lips press to his, again and again. "So, so sorry."

On unsteady legs, we rise from the pavement and wander back into the house. Devlyn's hand firmly holds mine as we wind our way to the living room and sit on the couch. He inches closer until it's difficult to tell where I end and he begins.

"Do you want a drink? Maybe some tea or water or juice," he suggests, tone antsy.

A fresh layer of guilt washes over me. I hate that my first instinct was to run away. To abandon Devlyn. What kind of person does that? *You were scared and so was he. And you both process fear differently.* Internally, I hang my head and berate myself.

"Some tea would be nice," I whisper, and he nods. Then he is off the couch and dashing to the kitchen.

While Devlyn prepares us drinks, I mull over what to say when he reenters the room. I feel the need to apologize until I lose my voice. My actions were spontaneous and foolish, but my head was—is—a scrambled mess. And when I said the words aloud—*I'm pregnant*—Devlyn froze, then thawed, only to freeze again. I went from panicked to unreasonably hysterical in a heartbeat.

So I bolted.

But I can't run away from this, from us. Devlyn or our unborn child. It may be unplanned, it may throw both of our worlds completely off-balance, but that doesn't change anything.

I lay a hand over my still flat belly, close my eyes and take a deep breath. Tell myself it will be okay. That it will all work out. That everything happens when it is meant to.

When my eyes open, I consider how to broach the conversation again. This time with calmer heads and less anxiety. Hopefully.

I am—we are—pregnant and we will be parents before the end of the year. A baby… Devlyn and I are going to have a baby. Another human to love and nurture.

Mentally, I laugh at myself. Leave it to us—the fumbling virgin and almost virgin—to mess up condom usage.

Regardless, it is done. Neither of us can change the past. All we can do now is prepare for the future. But what does that future look like?

Devlyn wanders back into the living room with a mug in each hand. He sets them both on the table, drops next to me on the couch, and wraps me in his arms again. Eliminates every ounce of space between us with a fierce hug. Holds me like he fears I will bolt for the door once more.

And I hate that I did this. Inflicted him with this level of fear. Fractured the trust he has in me. Created doubt that I will stay.

I want to stay. For as long as he will have me, I want to stay.

"Sorry I freaked out. Sorry I didn't say anything right away." He tugs me into his lap and shifts his hold. Shakes his head as he burrows into my chest. "Sorry I froze."

I lay my cheek on his head, close my eyes and comb my fingers through his dark locks. "This isn't all you, so don't you dare try to take all the blame." My arms circle his shoulders and head. Cradle him in my hold. "I'm just as guilty. I shouldn't have packed my bags and jumped in the car." My lips press to his hair. "But I wasn't thinking. Not clearly."

Nose buried in my hair, Devlyn inhales deeply. On the exhale, he leans back and frames my face in his hands. "This is scary, for both of us, but I know we'll get through it." He lowers my lips to his and kisses me with newfound tenderness. "I love you, Shelly."

Tears sting the backs of my eyes. An emotional ball grows thick in my throat. I lift my hands to his cheeks, cup either side of his jaw, and stroke his cheekbones with my thumbs. "I love you, too," I choke out.

Time creeps by, our tea cools on the table, but neither of us move. For now, I simply want to breathe him in. Want to let all the madness from earlier fall away. Want to feel his arms and warmth blanket me in love. Want to give the news of us becoming parents a moment to seep in.

Pregnant. Me. The woman that plans all the big moments in her life. The woman that makes five-year plans and intends to stick to them. I am pregnant. *We* are pregnant. This was definitely not in the five-year plan. Finding love was in the plan, but not becoming a mother.

My mind drifts to the piece of paper pinned to the wall in my apartment bedroom. My current five-year plan. The biggest thing on the list… purchasing Petal and Vine from Elizabeth.

Oh, god.

I close my eyes and sink deep inside myself. Try to steady my rapid-fire pulse with steady breaths. Clear the worrisome thoughts invading my head.

Elizabeth won't be upset about the pregnancy. Knowing her, she will rejoice at having another baby to spoil. Be excited that her own grandchild will soon have a playmate. But her happiness won't erase the guilt holding me hostage daily as I delay her retirement. Something she has looked forward to for the past two years.

Will I still be able to purchase Petal and Vine when the time comes? Will I be able to run a business with a newborn in my arms or on my hip? It's silly to think such things. Plenty of women and families manage this all the time. But maybe they planned ahead. Had all their ducks in a row before the pregnancy test came back positive.

Then my thoughts drift to Autumn and Clementine.

Autumn's first pregnancy was a surprise. In a matter of months, she wasn't just a pregnant mother with an absentee father, she'd also been kicked out of her home. Abandoned in every way imaginable. Her family had been that cruel.

But she kept going. Never gave up. Moved forward and persevered. Found a place to live and got a job she loved. Thrived when some might fall. And if she can overcome such heavy obstacles—struggles much worse than the possible ones I will face—then I can do this. *We* can do this.

"You're so quiet," Devlyn whispers against my skin.

I shift off his lap, pick up my mug and sip the now cool tea, then take his hand. "Just thinking."

"About?"

Everything. "How much this will change our future."

He nods, then tucks a strand of hair behind my ear. "True." Glass-green irises lock on my blues while his thumb leisurely strokes my cheek. "But I know we'll make it work."

"How?"

For a beat, his eyes drop to my lips before meeting mine again. "I just know." He shrugs. "With you, I believe anything is possible." I raise my brows in question. "Shelly, I have been through hell. In more ways than one." He takes my hand in his, pulls it to his lap and strokes my skin. Slow and steady. His eyes on the movement. "The first round was young love gone astray. Although it sent me in a downward spiral, I'm grateful it happened. Without that loss, I wouldn't appreciate and love you the way I do."

"And the other?"

He sucks in a deep breath and speaks on the exhale. "That hell is still ongoing."

"Your mom?"

He nods. "Yeah. Not sure what to do about her." He shrugs and looks off in the distance. "Things with her… it's been brewing a long time." His chest expands as he takes a deep breath. "I don't want my past with her to affect our relationship or the baby." He trails the pad of his thumb over my knuckles. "Maybe I should talk to someone again. Get advice from a professional or someone who's been in a similar situation."

I squeeze his hand and he brings his attention back to me. "If that's what you want, what you need, I'll support you." I huff out a laugh. "Heck, maybe I should talk to someone." His eyes narrow. "About pregnancy. Motherhood. How to keep moving forward without feeling like I'm pulling everyone under."

"Shelly…"

The backs of my eyes sting and I hate how I am already so emotional. "Well, it's how I feel." I shrug. "Like I'm letting Elizabeth down." Tears well in my eyes. I take a deep breath and try to hold them at bay. "I'm supposed to buy the shop from her after this year." My jaw wobbles back and forth. "How will I be able to do that now? How will I run a business with a baby?"

"Hey," he says, voice barely above a whisper. "We'll figure it out. All of it." He chuckles and I look up. "Maybe I'll need to learn how to run a florist shop too."

I furrow my brows. "So you're not doing it alone." He presses a chaste kiss to my lips. "Because you aren't alone, Shelly." Another kiss. "Ever."

"Aren't we just a hot mess," I say on a laugh.

"Wouldn't want to be in a hot mess with anyone else." Devlyn rises from the couch and extends his hand. "Come. Let's go make something for breakfast." His eyes drop to my belly. "Need to feed you two."

And in a blink, life returns to a seminormal state. We bring our mugs to the kitchen and add a touch of hot water. I scramble eggs and cook sausage while Devlyn cuts fresh fruit and toasts bread. We move around the kitchen as if we have done this for years. Been in a relationship. Existed in the same space. Loved each other.

Speaking of space… Suppose our living situation will be one of many conversations we share in the near future. A new knot forms beneath my diaphragm. Twisty and tight.

When the time comes, when we talk about housing and what will work best, I hope we are on the same page. *Please let us be on the same page.*

two

Devlyn

PREGNANT. SHELLY IS PREGNANT. *WE* ARE PREGNANT. IN the not-too-distant future, I will be a dad. Another human will depend on me to care for them. Raise them, feed them, nurture them. Turn them into a respectable human.

Is this within my power? Can I raise a child? Am I capable of molding a mini human into a decent person?

God, I hope so. Just the mere thought of letting someone down—my own child, no less—scares me to death. Has my limbs shaking and palms sweaty.

But Shelly and I will get through this. Together.

While Shelly showers and gets ready for work, I search the internet. One tab loads results of psychologists in the area. A second tab loads results of how condoms fail. And on the third tab is what steps to follow after learning you are pregnant. To some, tabs two and three may seem asinine. To me, I just want answers.

An idiot I am not. Since high school health class

had a more than lackluster curriculum on sexual education, I did my own homework. At the time, I had no expectations with where my relationship with Kelsey would go, but I wanted to be prepared either way. Searching videos on how to properly roll on a condom at sixteen was awkward. After watching various oblong fruits and vegetables get sheathed, I considered myself knowledgeable enough. Kelsey never got pregnant, so I must have done something right.

Obviously that all went out the window when I rolled on condoms with Shelly. Either that or one of a handful of other factors came into play.

According to my brief research, the list of reasons why condoms fail is short. Poor manufacturing. Stored at the wrong temperature. Used after expiration date. Torn during removal from the wrapper. Wrong size. Not enough lubricant. Using the wrong lubricant, such as oil-based. The condom was rolled on incorrectly. Not pinching the tip before rolling it on. Snuggling after and going flaccid while still inside your partner.

Of all the reasons listed, two stand out the most. Two slap me in the face, hard. Snuggling and oil-based.

"Damnit," I whisper into the bedroom.

In no way am I upset with the pregnancy or Shelly. But as I read those two common reasons, I hang my head.

One—how am I *not* going to snuggle with Shelly after we have sex? Ever. After the most physically intimate moment, I will cuddle with the woman I love. Every. Damn. Time. Going forward—well, after the baby is born—cuddling will have to be after I pull out. We have time to sort out the finer details.

Two—the body painting. Although the paint never ended up between our legs, it coated my hands and pretty much every other part of our bodies. It's quite possible, I didn't clean everything off of my hands before I put the condom on. It's quite possible, I sabotaged that moment and unintentionally put us in this situation.

"Everything okay?"

I look up from my phone to see Shelly dressed in a pink, long-sleeve V-neck, light-blue denim jeans and pink Vans. Her toffee locks hang in loose waves down her back, accented with a pink headband. Her face is free of makeup, twilight eyes sparkling as they roam my face, a slight flush on her cheeks.

Not sure how it's possible, but she is more beautiful than ever.

"Yeah," I croak out, then clear my throat. "Yes. Was just researching stuff online."

Her eyes drop to my phone, then lift back to mine. "Find anything noteworthy?"

Yes. No. I shrug. "A little. Wondering what we're supposed to do next."

In slow, measured steps, Shelly closes the distance and steps between my legs at the edge of the bed. Her fingers trail up my chest, my neck, then settle in my hair. My eyes roll back and close as I get lost in her touch. Lost in the whirlwind she stirs beneath my diaphragm. Lost in the new rhythm she sets for my pulse, my breathing.

My hands find her hips. Fingertips bearing down on her denim-clad soft skin. Without second thought, I drag her closer. Sweep the tip of my nose along the column of her throat. Inhale her earthy, sweet floral scent. Allow it to soothe me in the way nothing or no one else has.

Shelly is my solace. The sunshine after the storm. We may be headed into unfamiliar territory, but so long as I have her, everything will work out.

"My guess is we visit a doctor." I lean back and look up at her. A soft smile tips up the corners of her mouth. "I know a few people to ask."

"Are you worried?"

What a stupid fucking question.

Her fingers comb through my hair as her eyes dart between mine. "Yes and no." I tilt my head in question. "It's a definite shock, but I'm surprisingly not worried about pregnancy. What I am worried about is how we'll balance our lives once the baby comes. Between the shop and your art, I worry we won't have the time or energy to do what we love."

I give her hips a gentle squeeze. "We'll find a way."

"How can you sound so sure?"

I laugh without humor. "There isn't much in life I'm sure of, Shelly. But when it comes to you, to us, I believe anything is possible."

A weighted sigh leaves her lips before she drops her forehead to rest on mine. For a moment, we just breathe each other in. Absorb this new path life has put us on. Settle into the realization that every day going forward, our lives will be forever changed. Entwined. Connected.

"I should head to work." She lifts her head and retreats a step. "Elizabeth was already worried when I messaged and said I'd be a little late."

Although I don't want her to go, I nod because she is right. This big news, this baby, will change everything we know, but we can't stop living life. And that includes going to work. "Let me walk you out."

It has only been a few hours since learning Shelly was pregnant, but it feels as if weeks have passed. Our minds are spinning, but we need to slow them as best we can. Try to focus on the day to day. Talk to those who can help us or tell us what to expect. Follow our current routines until we need to adjust them.

This may be new to us, but it's not new. With the countless number of people in Shelly's corner, we will have more support than imaginable. Support and love.

Shelly unlocks her car and slips in behind the steering wheel. She rolls down the window and I lean in to give her a kiss. "Come over after work?"

She nods. "Yeah. May be a little later. I should make up some of my missed time at the shop. Plus, I need more clothes."

"'Kay." I press my lips to hers once more. "Drive safe. See you tonight."

Shelly backs out of the driveway and waves as she drives off. This time I don't fear whether or not she will return. Don't crumble to the ground like a piece of my heart abandoned me. Deep in my bones, I know Shelly will always return. To me, to us.

I walk back into the house, wander to the living room and plop down on the couch. Pulling my phone from my pocket, I unlock it and go to the browser tab with the list of local psychologists. One by one, I click the links and read the doctor's credentials, what their area of focus is, and the frequently asked questions. In my notes app, I jot down the names and contact information of each that sounds like they may be a fit.

Visiting a psychologist is twofold. To face and conquer the demons of my past, and to make sure I don't pass my darkness on to my child. I accept that the darkness in my veins will never go away. It is part of who I am. But learning how to properly cope when it creeps in is essential. Learning how to not let the darkness win is mandatory.

Part of that darkness stems from my upbringing. The intricate ways my mother twisted my way of thinking. The type of love she taught me that wasn't love at all. I wasn't aware of her warped mindset years ago. Didn't know I was as much her pawn as anyone else.

It should hurt... the realization of who she is and what she has done. But it doesn't hurt. That part of me, the piece reserved for Karen Templar, is just numb.

Although I accept this, I want to move past the numbness. Not let her take up residence inside me any more than she already has. I want to let her go. Permanently. Not just for my own mental health, but so I can be the best version of myself for my child.

I refuse to let my past haunt my future.

The idea of my child not knowing part of their family hurts. But my family not assuming a role in this child's life is in the best interest of me, Shelly and our baby. Optimistically, I'd like to think becoming a grandparent may change my mother. That it could flip a switch inside her and she'd become a better person.

But I won't put my child in harm's way. Ever. My mother's poison slithered into my psyche for years. Her tainted words and cold actions deformed a piece of who I am. Skewed how I interpreted connections and life and love. Contributed to a mountain of untold damage. Damage I pray is reversible. Damage I hope to heal, on some level, before our baby is born.

My biggest fear is passing on the toxicity in my blood. The defect in my genetic makeup. Because like it or not, pieces of my mother live inside me. Like it or not, darkness taints my head and heart.

But Shelly… she is the one shining light in my darkness. The light leading me back to a place of love and hope. The light I refuse to let go of or lose.

Because without her light, I fear the darkness will take over. If that happens, I won't survive.

three

. . .

Shelly

Today feels a week long and it is only noon.

On the way to work, I called Cora and asked if she had plans today. Relief relaxed my bones when she replied with a firm *nope*. But the second she asked if everything was okay, anxiety rippled through me head to toe. I played it off. Said everything was fine. Then asked her to come to the shop for lunch and to bring Clara.

The second I set foot in Petal and Vine, Elizabeth showered me with a barrage of questions. I wanted to answer each and every one of them, but remained tight lipped. Told her I invited Cora for lunch and would answer everything then. Since then, I have felt her concerned gaze on my profile. Have seen her lips part—questions written in the soft lines of her forehead—before she snaps her mouth shut.

It's been torture.

Any minute, my best friend will walk through the front door of Petal and Vine, pushing a stroller and cooing with her angelic daughter. And then, the three of us will dig in on lunch as I spill the beans about my accidental pregnancy.

Since calling her, I've mentally rehearsed more than a dozen ways to say *I'm pregnant* without saying those two specific words. For some reason, saying more feels necessary.

I hate how I'm riddled with anxiety. About saying the words aloud. About telling my best friend and second mother news that will thrill them. Speaking the words to someone other than Devlyn makes it more real. Tangible. Legit.

Nerves aside, Cora and Elizabeth are the first two women I want to tell.

Mom will find out soon enough, but I need to be in the right headspace to share such big news with her. Hell, Mom doesn't even know about Devlyn. Doesn't know we have been in this weird friends-to-lovers relationship for months. Had she known, I would've heard an endless string of pleas from her. Daily texts asking for updates on my love life. Calls more than once a week, masked as her checking in but really searching for unspoken clues.

Ugh.

Sharing the news with Mom will be a blast—insert thick layer of sarcasm. I already hear the long list of questions on her roster.

"Why didn't you tell me you were dating someone?"

"When can I meet him?"

"You found someone and *you're pregnant?"*

"Did you find a doctor yet?"

"Can I go to your appointments?"

"How long have you known?"

"Why didn't you tell me sooner?"

"When are you moving in together?"

"Are you planning to get married?"

Of all the questions I picture my mother asking, the last is the one I fear most. Deep down, Mom only wants the best for me and Micah. But I am fully aware that, in her mind, love equals marriage and babies. If the solid relationship my parents have isn't proof enough, her reasons for starting family dinners more than a year ago is definitely hard evidence.

I love my mother. Love her big heart and desire to see everyone happy. Love that dreamy look she gives Dad. I only wish she understood happiness comes in different forms.

When Micah and Peyton announced they wouldn't start a family, Mom all but lost her shit. She didn't understand how or why they didn't want children. Because Nicole Reed doesn't look beyond her own experiences. Can't fathom anything other than her own way of life being great. With Micah and Peyton not wanting children, I pray her perspective changes.

The bell over the front door jingles. I plaster on a big smile and mentally prepare myself for the most adult conversation I've had in years. Then sag against the arrangement table when a man steps around the pails of loose flowers.

He holds up two large paper bags. "Delivery from See Ew Thai."

I step around the table, dig into the pocket of my

apron, hand him a cash tip then take the bags. "Thank you."

"Have a great day, miss."

As the man exits the shop, Cora walks in with baby Clara in her beast of a stroller.

Oh god. Something else to worry over. All the gadgets and gizmos we will need for a baby.

"Auntie Shelly must have big news if she's sweet-talking Mommy with Asian food," Cora coos at Clara as she sidles up to the arrangement table. Eyes wide, Clara slaps at a toy dangling inches from her face.

"Guilty," I say, bending over the stroller and lightly pinching Clara's toes. "How's my favorite niece today? Is Mommy spoiling you rotten?"

Clara makes an unintelligible noise and we both laugh. Elizabeth exits the storage room and gives Cora a warm, welcoming hug before removing her granddaughter from the stroller.

For a moment, I watch the three of them. Revel in their smiles and sweet talk. Relish the ease of this new change in their lives. Envy how simple Cora makes motherhood look, although I've heard the struggles she experienced.

My best friend may be new to parenting, but she does it like a pro. She isn't back to working full-time, but has taken a couple of small, scenic jobs this month. Her way of easing back into the norm at her own pace. Outdoor photo shoots of places and not people. That way, she can bring Clara along and not worry.

"It's not ideal, but I'd like to have lunch with all of us. At least for a few minutes," I say as I start carrying the bags to the back. Cora and Elizabeth exchange a look of concern. "I'll set things up at the table. We should be able to hear the bell if anyone comes in."

Before either of them gets a word in, I step into the office-slash-break room and set the bags down. One by one, I pull out the food boxes and set them on the table. Get everything in place. Ready for them to stuff their mouths while I confess my pregnancy and beg for advice.

I peek my head around the doorframe and spot Cora and Elizabeth fawning over Clara. Warmth spreads in my chest at the sight.

Later this year, that will be me and Devlyn.

Tears sting the backs of my eyes, but I blink them away before they well and fall. I inhale deeply in an attempt to settle the nerves fluttering in my belly. "Ready when you are," I say.

Cora parks Clara back in the stroller before she and Elizabeth wander into the break room. I point out their places at the table on either side of mine. We take our seats and open the boxes. Elizabeth dives into her pad thai while Cora bites down on a spring roll. The moment their mouths are full, I open mine.

"I'm pregnant," I blurt out.

To no surprise, both of them go into coughing fits. Okay, so waiting until they had their mouths full was a *bad* idea. I thought it would be a great way to keep them from screaming or squealing or blurting out words I'm not prepared to hear. Obviously, the method to madness is actual madness. Oops.

After a few hard slaps to the chest and half a bottle

of water later, Cora's skin looks a little less red and blotchy. Elizabeth continues to cough, but at least it's calming down.

"Sorry," I say on a wince.

Cora lays a hand on mine and shakes her head. "Don't apologize," she croaks out, then coughs to clear her throat more. "I knew something was up, but I didn't think it was that."

"But you said..." I furrow my brows. "At the hospital yesterday..." I drop my gaze to her box of garlic tofu. "You were joking..."

Why the hell can I not finish a damn thought aloud?

"Shell, it *was* a joke." She squeezes my hand and I lift my line of sight back to hers. "With Clara born only months ago, Ryker yesterday... I would've said it to Peyton, but I know she and Micah aren't planning to have kids." She shakes her head subtly. "Shell, I didn't mean anything by it." Concern mars her forehead. "Is that why you ran from the room? Why you disappeared?"

"Not just from what you said." I shake my head. "But it kind of sent me into a thought spiral. Before I knew it, I felt nauseous. So I ran for the bathroom."

The three of us sit at the table as I recant the rest of the evening and earlier this morning. My initial shocked state and Devlyn's after the call from the hospital. My moment of panic when Devlyn froze. How I thought that he didn't want to do this, that he couldn't do this. Be together. Have a baby. Any of it.

And then I tell them when the moment of realization hit. While I sat on the side of the road and cried until it struck me what I'd done. That I just got in my car and left. That I ignored Devlyn as he hollered for me to stay. Then when I turned around and drove back, how I found him in the driveway. Cold and shaking and in full crisis mode.

That was the second time I found Devlyn curled in on himself. I pray it is the last.

He looked so scared. In pain. And in that moment, I hated the spontaneous choice I'd made. Getting in my car and leaving had been irrational and juvenile. To just walk away without talking more, without listening…

I will never do that again. To him or us.

The bell rings out front and Elizabeth rises from her chair. "I'll be back." She bends and kisses my crown. "Keep talking, sweetheart."

Not a second after Elizabeth leaves the room, Cora rises from her chair, yanks me from mine, and pulls me into the tightest hug. "I don't know how you expect me to feel, Shell." She loosens her hold and inches back to look me in the eye. "But I'm happy for you." The corners of her lips turn up as she smiles brightly. "Things may be crazy for a bit, but you will be an amazing mother."

I purse my lips as my brows shoot up. "You say that now, but this gal"—I point to myself—"is freaking out. A lot."

She drops her hold on me and we park ourselves back in the chairs. Cora spears a piece of broccoli and tofu while I stab curried chicken. For a moment, we sit in amicable silence. We eat lunch like we would any other day. Me and Cora. Two best friends spending time together.

"I freaked out too," Cora says after a few bites. "Ask Gavin. We'd been back together barely two years. Irrational as it was, I thought he might leave again." She laughs without humor. "Although we were happy—are happy—I thought an unplanned pregnancy would send him away." She shakes her head, her eyes glassy. "But it didn't, Shell. He was so happy. So damn happy. I'd never seen him light up like that. It was that look, that one moment… I knew we'd be okay." Setting her fork down, she reaches for my hand again. "And you will be too."

I tighten my hold on her hand. "How can you be so sure?" I whisper-ask.

Her smile brightens the room. "Because he chased after you. Asked you not to leave. Cried in the driveway when you left. Then he opened his arms up again when you returned. He took you into the house and you talked. You made breakfast and plans."

For the umpteenth time today, my eyes burn with the promise of tears. When I walked out Devlyn's front door in a fit of anxiety, I was one step closer to messing all of this up. Ready to throw in the towel without giving him a chance. I didn't get far, thank goodness. It's almost as if fate intervened. As if something bigger than me stopped me from making a huge mistake.

"What do I do now?"

Cora points to my lunch. "Eat." She laughs. "Take a minute to breathe and soak it all in. Yes, it's big. Huge. Life changing." She picks up her own fork and takes a bite. "But it's also incredible, Shell." She looks over at Clara sleeping in her stroller. "There's good and bad days. And yours will be different than mine." Her eyes find mine again. "But it's all worth it. My first piece of advice—the only one I'll give today—is to talk to your gynecologist. If they're an OB-GYN, you're golden. If not, they'll direct you where to go next." She sips her water. "And the rest of us will always be here. You have us. And Devlyn."

For a first-time mother of an infant, Cora is giving me a confidence boost. She and Gavin still navigate being new parents, but her calm reassurances settle some of the anxiety. Instinct told me she and Elizabeth were the right people to tell first. And who knows, I may wait until after my first official doctor's appointment to mention anything to Mom. That will give Devlyn and I time to adjust a little more before Mom shrieks in joy and asks unnerving questions.

"Thank you," I say. "Somehow, I knew you'd alleviate some of my worry."

"You never have to thank me, Shell. That's what best friends are for. You'd do the same for me in a heartbeat." It's true, I would. "So, when are you telling Mama Reed?"

I wince. "Uh, not for a bit. I want to see the doctor first. Give myself and Devlyn a little more time to process this before the big reveal." I shake my head on a laugh. "Mom doesn't even know we're dating. Doesn't know Devlyn exists. So, not only will I be saying, '*hey Mom, meet my boyfriend, Devlyn.*' I will also be saying, '*and by the way, we're pregnant. Woo!*' I close my eyes and take a deep breath. "Swear to god, if the first thing out of her mouth is wanting to know when we'll get married, I will lose my shit." I startle and look to Clara. "I mean cool. Lose my cool."

Cora laughs. "Shell, it's okay. Clara has no clue what we're saying right now. Down the road, yes, the alternate swear words will be in full force. For now, you're fine." She scoops up another bite. "And I promise not to say anything to anyone else. Not until you give the green light."

Elizabeth walks back into the room and joins us at the table. "What'd I miss?"

Over noodles, rice and veggies, I share with Elizabeth everything I did with Cora. She, too, promises not to say anything until I give the go-ahead. Then she hugs me, tighter and harder than ever. She assures me everything will be fine. She tells me not to worry about the shop, that she will be here until I am ready and able to handle the change. Of course, I cry. Because today is the day to cry until my eyes puff like clouds.

And when lunch ends, I feel lighter and more stable on my feet.

After the call this morning, it felt like someone had grabbed me by the ankles and held me upside down. Now, I feel strong enough to walk. To move forward. To handle this big change in my life with more confidence.

four

. . .

Devlyn

"How does that make you feel?"

I love and loathe therapy. Getting in my car twice a week to drive to an office across town to talk about my feelings, about my past, about what makes my blood boil and my mind abandon reality is just... awkward and relieving and unnerving.

I thoroughly enjoy the opportunity to vent. To expel the darkness that has plagued me longer than I allowed myself to realize. To shed weight I didn't realize I carried.

What I don't like is the aftermath. The emotions stirred up during each session. Emotions I walk out the door with and sort through in the days between sessions. Emotions I must process, but don't want to expose to Shelly.

The first session after my consultation, I left the office in a mass of confusion. We'd barely scratched the surface, but my mother had been a huge topic of discussion. It *hurt* to talk about her. Not just my head, but also my heart. Because the more I talk about her, the more it registers how much she *doesn't* love me. Her definition of love is warped. Whatever makes her feel important, puts her in the spotlight, has people fawning over her… that is her version of love. For Karen Templar, love has a price tag.

How sick and twisted. And sad.

During our first session, after my need to pause and take several deep breaths, Dr. Prince had said, *"You can't move past this if you don't process it."* I have to let in the feelings I concealed for years. Unearth all the memories that once seemed loving and innocent, so I can dissect and process them with a fresh perspective.

So that is what I have been doing. Processing.

And processing hurts. Profusely.

"Afraid," I answer.

Dr. Prince tilts his head and reads my expression a moment before jotting something on the notepad in his lap. "Can you elaborate? Share why you feel afraid."

Elaborate. I don't *want* to elaborate. But I *need* to open up and expand. Spread my wings. Peel back the layers and expose my heart. Let the poison spill from my veins so I can move on, move past my fears. Move forward.

My eyes shift to the window, to the somber gray sky through the cracked wooden blinds. To the semibare branches of a tree. The day as moody as I feel. For two deep breaths, I close my eyes. Give in to my fears and let them take over. Give myself permission to voice the thoughts haunting me since learning Shelly was pregnant.

I am safe here.

"What if I become her?" I open my eyes and meet Dr. Prince's gaze. My fingers toy with the bottom of my hoodie while my leg bounces uncontrollably. "What if I do to my own child what my mother has done to me? Suppress them. Make them feel less important, less than human. Worthless. Trivial."

Dr. Prince scribbles on his notepad. "Tell me an occasion when you felt suppressed or worthless."

A fist wraps around my heart. Squeezes the pounding organ until it quivers, until it begs for relief. I rock slowly in place on the sofa. Take a deep breath. Then another.

I hate this. Digging up my demons and letting them trample over my soul. Letting them sink their claws a little deeper. Chip away at what heart I have left before I vanquish them.

I get it. The process is a necessary evil. But *fuck*… it rips me apart.

"When I was eight, my school hosted an art fair for students in third through fifth grade. We'd been working on a special project since the start of the school year. Each student drew a word from a hat and was told to create something that made them think of that word. We could draw or paint or paste magazine clippings. Whatever we had access to. Whatever called to us. My word, ironically, was love."

I clamp my lips between my teeth, take a deep breath then continue.

"Love means something different to each of us. My eight-year-old brain had difficulty processing the term.

Had difficulty explaining love in the form of art. Even at that age, art was the one thing I loved most." The backs of my eyes sting. "I don't think I really knew human love. I had a warped perception of it."

Leaning forward, I swipe my bottled water from the table and take a sip. "On the night of the art fair, I was giddy for my mother to see my artwork. Far back as I can recall, she's worked in museums. Art existed in her life each day. I'd been so proud of my mixed-medium painting. The clipping of two people smiling at each other. I'd added various shades of red. Painted over the magazine page around the people." I laugh without humor. "For my age, it was remarkable. My teacher raved over the piece and instilled me with so much hope. Told me how talented I was. That I'd be an incredible artist one day. Have my work on display for the masses." I tip my head back and blink a few times before leveling my gaze. "That teacher made me feel loved. More than my own mother."

I lift my hand to my hoodie strings and fiddle with the strands. "We made our way around the room and my mother criticized each piece harshly. As if children should be perfectionists. As if children shouldn't create art unless it will win awards and sell for thousands of dollars." My vision glazes over. "She didn't even know she was degrading my piece until she finished speaking."

The only words I remember hearing that night were trash and sloppy and hideous.

"When her eyes dropped to the small paper placard and she saw my name, I'd never seen my mother so disgusted. Her lip curled as she looked down on my wilting frame. She said, *'I'm disappointed, Devlyn. I expected better from you. You know what real art looks like. I never want to see such trash again. It's embarrassing. You're a Templar. Remember that next time you pick up a brush or pencil. Don't throw my name in the garbage.'"*

The first round of tears this session spills down my cheeks. The salty drops sear my skin as they trail to my chin. I swipe them away and shift my gaze to the window again. To the gloomy sky that matches my mood. Mercurial and lusterless and meh.

"I know sharing that moment wasn't easy, Devlyn. Thank you for being brave enough to share it with me." I nod and swing my gaze back to him. "Processing years of pain will take time. But each time you choose to come here and speak with me, it's a step forward. One step closer to healing." His pen scratches against the pad of paper. "How've things been with Shelly?"

My soul sighs and breathes easier with the subject change. The heavy thoughts from a moment ago drift off. Fade to background. Make room for the light to enter. My peace. My heart.

"Great." My cheeks sting as my lips stretch into a wide smile. "We have our first appointment with the doctor today."

"That's wonderful, Devlyn. Have you and Shelly talked further about the future? What either of you want it to look like?"

At the end of my Thursday session last week, Dr. Prince gave me a *homework assignment*. To sit down with Shelly and talk about my feelings. Not just the way I feel about her, but how I feel about all the changes happening in both our lives.

He also asked me to voice my desires. What I want my future with Shelly to look like.

Three months have passed since Shelly and I officially started dating. The two months prior were a bit rocky. Unstable due to my uncertainty more than hers. But in the past five months, I have never been more in tune with someone. More certain of what I want. More confident of the path I want to walk in life, with Shelly at my side every step of the way.

What I don't know is if Shelly is ready to walk the same path.

"Yes and no." When I don't expand, Dr. Prince asks me to elaborate. Secretly, I think *elaborate* is his favorite word. "I told her I want to be involved during the pregnancy. That I want to be there for her. The things left unsaid, well… I fear she may panic if I say them aloud."

"Like what?"

My fingers toy with my hoodie strings once more. "Am I crazy for wanting to ask her to move in? Is it too soon in our relationship?" I zero in on the fraying end of the string and sigh. "I don't want her to think the only reason I'm asking is because she's carrying our baby." I drop my chin to my chest and close my eyes. "It's not the only reason."

As many notes as Dr. Prince writes during our sessions, he'll undoubtedly have a novel before the end of the year. His notes are a point of reference, a way to chart my growth. I know this. He told me this. But sometimes I wonder if he takes medication after our sessions. If my long list of issues is too much for even him. He never seems put off or out of sorts, but I still wonder how he manages to breathe after such intense talks.

"First of all, not all relationships evolve at the same pace. Some couples wait years before living together. Some want to marry beforehand. And others move in together and get married in under six months. No two relationships are the same, Devlyn. There is no rule book on when to take the next step. Whether it's sex or cohabitating or nuptials. You and Shelly have to go at the pace that feels right for you both. In order to know the pace, you have to communicate." He glances at his watch and notes we only have another five minutes. "Before our next session, I'd like you to talk more with Shelly. Voice your fears with her. As many as you feel comfortable sharing. Then ease into the conversation about where you want your future to go with her."

Expose my fears and tell Shelly I want her to move in.

Nausea rolls in my stomach. My mind screams to back down. My heart begs me to wait. To hit pause. Because the last time I was so utterly vulnerable to someone I loved, they squashed me with pointy heels.

"I'll do my best," I say with a nod, as if to assure myself.

"There's no pressure, Devlyn." He sets the pen and pad of paper on the table. "If you go to bring up the future, but the timing doesn't feel right, drop it. This isn't a race. There's no prize for reaching the finish line before others. This is about progress. About letting go of what doesn't serve you and making room for what you want in your life. It won't happen overnight. And you shouldn't expect it to."

Let go of what doesn't serve me. I never thought about anything that way, but I like how it sounds.

"Thanks, Dr. Prince."

We both rise from our seats and he walks me out. "See you in a few days, Devlyn."

I unlock the car, slip into the driver's seat and crank the engine. While the cab warms, I recall Dr. Prince's words. *"This is about progress. About letting go of what doesn't serve you and making room for what you want in your life."*

To let go of my mother and all the subliminal pain she inflicted over the years, I need to rehash the memories that hold me prisoner. The memories that diminish and suffocate. The memories that make me feel less than worthy. That makes me feel undeserving. That hinder me from moving forward, from growing.

I need to let her go so I can let Shelly in fully. Let her shine her love and light on all the dark places. Cast away the demons and shadows. Replace the hurt with affection and passion. Help me heal and grow and move forward.

And if I am lucky enough, Shelly will say yes. When I ask her to move in, she will agree with my favorite smile and a resounding yes.

five

. . .

Shelly

THINK I'M GOING TO BE SICK.

I pause at the entrance of the doctor's office. Brace my hand on the wall. Take a deep, cleansing breath. Then another. Close my eyes and allow the cool air to settle the chaos in my stomach. After a third deep breath, the nausea subsides. A little. Enough for me to stand straighter and trudge forward.

Do all medical facilities use the same lemon-scented bleach?

Ugh. This is going to be a long, *however many months I have left* pregnancy.

At least I haven't thrown up since the day at the hospital. Puking is the worst. The. Worst. Need someone to hold your hair while you hurl into the porcelain throne? I am *not* the gal to ask. Don't care how tight we are, don't care how many years we have known each other, if you bow to the porcelain throne, I will run the other direction.

I check in at the reception desk and am handed several pages on a clipboard with a pen.

When I called to set the appointment with my regular gynecologist—who also specializes in obstetrics, lucky me—the woman on the phone told me new paperwork is necessary. Standard form updates plus new documents for the pregnancy appointments and a more thorough family history.

I'd rather fill out new paperwork than have to visit a new doctor.

Halfway down the first page, the door to the office opens and Devlyn walks in. The remaining bit of my nausea vanishes at the sight of him.

Slipping off his sunglasses, our gazes lock. A brilliant smile lights his face as he walks in my direction. Warmth embraces me in an everlasting hug. He takes the seat next to mine. Curls his fingers around my elbow, leans in and presses his lips to mine.

Damn, I will never tire of him. Not the smile he reserves only for me. Not his gaze that heats my blood. Nor the simple yet potent way he caresses my skin with his masterful hands.

Not sure if I can pinpoint what it is about Devlyn that calls to my soul, but he quiets the noise. Grants a sense of peace I didn't know existed until him. Bestows me with love I hoped was possible, but never experienced until he entered my world. And he just makes me feel… alive.

"Am I late?"

I shake my head as I work to calm my heart. "No. I got here a few minutes early to fill out paperwork." I hold up the clipboard. "Should finish before they call us back."

"Need help?"

"Maybe with health questions when I get to the family history section." He nods, then sits back and wraps an arm around my shoulders. His thumb paints small circles on my upper arm, distracting me from my task.

Devlyn is my favorite distraction.

I trudge through most of the paperwork on my own. When I reach the family history page, Devlyn chimes in with what he knows about his family. High blood pressure on his father's side. Ovarian cancer on his mother's side. For the most part, my family history is boring. Grandma Reed had diabetes, but not until later in life. Other than that, our slate is pretty clean.

"Shelly," a female voice calls out. I peer up from the clipboard to see a nurse at the doorway leading to the patient rooms. "Come on back." Devlyn and I rise from the seats and walk toward the nurse hand in hand. She steps aside to let us pass, then closes the door behind us. "Hi Shelly, I'm Ramona. Don't think we've met yet." She extends her hand to me, then Devlyn. Next, she hands me a small plastic cup with a sealed lid. "We need to collect a sample before heading back."

This part of the visit isn't new.

I take the cup from Ramona, ask Devlyn to hold my purse, then enter the restroom to the right. Once the cup is full and the lid secured, I set the sample in the pass-through box in the room, wash up and exit.

Outside the restroom, Ramona has me step on a

scale, measuring my weight and height. After noting the numbers in my chart, she walks us to the patient room and closes the door behind us. Paper crinkling echoes in the room as I sit on the exam table. Devlyn parks himself in the extra seat off to the side while Ramona sits on a wheeled stool after washing her hands.

"How has your health been since your last visit, Shelly?" Ramona asks as she wraps a blood pressure cuff around my bicep.

"Good. No changes. Except the obvious," I say on a nervous laugh.

She peels the cuff away and jots numbers down in my chart. "Blood pressure looks good." Grabbing the thermometer from the counter, she holds it a couple inches from my forehead until it beeps. "Temp is normal."

Her warm gaze lifts from the stack of papers in my file and meets mine. Over the next few minutes, Ramona asks a series of questions. Most of which I am used to answering at my regular checkups. Today, though, new questions get added to the mix. Questions about sexual partners and methods of protection and what changes I have noticed in diet, sleep and mood. The questions aren't awkward or uncomfortable. Devlyn knows the answers as much as I do.

Ramona rises from the stool and tucks my chart under her arm. "Dr. Webster will be in shortly." Then she exits the room.

Wood squeaks against the linoleum as Devlyn scoots

his chair closer to the exam table. He wraps my hand in his, then lifts it to his lips. "Doing okay?"

My blues lock onto his greens as a small smile plumps my cheeks. My shoulders lift in a half shrug. "Yeah. It's just a lot." I lift my free hand to cup his cheek and he leans into my touch. "But we got this."

He rotates his head and kisses the inside of my palm. "We do."

A soft knock on the door interrupts our quiet moment. Dr. Webster enters the room with a cheery smile on her face. Not a single visit to her office goes by without her beaming disposition.

Before I found Dr. Webster, I'd visited a couple other gynecologists in the area. Of the three doctors, Dr. Marianne Webster made me the most comfortable. Her office and staff were warm, inviting and relaxed yet still professional. Every time I walked through the doors, I never felt like a number or just another patient to cash in on. And that stood out the most.

"Hi, Shelly." She smiles brighter then shifts her attention to Devlyn. "And you must be Dad. I'm Dr. Webster." She extends her hand and Devlyn freezes for two breaths before taking it.

Dad. She just called him Dad. Cue the waterworks.

"Devlyn," he chokes out before clearing his throat. "Excuse me. Devlyn. It's nice to meet you."

The next thirty minutes are filled with more questions—from Dr. Webster and us—answers and too much information. Of all the details she shares, one piece sticks out the most. Roots itself deep in my memory. Imprints itself on my heart. My expected due date.

September twenty-first.

The moment Dr. Webster says the date, Devlyn squeezes my hand a little tighter and we share similar smiles.

Dr. Webster tells us the date can change from one appointment to the next, but based on dates in my paperwork, September twenty-first falls in line. Next, she goes over what to expect in the coming months. The number of appointments and what to expect during visits at specific week markers. When she will order the first ultrasound. Changes I will experience, if I haven't already, physically as well as emotionally and mentally. She discusses diet and exercise and creating healthy habits now. Vitamins and changes I should experience in the first trimester.

Information overload is an understatement, yet I feel as if I need more.

She removes a gown from the cabinet, asks me to dress down for a pelvic exam and excuses herself from the room. While I disrobe, Devlyn looks at his fumbling hands in his lap. Although we've had sex several times, his timidity as I peel off my clothes in the doctor's office comes as a surprise.

Back on the table, I reach for his hand and lace our fingers together. "Doing okay?"

He nods and gives my fingers a gentle squeeze. "Yeah. Just trying to remember everything she said." His eyes widen for a beat. "It's a lot of information."

I chuckle and he joins in. "Agreed. Lucky for us, we'll walk out with a folder full of brochures."

Leaning forward, Devlyn kisses my temple. "Love you."

I tighten my hold on him as his words wrap around my heart. "Love you, too."

Dr. Webster performs a routine pelvic exam and Pap smear since my last appointment was more than six months ago. Since I had a blood panel done at the hospital and provided a copy with my paperwork, I luckily get to bypass more needle sticks.

Just when I think Dr. Webster is going to exit the room and let me redress, she rolls a cart closer to the exam table and grabs a tube of gel.

"Seeing as you're roughly five to six weeks, I don't want to set any expectations." My brows pinch together as she holds the gel tube over my abdomen. "Going to see if we can hear a heartbeat yet."

My own pulse kicks up a notch and whooshes behind my ears. In my periphery, Devlyn rises from his seat and inches closer to the exam table. His hand seeks mine once more and clutches it tightly.

This is really happening. I'm pregnant. With Devlyn's baby. Our baby. And we may hear a heartbeat.

"Just relax," Dr. Webster says, and I take a deep breath. "This might be a little chilly."

She squeezes a dollop of gel onto my lower abdomen and I startle. Devlyn strokes his thumb over my knuckles. Back and forth. Again and again. Settling my nerves and steadying my heart.

Dr. Webster picks up a wand attached to the

machine on the cart and presses it to the gel on my belly. For three breaths, the room falls completely silent. Not a peep as the goop smears my belly. And then a strange but quiet, pulsing sound filters through the air.

Whoosh. Whoosh. Whoosh.

Such a strange sound. Like the rapid push and pull of water.

I look up at Dr. Webster in question. Her beaming smile is all the answer I need. The whooshing sound…

"Is that?" My gaze shifts to Devlyn and I see the same question in his eyes.

"Your baby's heartbeat?" Dr. Webster finishes and we both nod. "It is." She moves the wand and the sound intensifies. "Definitely six to seven weeks along." Then the sound vanishes as she removes the wand. She wipes the gel from my belly and closes the front of the gown. "I'll step out and let you change. Then we'll go over what to expect at your next appointment before you leave."

After I redress, she comes back in with a large envelope filled with brochures and resources. She shares what to expect at my next appointment in a month. And before she steps away from the checkout area, she gives me a brief hug and congratulates us once more.

With my next appointment scheduled, Devlyn and I exit the office hand in hand. He walks me to my car and pauses near the driver's side door.

"Hungry?"

My stomach grumbles as I say, "Yes."

"Why don't you head to the house and I'll stop at the store. Any requests?"

I shake my head. "Surprise me."

Devlyn dips down and presses his lips to mine. "I'll be quick."

As I settle in the driver's seat, Devlyn jogs to his car. I wave to him as he drives off. And then, for a moment, I sit in the parking lot and absorb the reality of today.

Yes, I knew I was pregnant. But after hearing the heartbeat… the reality of it *really* sank in.

"I'm going to be a mom," I whisper to myself. My hands settle on my lower abdomen and cradle the still flat area. I breathe deeply and close my eyes. "Wow."

Then, my little bliss bubble pops.

Time to buck up and tell Mom. *Please… someone save me.*

six

. . .

Devlyn

"I'M SORRY, WHAT?"

A loud clang vibrates the air as Shelly's fork falls to her plate. Her brows pinch at the middle and eyes narrow as she regards me across the table. My heart beats a vicious rhythm while I internally cringe.

I set my fork down, take a deep breath and lift my line of sight to hers.

Remember Dr. Prince's suggestion. Talk with Shelly. Share my fears. Tell her my desires for the future.

"I'd like us to move in together," I say, my voice quieter. Smaller. Meek. My palms damp and fingers twitchy as I swipe them over my denim-clad thighs.

The room fills with eerie silence. Across the table, Shelly sits frozen in place. No shift in posture or facial expression. Her eyes still on mine, but unmoving. Unyielding. I don't sense anger—which settles my anxiety a degree or two—but, for the life of me, I can't pick up what exactly she *is* feeling. Her stillness, her voicelessness, the uneasy energy around her… it has me concerned. Off balance. Scared. Lost.

If I were in my studio upstairs, painting her in this very moment, she'd be haloed in burnt orange—a color I don't typically associate with Shelly. Not due to indignation. No, the color would represent the disorientation pulsing off her. And perhaps a hint of fear.

It's okay. I'm afraid too.

"Please say something," I say just above a whisper.

Her chest rises and falls as she inhales a deep breath. She licks her lips, traps them between her teeth a moment, then releases them on a swallow.

"Devlyn, I…" Her eyes lose focus for two breaths before she blinks a few times. "Isn't it too soon?"

I twist my hands in my lap beneath the table and ask myself the same question for the hundredth time since learning Shelly was pregnant. *How soon is too soon to live together?* Dr. Prince said there are no written guides to dictate when couples take the next step. Only we determine our time line. Our future.

My shoulders rise and fall. "It doesn't feel wrong."

Wanting Shelly in every aspect of my life has never felt so *right*. Is moving in together after dating three months a premature decision? Probably. Considering I let no one in for four years after Kelsey, this change may be deemed irrational and foolish and swift. A decision made in the heat of the moment. An open invitation to doom our relationship.

But I don't care what other people think. I only care what Shelly thinks. What she wants.

"Can I think about it?"

Every joy-filled cell in my body plummets. Wilts. Turns cold. "Yeah. Sure. Of course."

What else can I say? Shelly is her own person. Makes her own decisions. I need to let her make this decision as well. Having a baby together doesn't automatically equal cohabitation. It doesn't mean our romantic relationship will last forever.

But I want it all with her.

Taking a deep breath, I remind myself that she loves me and I love her. Her asking for time to make a decision is better than her shooting the idea down immediately. Not like I haven't mulled over the idea for days. Only fair that I let her do the same.

She could've said no and walked out the door. Give her time.

After a beat of silence, she picks up her fork and I mimic the action. We eat dinner in companionable silence for a few bites. In my periphery, she sips her water, then gingerly sets down the glass. Her fingertips swirl over condensation droplets, her eyes zeroed in on the action.

"While I consider the idea of moving in" —I lock onto her mesmerizing eyes and stop chewing— "will you think about meeting my parents?"

The bite of chicken in my mouth lodges in my throat. I smack my chest and cough violently. My face and neck and chest go hot as I attempt to dislodge the food from the wrong pipe.

"Oh god."

Shelly evacuates her chair and dashes to my side. *Whack.* Her palm smacks between my shoulder blades with force. *Whack. Whack.* I cough harder and the food clears my windpipe.

"Are you okay?"

I nod as my lungs burn and beg for air. Grabbing her hand, I bring it to my lips and kiss her between coughs. "I'm—" *Cough, cough.* "Fine." Tears spill down my cheeks as I hold up a finger, asking her to give me a moment.

Her hand rubs small circles between my shoulder blades. The gentle motion calming, soothing. And soon, my lungs settle. My throat stills. I take a sip of water. Then another.

"Better?"

I nod. "Yeah." My voice like froggy sandpaper. I swallow a bigger gulp of water. "Much."

Shelly settles back in her chair and shakes her head. "I seem to have a talent for saying things at the wrong time." I cock my head as my brows scrunch together. "When I told Cora and Elizabeth I was pregnant, they both nearly choked on their lunch." She rolls her eyes and laughs under her breath. "Really should work on *when* to say certain things."

Setting my glass down, I lay a hand on the table, palm up. She places hers atop mine and I sigh.

My skin warms and tingles at the point of contact. Our connection a live wire. Buzzing. Sparking. White hot and a constant burst of light.

The pulse never dulls. The magnitude never fades or

shrinks. If anything, what I feel for Shelly, the connection we share, it continually expands. Like the birth of a new galaxy. Mighty and endless.

This… her hand in mine… this is all I need.

"It's okay. Maybe next time, ease into it." We laugh until the reason I started choking circles back. "I'd love to meet your parents, Shelly. Whenever you're ready. Wish mine were worth meeting," I say with a hint of solemnity.

Shelly squeezes my hand and my eyes dart to hers. "Me too."

We finish dinner and talk about the first of many visits to the doctor's office. After I clear the table, Shelly and I snuggle on the couch and watch television. Her head on my shoulder, it isn't long before she falls asleep and I carry her to bed.

As she sleeps in my arms, I lie in the dark and mentally paint a picture of what our life will be like. When the baby comes and the years that follow.

I see it all so clearly. As if it already exists, but I have yet to live it.

Shelly and I existing in the same space. Living together. Loving each other. I see her brilliant smile and flushed cheeks as we hold our child for the first time. How she will turn my house into a home. Paint the walls with her warmth. Add small touches of joy and hope. Introduce a level of love that only exists within her. Love I want, crave, live for each day.

The mental picture soothes my soul in an unfamiliar way. Settles the unease I have over Shelly not instantly agreeing to move in together.

And as I drift off to sleep, one thought plays on repeat. I will do whatever it takes to make the image in my head a reality.

Whatever it takes.

seven

• • •

Shelly

WHY DOES IT FEEL LIKE EVERY DAY SOMETHING MAJOR happens? Where the hell did all the simple days go? Get up, go to work, eat, sleep, rinse, repeat—plus time with friends and Devlyn.

Since the day my phone rang and the nurse from the hospital told me I was pregnant, every day is filled with some form of chaos.

Okay, not exactly chaos. But is there an actual term for the craziness scale? Lunacy level. Madness meter. Deranged degree. Psycho scale. There is probably some technical term, but I have no clue what it is.

Most of my life, I have been in the chill zone. Low key. Easy, peasy, lemon squeezy. But now… now everything is pure madness. Constantly midscale or higher.

Tonight, life is reaching the high end of the scale. And I'm not sure how much more crazy I can handle. Tonight is dinner night with the family. With my *when will you get married and have two-point-five kids* mom and my dad that looks at her as if she does no wrong.

Someone… *please* help me. Help us.

Poor Devlyn is sweaty and pale, and it's maybe sixty degrees on my parents' front porch as we hesitate to step inside. Thank god, Micah and Peyton are already here. Although neither of them know about the pregnancy, at least they have met Devlyn. Not everything will be a complete shock with them.

I lace my fingers with Devlyn's and inhale deeply as I glance up at him. "You ready for this?"

His eyes meet mine as he squeezes my fingers tighter. "Yes. No." He pinches his eyes tight for a beat. "Yes. Your parents are a million times better than mine. Guess I'm just worried about your dad or brother choking me after the news." He gives me a sheepish smile.

Pushing up on my tiptoes, I kiss his cheek. "I'll keep you safe." A promise I plan to always keep.

"Pinkie promise?" He offers me his little finger.

Without hesitation, I hook my pinkie with his. "Promise."

Devlyn has yet to divulge all the secrets of his past. Can't say I blame him. It's a lot for him to unpack, to relive. But he has shared bits and pieces, and that is enough. The strength it must take to share such truths… his bravery astounds me daily.

In twenty-two years, he has endured a lifetime of heartache. Most of which occurred in the four walls he called home. The saddest part of all, he didn't comprehend how catastrophic his homelife had been until he left for college. Until he lived in and experienced the world. Gained new peers that came from loving homes.

Met friends' parents and professors that never said an untoward or demeaning statement.

Devlyn had been hurt in ways I will never fathom. I don't know and couldn't possibly understand the hardships he experienced. With all he's dealt with, I also refuse to pressure him to share. In his own time, when he feels safe doing so, he will give me those pieces of him. And until that day arrives, I will stand by his side. Be a pillar of strength when he needs someone to hold him upright. Give him time and space when his mind won't quiet. Hug him impossibly tight for hours when it all feels too much. Lend an ear and a shoulder when he chooses to spill his bottled-up pain.

Digging up demons is no easy feat. Fighting those same demons alone is your worst nightmare times a hundred.

He won't fight his demons alone. I refuse to allow it. Not now. Not ever.

As my hand reaches for the handle, Devlyn lifts his free hand to my cheek. His thumb strokes my cheekbone and I sigh, leaning into his touch. He leans in closer and I breathe him in. Inhale the earthy scent on his skin that reminds me of his studio, his drawings, the way he sees me. Then his lips are on mine. Slow and steady, soft and warm, bestowing me with unrivaled comfort and peace.

"Love you, my Andromeda," he whispers on my lips.

"Love you too." I take a deep breath. "Here we go."

I open the front door and lead us inside. As we toe off our shoes, a pungent smell hits my nose and my stomach rolls. My eyes fall shut as I inhale deeply and exhale slowly. Again and again.

Devlyn takes my elbow in his hand and brings his lips to my ear. "What's wrong?" Concern evident in his whispered tone.

I straighten and lift a hand to cover my nose and mouth. *Jesus. What the hell is for dinner?* Please do not let pregnancy ruin all the foods I love.

"Just the smell," I say as I drop my hand. "I'll be okay in a minute. I hope."

Thankfully, no one has caught wind of our entrance. We stand by the door as I take more breaths to settle my stomach. The nausea subsides for the most part. I slide my hand into Devlyn's and lace our fingers in a silent ready signal.

Now that my stomach is calmer, I zero in on the chatter and laughter spilling from the kitchen. No doubt, Mom has Micah cooking again while Dad and Peyton watch the show.

My brother has been such a trooper through it all. A year ago, he would have burned the house down making dinner for the family. But through his persistence and desire to be a better man for Peyton, he learned to navigate the kitchen like a certified chef. Mom was on standby, in case he needed help, but mostly stood there with a smile on her face. Pride in her eyes as she watched her son accomplish a task he never cared for until he met his wife.

On quiet feet, Devlyn and I round the kitchen island near Dad and Peyton. Peyton spots us first and spins on her stool, a warm and welcoming smile on her face.

"You haven't missed much of the show," she says as she slides off her stool and pulls us in for a hug.

"Good. I need these moments for posterity," I say on a laugh.

Peyton hugs Devlyn briefly before everyone catches on to our arrival. "Nice to see you again," she tells him. "No need to be nervous. Promise."

My favorite smile softens Devlyn's face as he thanks Peyton. Then Mom and Dad are footsteps away. Dad appears cool and collected. Mom, on the other hand, looks as if she is about to squeal like a tween at a boy band concert.

Please, I beg you, universe, don't let Mom scare Devlyn.

"Mom, Dad, this is Devlyn." I gesture to Devlyn, his arm snugly hooked in mine. "Devlyn, these are my parents, Nicole and George Reed."

Dad offers a warm smile and extends his hand. "Nice to meet you, Devlyn."

"You too, sir." Devlyn takes his offered hand and shakes.

Before their hands separate, Mom steps in and wraps her arms around Devlyn. My eyes widen more than Devlyn's as he looks to me for help. He doesn't *not* hug her back, but the embrace looks awkward from where I stand.

"Mom," I admonish. "Please don't frighten Devlyn."

It's a half joke. A way to lighten the mood, but also tell my mother to take her enthusiasm down a notch. She just met him for crying out loud. Yes, my mother is an exuberant woman, but I damn well know she doesn't hug strangers like this. Devlyn may not be a stranger to me, but he is to them.

She drops her arms and takes a step back. Then another. "I'm so sorry, Devlyn. Where are my manners?" Pink stains her cheeks. "Please, excuse my outburst. It's just—"

"Nicole," Dad says, resting a hand on Mom's shoulder. "Give the guy a moment to breathe."

"Yes, of course." She winces. "Sorry."

Well, well, well. The hug could have been predicted, but the embarrassment and apology, not so much. Not that Mom doesn't apologize when necessary, she does. In this circumstance, though, I expected her to wave it off like it was no big deal. To throw out some excuse as to why it'd be acceptable to embrace Devlyn so fiercely.

Hmm. How intriguing.

Stirring a pot on the stove, Micah glances over his shoulder and smiles at Devlyn. "Hey, man. Good to see you again."

Devlyn nods. "You too."

Mom resumes her spot in the kitchen near Micah while Dad and Peyton return to their stools. Devlyn pulls out the one beside Peyton and gestures for me to sit. After I do, he steps up behind me, wraps his arms around my waist, rests his chin on my crown and sighs. I rest my hands over his and give him a gentle squeeze, silently asking if he is okay. He answers by hugging my middle tighter and kissing my crown.

"What's for dinner?" I ask Peyton.

"With St. Patty's around the corner, Momma Reed

thought corned beef and cabbage were a good idea. We're also having roasted carrots and potatoes."

Sautéed cabbage. That must have been what I smelled when we walked in the house.

Don't get me wrong, I love cabbage. Coleslaw, in salads, cooked. To be honest, I love most foods. But something about the cabbage scent when we walked in… it was foul. Maybe they added different seasoning to it.

It isn't long before Micah pulls the corned beef and roasted vegetables from the oven. Mom sets the serving dishes on the dining room table as Dad, Peyton, Devlyn and I rise from the stools.

The six of us sit around the table. Mom and Dad in their usual seats. Micah and I on the same side we've sat on since childhood, only now with someone special next to us.

As we fill our plates, I bypass the cabbage and pray it finds a resting place far from my seat.

"So, Devlyn," Mom starts. "What do you do for work?"

This is not an interrogation. This is my family getting to know Devlyn.

"Artwork. Oil painting, pencil drawings, charcoal. Whatever calls to me for the piece."

A flicker crosses Mom's face before her eyes widen. She stares at him for two breaths before her eyes dart between the two of us. "Oh my goodness." She sets her fork down and brings her hands to her lips in prayer. "Are you Devlyn Templar?" she asks, her tone filled with awe.

Devlyn spears a potato and nods, acting as if her local celebrity moment is no big deal. "Yes, ma'am."

Mom's eyes dart to me, then back to Devlyn. This happens three times before she finds her words again. "How long have you been dating?"

I know why she asks this question. The drawing she gifted to me for Christmas. She bought it off a local artist's website. My reaction to the piece. Peyton's reaction. The pieces are slowly clicking into place in her mind.

Please don't let her give me grief for not broadcasting my relationship sooner.

"Since early December," I answer. "But we met back in October." My gaze shifts to Devlyn as I lay my hand on his thigh beneath the table. "He did some artwork at Petal and Vine."

For a split second, Mom's face falls at the time line. It doesn't take a genius to do the math. Devlyn and I have dated nearly three months. Have known each other five. That isn't what makes her face temporarily wilt. She doesn't have to say it, but I know it's because I didn't share the news sooner.

The Reed family isn't big on secrets. We share important details about our lives on a regular basis. But just as my brother didn't come right out in the beginning and tell our parents he and Peyton were dating, I followed suit. Not to hurt my parents. More to give myself time to adjust to the change. To see where our relationship went.

After what happened in my apartment the night of Devlyn's art show, had I told my mother sooner about a potential relationship, the update of our weeks apart would've been harder. Mom would have brought Devlyn up more often than not. Asked questions I wasn't prepared to hear or answer.

And my heart would have snapped sooner.

I love my mother, but she can be a handful at times.

"Oh." Two letters. One word. That is all she says as she picks up her fork. Then she blinks a few times and swallows. Pierces the beef on her plate and cuts off a smaller piece. "And the drawing we gave you at Christmas..." She doesn't finish her question before she shoves the fork in her mouth and meets my eyes that match hers. A coincidence she probably never considered when the art was purchased.

I squeeze Devlyn's thigh as he sits quietly at my side. "That's me," I say with a little too much exuberance, then laugh under my breath. "Well, it's mostly my eye. But you know what I mean." Across the table, Micah bites back a smile at my rushed words while Peyton's eyes drop to her plate. "What're you smiling at, *starlight*?" I tease my brother with an arched brow.

"Starlight?" Dad chimes in. "What the hell does that mean?"

Peyton and I burst out laughing while Micah and Devlyn pick at their dinner and my parents sit in a cloud of confusion.

"Dad, you of all people should understand. Between Micah's nickname and the drawing with the constellation in the iris." I gesture toward Mom. "Have you not noticed how identical my and Micah's eyes are to Mom's?"

Dad stares at Mom across the length of the table for two breaths. Then a soft smile plumps his cheeks. "Her eyes always remind me of the nights we used to camp in the woods. When there wasn't a light for miles. All you could see were thousands of stars." His eyes glaze over as his memories flood in from years past. "She's always been my favorite starry night."

My heart melts as I listen to Dad speak with so much love for Mom. After more than thirty-five years, they are just as in love today as they were back in their teens. If not more. And it is a beautiful and envious thing.

Dinner continues with less intense conversation. Talk about Micah and Peyton and business at Roar. Dad mentions his time line for selling the insurance firm in the next three to five years. He has an eye on the market and wants to make sure he sells before a downshift. Mom talks about trends she has noticed in marketing and the shift on how to advertise. She mentions helping me when I take over Petal and Vine at the start of next year.

At this, Devlyn fidgets in his seat. His leg bouncing beneath my hand.

Mom and Dad clear the table and suggest we head into the living room for dessert. While they are in the kitchen, we meander to the living room and sit on the love seat.

"What's going on?" Micah whisper-shouts from his seat on the couch.

Leave it to my brother to detect the blip in my radar. He may not be the most intuitive person on the planet, but when it comes to me, he knows when something is off.

"I'll explain when Mom and Dad come back." His eyes narrow. "Micah, please," I plead with him.

Devlyn wraps his arm around my shoulder and kisses my temple. "Deep breaths," he whispers in my ear. Inhaling deeply, I rest my head on Devlyn's shoulder, eyes still on Micah.

"Please," I whisper.

Mom and Dad enter the room with a loaded tray. Small portions of peach cobbler and a scoop of vanilla ice cream. They hand out dessert and spoons, then take their seat on the couch.

It's now or never. Devlyn's here. You can do this.

I set my bowl down on the table, not a bite taken. Mom looks at me with a furrowed brow and questions on the tip of her tongue.

"Mom, Dad." My eyes shift from them to Micah and Peyton then back. "Devlyn and I have some news." Unlike the last few times I announced something important, I wait until no one has food in their mouth.

"What is it, sweetheart?" Dad asks as he sets his bowl on the table.

I *feel* Micah's intense laser focus on me, but ignore it and push forward. Taking Devlyn's hand, I intertwine our fingers and form an invisible barrier to keep us strong.

"I'm pregnant."

The room goes silent. Scary silent. No one moves. No one says a word. But four sets of eyes *stare* at us.

Hard. As if searching for answers as to how and when and why.

I understand why they're in shock. Hell, we were in shock too. But I at least expected Mom to be a bit more vocal and bouncy. How long has she been harping me and Micah for grandchildren? Close to two years.

My eyes land on her face and all I see is confusion and emptiness. And it is so disconcerting.

"Someone please say something," I whisper, although it filters through as a scream.

Of all the people I expected to speak up first, it wasn't Peyton. "Congratulations." She rises from her seat, sets her bowl on the table and walks across the room. Bending at the waist, she hugs me and Devlyn in turn. "Just give them a minute," she whispers between us and I nod.

The second she lands in her seat, it is as if a switch flipped. Micah pipes up next, his eyes glassy as he searches mine. "Are you happy?"

I love that this is his only concern. After all our conversations about relationships, my virginity, and how we both felt about the future, neither of us spoke deeply on the topic of children. Before Peyton, both of us were unsure. Once he and Peyton were serious, they'd decided to forgo starting a family. I fully supported my brother and Peyton's decision. Mom was harder to convince.

Last Micah knew, though, I was a virgin. Devlyn and I had been dating, but my brother knew I wouldn't take that major step easily. So this news also tells him how deeply I care for Devlyn. That he is much more than just another guy to date. After several conversations about my love life, or lack thereof, he knew no one fit the bill. Made a big enough impact for me to want more. My brother knew I'd been waiting for the right person.

"Yeah, big brother." I twist and lock onto my favorite shade of green. Lift Devlyn's hand to my lips and kiss his fingers. "I am."

"You know I had to ask."

I face him and smile. "I know."

"Are you getting married?"

Beside me, Devlyn stiffens. Can't say I blame him. If I were in his shoes, I would too. Mentally, I was prepared for such radical questions. Mom had peppered me and Micah with them for years. But I didn't quite prepare Devlyn, and that is on me.

"Nicole!" Dad shakes his head as his eyes widen at her. "Not the time."

Thanks for the rescue, Dad.

I lean into Devlyn and wait for his frame to relax. One, two, three breaths pass before his muscles soften beneath my touch.

"Better?" I whisper and he hums. "No offense, Mom, but Devlyn and I have more important priorities to consider right now." My tone is gentle and nonconfrontational. "We're still adjusting to the news ourselves."

"Have you been to the doctor?" she asks, her eyes softening at the edges.

This we can handle. Simple conversations about the pregnancy. Without asking, my parents have to know I am not that far along. Even if Devlyn and I had gotten pregnant early in December, I'd only be a few weeks further into pregnancy. Not enough for the naked eye to notice.

For the next hour, we finish our dessert, discuss doctor's appointments, and how pregnancy was for Mom. My pregnancy may be completely different from Mom's, but knowing her experiences gives me insight on how mine may go. After all, I favor her more than Dad.

When it's time to exchange hugs and goodnights, Mom makes me promise to check in after each appointment. She also tells me to update her more often. She won't admit it outright, but the double whammy tonight—meeting Devlyn and learning about the baby—caught her off guard. Probably bruised her heart.

My intention wasn't to hurt her. I wanted to wait until the time felt right for me and Devlyn. In this one thing, I should get to be a little selfish. Devlyn too.

After an endless hug from both my parents at the same time, the four of us head for our cars. We stop between the two cars and fumble over what to say next. Surprisingly, Devlyn is the first to break the silence.

"You should both come over for dinner one night."

Micah looks at me for a split second. Questions and emotions flit his expression. Although he won't come out and ask right now, I know he wants to ask if we are living together. Months have passed since the two of us last sat down for lunch and sibling catch-up. After tonight, it wouldn't shock me if he texts and sets up a brother-sister date.

"Sounds nice." A smile brightens Micah's face as he wraps an arm around Peyton's shoulders. "Just let us know when. Shell knows our schedule."

"Wonderful."

Devlyn's shoulders round as he visibly relaxes next to me. I hate how stressful this night must have been for him. Nervousness over meeting my parents. Worry over whether or not they'd like him as a person and approve of him to date their daughter. Unriddled anxiety over sharing news about the baby.

It had to have been a lot for him. He hid the tense moments well.

We exchange hugs one last time, get in our cars and go our separate ways.

I lace my fingers with Devlyn's and hold his hand the entire drive to the house. Keep my eyes on his profile and watch him as the streetlights zip past. Breathe in his earthy scent that has quickly become my favorite comfort. And fall for this beautiful man a little harder.

It may be too soon, but my answer is yes. Yes to moving in with Devlyn. Yes to sharing a home and life with him. Yes to everything us and our future.

But first, I need a minute. A little time to sort things out. To talk with Elizabeth about the shop and new time line for the sale. Talk with the apartment complex manager, seeing as I renewed my lease six months ago. And maybe I should talk with myself. Mull over what this next step means, not just for me but also Devlyn.

I just need a minute to breathe. Because this baby… they will change everything.

eight

. . .

Devlyn

"Can we stop at the store?"

I lift Shelly's hand to my lips and kiss her knuckles. "Of course. What do we need?"

"Antacids and more dessert."

Chuckling, I shake my head. "Sounds like a winning combination."

I steer the car into the grocery store parking lot and park in a spot near the front. With the lot almost empty, Sunday evenings at the supermarket look to be the best time for shopping. Good to know.

We hop out of the car and walk to the door hand in hand. The automatic doors whoosh open and I pick up a handbasket from the stack. Shelly guides us to the healthcare aisle first, grabbing the largest container of Tums from the shelf and tossing them in the basket.

She shrugs. "Probably going to need them all." I wouldn't care if she threw ten bottles in the basket. If she needs them, I will buy them.

"Any dessert in particular?"

"Maybe peanut butter cups and ice cream."

We stop in the aisle loaded with candy and chips next. I stand back and observe as Shelly eyes the Snickers and Reese's and Baby Ruth bars. She taps a finger against her lips. Darts her eyes from one to the other over and over. And when she finally decides, I laugh because she puts all three in the basket with a radiant smile on her face.

The ice cream aisle carries the same level of indecision. But after I add a pint of cookie dough in the basket, she reaches into the case and fetches a tub of the nondairy Ben and Jerry's P.B. & Cookies. I sense of trend. Lots of peanuts or peanut butter.

It's cute.

She is cute.

Damn, but I got lucky with Shelly. Our relationship could have ventured so many different directions from the path it took. But it didn't and I thank my lucky stars every day.

After experiencing heartbreak, I never pictured myself in this place. Happy. Excited about life. Eager to spend each day with another person. Loving someone again. Yearning for the future.

But here I am, ready for it all. Ready to share my future with someone I love. And I have never felt better.

With our dessert loaded into the basket, Shelly and I stroll hand in hand toward the checkout. We round the end of the ice cream aisle and I skid to a stop after one step. Shelly jerks back and looks at me over her shoulder.

She tugs on my hand. "Dev?" Her fingers squeeze

mine tighter. "Are you okay?" I'd answer, but my lips won't move. My tongue refuses to form words. My voice box forgets how to vibrate the proper sounds. Shelly steps into me, frames my face with her hands, and looks me square in the eyes. "Devlyn," she whispers, a breath from my lips. "You're scaring me. What's wrong?"

After a beat, I blink. Take a slow, methodical breath. Swallow past the bubbling anxiety clawing its way up my throat. Shift my gaze and lock onto Shelly's starry-blue irises. Eyes that soothe me in ways nothing else does.

"My mother is here," I whisper almost inaudibly. Shelly starts to turn her head, but I grab her elbow. Switch her focus back to mine. "Please don't turn around." A surge of fear spreads through my bones and rattles me head to toe. The need to protect Shelly from her floods my veins.

"Where is she?" Shelly whispers.

"Two aisles down." I shake almost imperceptibly. "Don't think she saw us, but can't be sure." I close my eyes for two breaths. *Why is she here? She doesn't live on this side of the bay. So why is she shopping* here? "Just please… please wait a minute. I'm sure she'll—"

My words get cut off as my mother sidles up to us. "Devlyn, what on earth?"

Hours of therapy turns to dust in my head as my mother stares down at me with black eyes. In a blink, all rational thought leaves my body. And in its place… the scared little boy living inside me emerges. I don't speak. Don't know the first response to the situation. All I know is, I don't want to be here. I don't want to exist in the same space as her. Don't want to breathe the same air as her.

I need to leave. *We* need to leave. Now.

When I don't respond, she tackles me verbally. "I have been calling and texting and stopping by the house. What is the matter with you?" While she babbles on about how my lack of contact bothers her, I take note that she has yet to acknowledge Shelly. "Your father and I have been worried sick. Your behavior has made me absolutely sick."

I tighten my hold on Shelly and nudge forward, hoping she catches my signal to leave. I take a step and Shelly falls in line beside me. Then, she is the one tugging us faster to the checkout. As if she senses my absolute need to leave. To get out of this store and away from my mother, sooner rather than later.

All the while, my mother is on our heels, berating me loud enough for the entire grocery store to hear.

"You will not walk away from me, young man."

Shelly and I dart into the express line, toss our snacks on the belt and face the cashier with pained smiles.

"Look at me when I speak to you," she demands, but I don't comply.

Per Dr. Prince's advice, I carry on and try to push past the cold demands. Ignore the words that are meant to sound sad, but are actually a ploy to crush me with her pointy, overpriced heels.

The cashier scans our groceries and bags them quickly. *Thank you.* I slip my card into the reader and press the appropriate buttons to pay the bill. As soon as the receipt is in the bag, I swipe it from the counter, take Shelly's hand and dart for the exit.

"She'll leave you. Just like the last one did. Who will be there when she abandons you?"

I freeze just before the door. Close my eyes and grind my molars. Remind myself to breathe. Remind myself that she will use whatever manipulation tactic necessary to keep me exactly where she wants me. Alone and at her mercy.

Never again.

Shelly squeezes my hand. Snaps me back to the here and now. Reminds me of why I need to make a change. Why I need to vanquish the pain and hurt and misguidance of my past. For her. For our baby. A baby my mother will never know about. Ever.

"Let's go." Shelly's thumb strokes the top of my hand. "I got you." Without a backward glance, Shelly and I exit the store. When we reach the car, she makes me sit in the passenger seat. "It's better if you don't drive right now. You need a minute."

Behind the wheel, she cranks the engine, clicks her seat belt into place and throws the car in reverse. We zip out of the lot and drive slightly over the speed limit the entire way home. If we get pulled over, I'll gladly pay the fine to avoid one more second in the same space as Karen Templar.

Shelly parks the car in the driveway. And it's not until we are in the house, door locked and alarm set, that I finally take a full breath. Finally let everything that just happened sink in. I shiver from head to toe.

Shelly drops the groceries at her feet and wraps her arms around my chest. She hauls me forward until not a breath of air resides between us. Then she hugs me with unimaginable force. It isn't strength. More like warmth and love and a promise to always pick me up when I fall.

Right there, near the entrance of the kitchen, I hold on to her as if my life depends on it. I hug her and cry into the crook of her neck. Sob and shake as years of pain and hurt spill from my body, from my soul.

"Let it all out." One of her hands is in my hair, the other squeezing my middle. "I got you." She kisses my shoulder. "I always have you."

When my tears slow, I lean back and cup Shelly's cheeks with my palms. "Love you so much." I press my lips to hers. Kiss her with unimaginable tenderness. "Don't know what I'd do without you."

A soft smile dons her lips and lifts the corners of her eyes. "Good thing you'll never find out." She kisses me chastely. "I love you more."

I highly doubt that.

nine

. . .

Shelly

The bell jingles over the front door of Petal and Vine. I peek up from the arrangement in front of me to see an older couple. "Good afternoon," I greet them and lift my hand to wave.

They return the greeting with bright smiles, then wander the perimeter of the store. The woman runs her aged fingertips over the dried flowers and wispy grasses. Her eyes scan the bins before she leans forward and inhales the dried lavender, followed by the eucalyptus. The man with her follows two steps behind, hands clasped behind his back, eyes on her. A small smile highlights his weathered skin as he watches her with love in his eyes.

My first thought is that may be Devlyn and me one day. Meandering a store, one of us shopping while the other observes in companionable silence. Simply happy because we exist in the same space.

Then I shake off the errant thought.

My relationship with Devlyn hasn't broached six

months yet. Although things are progressing quicker than imaginable, thinking about us together with gray hair and a hobble in our step is a bit of stretch. Although I don't foresee a day without Devlyn in my life, flashing forward to our retirement years isn't ideal.

While the couple scans the flower selection near the meadow painting, I covertly—at least I hope it's covertly—watch them. Watch the way she plucks stems from the pails and lifts them to smell before deciding whether to put it back or hold on to it for purchase. Then I shift my gaze to him. Watch the way he stands just a step back and off to the side. Watch the way he studies her every move with a keen eye and slightly leans in her direction. The longer I stare, the more my heart melts at the sight.

I *do* want that. The simple happiness of existing in the same space as someone you love. To find joy in the small things, like the way they look at a flower or brush the hair from their face.

"Brought you lunch."

I jump back, slap a hand to my chest and nearly knock over the vase of flowers I'd been working on. "Holy sh—" I pivot and catch sight of Devlyn. "Jesus. Make noise or something." Planting my palms on the table, I take a deep breath and give him my sharpest side-eye. "Scared the sh— crap out of me."

He leans in and kisses my temple. "To be fair, I did call your name. Twice, actually." His gaze drifts to the older couple. "But you were preoccupied."

"You did?"

A soft smile turns up the corners of his mouth as he

notices what had my attention. "I did." His eyes drift back to mine as his smile deepens. "But I see why you were distracted. They're adorable to watch."

"That they are." I twist to face him fully. "You brought me lunch?"

He holds up a white paper bag. "Yes. Sandwiches from the deli. Hope that's good."

I nod as my stomach groans in agreement. "Let me go find Elizabeth so we can take lunch."

"Already done." Devlyn leans his hip on the heavy arrangement table. "When she let me in through the back, she said to give her a minute."

The words leave his lips just as Elizabeth enters the shop from the storage room. Sidling up to me, she lays a hand on my shoulder. "Go enjoy your lunch." I start to argue about not finishing the arrangement, but she sweeps it from the table and stows it in the storage cooler. "It'll be here when you're done. Now go."

Is this how it will be throughout pregnancy? Being parented, but not, all over again. Family and friends treating me as if I am fragile. Earlier, I went to pick up a box and Elizabeth rushed to my side. Told me not to lift it. The box weighed maybe seven pounds, which is nothing. Hell, most babies weigh that much when they are born.

I wish everyone wouldn't handle me as if I am breakable. Yes, I carry precious cargo, but my body is quite capable of physical activity. And while it's still possible, I'd like to do what my body will allow.

In the pamphlets I'd read, exercise and routine fitness are encouraged during pregnancy. Obviously certain movements and higher weights are off-limits, but lifting is permissible unless otherwise instructed by the doctor.

Inhaling deeply, I move past the notion that everyone will treat me with kid gloves. I remind myself they are looking out for me and the well-being of the baby. Their actions aren't meant to offend or suggest I am incapable. They love me and want the pregnancy to progress without hiccups.

"Got you the same sandwich as last time," Devlyn says as he pulls the food from the bag.

"Sounds perfect."

We take our seats and peel back the butcher paper around the sandwiches. Take the lid off the fruit cups. Dive into our sandwiches and enjoy the first bite as the flavors hit our tongues.

Except mine doesn't taste right. Or smell right.

I swallow the bite as my nose bunches. Slowly, I lift the sandwich to my nose and sniff. An odd tang hits my nasal cavity and I push away the offending scent. Set the sandwich on the butcher paper and peel back the bread. Inspect the cheese as if it were a suspect in a murder investigation. Narrow my eyes at the offensive smell.

"What's the matter?"

"The cheese smells off."

Devlyn sets his sandwich down and picks mine up. Lifting it to his nose, he inhales the unpleasant odor, only he doesn't seem as perturbed. He sniffs it again. Then again. No wince or offensive look. No puckered nose indicating disgust. Devlyn just appears… normal.

Damnit.

Please, please, please tell me this is not a pregnancy thing. Because not being able to eat the foods I love is unacceptable. I love cheese. All the cheeses.

"Smells okay to me," Devlyn says with an edge of uncertainty in his voice. "Want mine?"

I stare at his Cuban sandwich and my stomach grumbles. They have never been my thing, but maybe because I haven't tried one in years. Plus, Devlyn takes off the mustard and pickles. A win, if you ask me.

"I'll give it a try, but only if you don't mind."

Devlyn lifts his hand to my cheek, sliding it down until he pinches my chin between his thumb and finger. "Wouldn't offer otherwise."

We switch sandwiches and I take a hesitant bite. Worried the cheese from the Cuban will offend too. But as I chew the bite, as all the flavors hit my tongue, I moan. Then I take another bite, close my eyes and savor the taste. Dare I say, I love this sandwich more than my favorite.

"Better?"

I nod with a little too much enthusiasm. "Much, thank you."

"Think it's pregnancy related?"

Setting my sandwich down, I eat some of the fruit. "Probably." I swallow a bite of strawberry. "I read in one of the brochures that diet changes are different for each expecting mother. Some women don't experience any, with the exception of eating more. Other women crave foods they hated and dislike foods they've loved." I pierce another strawberry and blueberry and point to the sandwich in Devlyn's hands. "Hope that's the only issue."

"Me too."

Most of lunch goes by in relative silence. A little more than a week has passed since the Karen incident at the grocery store. The first two days post-Karen were iffy. I kept an eye on Devlyn every minute humanly possible. Watched for signs of detachment. Held him often so he didn't shut down and curl in on himself.

But being with him twenty-four seven is impossible. Life and work continue to demand our time.

Thank goodness he had an appointment scheduled with Dr. Prince two days later.

Although I want Devlyn to share everything with me, I know he needs someone else's guidance when it comes to this piece of his past. One day, when he is in a better place with it all, he will share.

Until his appointment, Devlyn and I spent every available minute together. When I worked, he was in the studio. Loud, angry music vibrated the walls when I walked through the front door every evening. The music wasn't offensive, but more like a key to his mood. A glimpse at what I was walking into each day. And with each passing day, the music became less harsh. Less *I want to throw shit at the wall* sounding.

I want to smack Karen Templar. Dig my nails in her skin and listen to her cries. Get in her face and scream obscenities. Tell her she doesn't deserve to have someone as wonderful and extraordinary as Devlyn in her life. Make her feel an inkling of the pain she inflicted on her son.

But I won't do any of the above. Physical altercations and acts of violence wouldn't help. Not me or Devlyn or the situation as a whole.

This is Devlyn's battle. One I will help him with, whatever that looks like, but only as he needs me to. I need to be strong for him. Hold him up when his knees buckle. Tell him how much I love him. How I will be there for him always. And if he needs me to step up to the plate, if he needs me to be his voice or his shield, I will do exactly that.

The butcher paper crinkles as we finish lunch and toss our trash in the bin. We tidy up the table and meander back out to the main room of the shop. The older couple from earlier is long gone. A man lingers near the cooler of prearranged vases while a woman wanders near the loose flowers in the customer walk-in.

"See you after work?" Devlyn leans his hip on the arrangement table, his eyes wandering the lines of my profile, heating my skin.

I nod. "Yeah. After I stop by the apartment first."

He straightens, then leans into me. Presses his lips to my temple. Drops his lips to my ear. "Love you, Andromeda." He tugs the loose length of my hair. "See you in a bit."

I reach out, pinch the bottom hem of his shirt as I twist to face him, and kiss him for all to see. The kiss isn't obscene, but the gentle press of my lips to his lingers. The moment his lips leave mine, I want to dive back in for another. But I resist the urge. Remind myself there is plenty of time for that later. After work.

"Love you too. I'll text when I'm on my way."

With one last kiss, Devlyn weaves his way through the back of the shop and out the employee door. I miss him the second the door clicks shut. But his earthy scent and the tingle from his kiss remains. For now, it will have to do.

Elizabeth takes lunch while I man the shop. I wrap a mix of flowers in brown paper and tie them with twine for the woman. She pays and exits the shop.

I snag the arrangement I worked on before lunch and pick up where I left off.

As I finish up the bouquet, the man steps up to the table and asks for help. He wants to send flowers to a friend who lost a loved one. Sifting through the available options, I opt for a small bundle of lilies, add them to a vase with some greenery and give him a small card to fill out for the bouquet. After he pays and exits, the shop is quiet. Too quiet.

I start a new arrangement. Grab a fresh vase and an array of colorful flowers. Add a handful of stems, various greenery and some baby's breath. As I place it in the prearranged cooler, the bell over the door jingles. Tipping up the corners of my mouth, I pivot on my heel and open my mouth to greet the next customer.

But no words leave my lips. My whole frame stiffens and I forget how to speak.

Twenty feet from where I stand, not facing me head on, is Devlyn's mother.

What the hell?

Much as I'd love to give this woman a piece of my mind, much as I'd love to shove her out the front door and tell her to never return, my lips refuse to move. Words refuse to form on my tongue.

And before she sees me, I spin around. My feet trek across the floor and toward the break room. Elizabeth hasn't been back here but maybe ten to fifteen minutes, and I hate that I will interrupt her time. But I swear to make it up to her. Give her extra time, let her come in later on a different day. Whatever she wants.

Anything but be in the same room as Karen Templar, forced to interact with her. Not on my own. Not anytime soon.

"I need a favor," I say as I enter the room.

Elizabeth looks up from her book, finishes chewing and swallows. "What's the matter?"

I pick at the pocket of my apron. Twist my lips between my teeth. "Devlyn's mother is out front." Elizabeth's brows pinch at the middle. It isn't my place to share Devlyn's past, but I need to give Elizabeth something. Some indication as to why I refuse to be in the same room as her. "It's a sticky situation." That's putting it lightly. "Things aren't good with Devlyn and his parents, and we bumped into her the other night. It was bad."

Tucking her bookmark between the pages, Elizabeth rises from the table and wipes her mouth with a napkin. "Say no more." She sidles up to me and rests a hand on my shoulder. "Stay back here. I'll come back when she leaves."

My entire body deflates. "Thank you."

Not a minute after Elizabeth exits the room, my stomach starts to roll. *Nerves or morning sickness?* It's long past morning, but I read the nausea happens at all hours. Most women just happen to get it in the morning.

I lock myself in the bathroom, crank the cold-water knob on the faucet and soak a paper towel. Then I park myself on the lidded toilet and dab my cheeks, forehead and neck with the towel. Bend at the waist and tuck my head between my knees.

As a child, I passed out quite often. My blood sugar and iron levels were never where they were supposed to be. At an early age, I learned the signs leading up to a fainting spell. The doctors told me if I felt that same woozy feeling, felt like the world was too wobbly beneath my feet, I needed to sit in a chair or on the floor. Somewhere safe. That I should tuck my head between my knees and take slow, deep breaths. In through the nose, out through the mouth. Help the blood and oxygen flow to my head. It wasn't an immediate fix, but it helped.

After the third deep breath, I slowly sit straighter. Open my eyes. Focus my thoughts on something calming.

Nights snuggled with Devlyn on the couch. Just me, him, good food and whatever show we're currently watching. His warm arms around my waist. The stroke of his fingers on my skin.

Another deep breath and the nausea passes. "I got this," I whisper with renewed confidence.

A knock on the door startles my peace. "Shelly? Everything alright?"

I rise from the toilet and toss the paper towel in the

bin. Twisting the handle, I open the door to see Elizabeth, her face etched with concern.

"All good. Felt sick for a moment, but it passed."

She rubs my back between my shoulders as I walk out. "Glad it's better. May need to keep some ginger ale and saltines on hand." A gentle smile dons her face. "Just in case."

"Not a bad idea." My eyes dart to the doorway, then back to Elizabeth. "Did she… uh…"

"She left. Didn't buy anything, actually. She wandered the shop for a few minutes, then started asking questions."

"About the shop?"

Elizabeth shakes her head. "Not one. She asked questions about Devlyn." She pauses to swallow. "And you."

Shit. I hoped she wouldn't remember my face from the shop. She'd only been in here the one time, well over a year ago. I wasn't even the one to help her.

Obviously, Karen Templar has a fantastic memory. One I'd like her to forget.

"What did she ask?"

I hate that Elizabeth is suddenly in the middle of our mess. It isn't fair to her.

"At first, she asked about the new piece on the inside wall. The meadow." *My meadow.* "Asked if Devlyn had painted it." My eyes widen. "And when he was here last." A light layer of sweat dampens my skin as the nausea starts to make a comeback. "Since I hadn't seen her in a while, I told her Devlyn painted the inside when he'd done the exterior more than a year ago."

Thank god.

The last thing I need is this woman constantly snooping around the shop. Barging in at any given moment and pestering me or waiting for Devlyn to show.

"What did she ask about me?"

An audible exhale leaves her lips as Elizabeth takes my hands in hers. In that small touch, I feel every ounce of her love and concern. "Please tell me you are safe, Shelly." Her gaze pierces mine with a fierce level of protectiveness. "If that woman is harassing you…"

"For now, everything is okay." I nod imperceptibly. "There's just been some recent events with her and Devlyn." My eyes fall to our joined hands. "Wish I could share more, but it's not my place."

"I know, sweetheart. Just promise me one thing." I lift my eyes back to hers. "If it gets too bad, if you or Devlyn are in harm's way, don't keep this secret." Her gaze drops to my belly briefly. "It's not just the two of you anymore." Her eyes dart between mine. "It's okay to ask for help. Especially with this."

"I promise," I whisper.

Elizabeth's shoulders visibly relax. "She asked if the young blonde girl still worked here. I didn't answer. Just deterred her and asked how I could help. The way she left…" She shakes her head. "I don't think she'll return."

I pray she is right. The last thing any of us needs is to be on the receiving end of Karen Templar's wrath.

"Thank you." I pull Elizabeth into a hug and hold on tight. She squeezes me until I have to tap out of the embrace. "Sorry I interrupted your lunch." I point to the table where her sandwich sits. "Take all the time you need."

Before she rebuts my courtesy, I dart from the room.

The last few hours of the day go by uneventfully. But as I compile online orders and start arrangements for deliveries, the thought of that woman in here, in *my* shop, gazing at *my* meadow, eats away at my happiness.

She may not have said one word to me, but her presence alone sucked the life from one of my happy places. And I intend to get it back.

I will not let her stomp all over me or Devlyn. Will not let her ruin the love and joy we have found together. And I downright refuse to be bullied and squashed by anyone, especially that wicked woman.

Not today. Not tomorrow. Not ever.

ten

• • •

Devlyn

DIFFICULT AS IT IS, I TRY NOT TO SPEND MOST DAYS HATING my mother. Dr. Prince says I should focus on how to relieve myself of the trauma. Find new ways to dispel the pieces of my past that affect my present and possibly my future. That I should forgive my younger self for not knowing or understanding the influence my parents had on me at such a vulnerable age.

It is okay to forgive past me. It is okay to let go of things I had no control over.

Forgiving and letting go of the past opens up space for the future. Is silent permission to love without fear of repercussion. To hope for the things I want in my life. To experience happiness without apprehension.

In order to move forward, in order to work through all the parts that eat away at my soul, I have to learn to forgive. And forgiving the woman who should have loved me more than anyone, but didn't, is difficult.

I *want* her love. I *want* her approval.

Knowing I will never have either is the hardest part. But knowing I will never have either also helps.

When I argued with Dr. Prince, told him I didn't have the energy to forgive my parents, he countered my rebuff. Said forgiveness and release don't need to be done face-to-face. It's more about letting go of the piece of them that still takes up residence inside me. It's about discovering a way to dig up the painful parts, dissect each moment on its own, make peace with the hurt, and then let that piece of the past go.

Weeks ago, he'd said, "Mental and emotional trauma leaves invisible scars. Healing those scars will take time. It's not something that can be rushed. We all heal at our own pace and in our own way. Grant yourself the time your mind needs. Be open to expelling the past and making room for the future."

So, one session at a time, one relived memory at a time, I learn how to forgive and let go of my parents.

During an early session, I argued with Dr. Prince that my father was not to blame. He'd never said an unkind word. Never raised his hand in physical threat. Never belittled me in private or public. It had always been my mother who'd done those things. My mother was the villain.

After my counterstatement, Dr. Prince asked how my father acted while my mother behaved in this manner. For minutes, I stared out the window of his office. Watched the birds flutter around the tree branches and chase one another. Got lost in the fluffy white clouds as they floated in the Mayan-blue sky.

Drifted away mentally with the breeze, wishing it was easier to escape the disasters of my past.

It was then that I realized what he'd meant when he said my father had also been part of the problem. Because James Templar never did a damn thing. Not to help me, anyway.

He'd coddled my mother. Admonished me for upsetting her. Told me to be on my best behavior. All with a pained look on his face.

To this day, I don't know if that pained look was because my mother was upset. Or because he suffered her wrath as well.

The more I dug into my past, the more I paid attention to the little moments over the years, the more I saw it. Although my father was a victim, it wasn't the same. He *chose* to stay. He *chose* to elevate my mother. To put her on the pedestal that slowly lifted her higher and higher with each passing day.

My father fed—feeds—my mother's narcissism. He fuels her by never telling her the words she speaks or actions she takes are harmful. And together, they buried me in hurt and confusion and emotional detachment.

"Is she still attempting contact?" Dr. Prince asks from his plush leather chair.

Three months have passed since my first session. In those three months, a lot has been brought to light. A lot has been picked apart and evaluated with a new lens. But with each session, life moves forward rather than backward. With each session, I learn how to heal.

Not long after seeing my mother in the store, when she blew up and made a scene, she stopped by Petal and Vine. She'd missed me by mere minutes. Thankfully, Shelly escaped to the back and avoided another interaction unscathed. My mother probed Elizabeth with questions, but got no answers.

Surprisingly, it has been quiet since.

No constant calls or voice mails. No text messages. No incessant emails.

Almost as if Karen Templar vanished without a trace. And that has me on edge.

"No." I shake my head as I scoot to sit straighter in my seat. "Is it weird for me to be worried by her silence?"

Dr. Prince scratches a note down on his pad of paper. "Not weird at all. Oftentimes, in situations such as yours, it's alarming to feel free after years under someone's thumb."

"I just know my mother." I laugh without humor and drop my gaze to my lap. "She never lets anything go. She always has a plan. A way to come out the *winner*, whatever that looks like in her eyes." I lift my gaze and lock on Dr. Prince's steely irises. "My mother isn't the type to throw in the towel. Walking away isn't her style."

"What do you worry about most when it comes to her silence?"

I don't hesitate. "Shelly."

"Can you be more specific?"

Weeks of silence from my mother bother me more than her deranged display at the store. Since that night, I have agonized over Shelly's safety, and the baby. After days of deep breathing and mental reflection, I can't dislodge the twisted feeling in my gut. That the worst is yet to come.

"I worry Shelly will get caught in the cross fire. That my mother will do something unpredictable and Shelly will be hurt physically. And so will the baby."

"Do you believe your mother is capable of physically harming others?"

I shake my head and laugh again. "At this point, I believe my mother is capable of just about anything. She may not wield that weapon, but she is the one responsible."

Dr. Prince sips his water, then jots more notes on his pad of paper.

God, he has to have a ream's worth of paper in my file by now. Not sure if that is good or bad. Maybe a bit of both.

At least I have an outlet for my thoughts and emotions. A safe place to get everything off my chest. A safe person to help me make sense of it all so I can grow past it.

But how does this man sleep at night after hearing such stories?

"Has Shelly responded to your request for her to move in?"

Another item on the list that has me restless.

Months have passed since I asked Shelly to move in. I haven't pressed her for an answer and she hasn't hinted one way or the other. Yes, my asking was premature in our relationship and during a sensitive time. But I meant every word. Wanting Shelly in my home, at my side more often than not, hadn't been an irrational idea.

I still want us to live together. Still want a future with her.

I mean, she practically lives in my house already. With each passing week, more of Shelly's belongings find a new home in my house. Small touches of her invade each room.

Her clothes hang in the closet and fill the drawers of the dresser, adding softer tones and a splash of pink. The little bit of makeup she uses lies on the vanity in the master bathroom. Her sweet but earthy floral scent is now a permanent fixture in the bedroom. *Our bedroom.* Her favorite throw blanket, the one she had draped over the couch in her apartment, now lies over the back of my couch. *Our couch.* She even brought over the container she keeps on her kitchen counter with all her favorite teas.

Whether Shelly realizes it or not, we live together. It just isn't official.

She still pays rent on the space she doesn't frequent often. A space now filled with barely used furniture, slowly emptying cabinets and less of Shelly's personal possessions. In the past two months, she has added life to my home—*our home*—as her old apartment becomes a vacant shell.

"Not yet." I pick at my cuticles, then force myself to stop. "I want to ask again, but I don't want to upset her."

"Why do you think asking would upset her?"

Great question.

Anymore, I feel like I don't have answers to any questions. That I am just going through the motions most days. Trapping myself in the studio and mood painting. Impatiently waiting for Shelly to walk through the front door with a smile on her face and arms spread wide. To bring me further into her light.

"A lot has happened in such a short period. I often question if my intentions *are* out of impulse. I wonder if she thinks I'm only asking because she's pregnant."

"Are you?"

"Am I what?"

"Asking Shelly to move in because she's pregnant?"

Guess I shoved myself into this corner.

The baby isn't the chief reason I asked Shelly to move in. I asked because I love her. I asked because she matters more than anyone. Is the baby a secondary factor? One hundred percent, yes.

I don't doubt Shelly's ability to handle herself. She is incredible and strong and lovable. But she is not alone. Not in life or love, and definitely not when it comes to the baby. *Our baby.*

"No. With or without the pregnancy, I would've eventually asked her to live together. We just click. Can't put it into words, but there's something about her that I connect with on a base level." Long before we were together, Shelly had been my muse. When I saw her again after nearly a year, she reignited that spark inside me. "When we're together, it all just locks in place. Flows smoother."

With Shelly, life isn't a chore. I look forward to each day. To seeing her, holding her, being with her. She breathes life into my soul and elevates me in an incomprehensible way.

Dr. Prince glances down at his wrist. "Homework time," he says with a hint of laughter. The homework term has become a little joke with us. Don't know if he uses the same word with his other patients, but we laugh at it. Make it lighter and less about actual work.

"Ask Shelly again?" He nods and scribbles on the notepad. "Will do."

"Remember Devlyn, asking for what you want shouldn't be a chore. Don't treat it as such. It's normal to ask for what you want. The delivery is what makes all the difference." He rises from his seat and I follow suit. "Mull it over before you ask. Think of how you want the question to come across—out of a place of love and not need—and practice how you think that should sound. When it feels right, ask."

He makes the task sound so simple. Like taking a breath or painting what I feel. If only.

I don't fear Shelly. I don't fear the love she has for me, for us. What I *do* fear is rejection. Especially from her.

For years, I handed out rejection like Halloween candy. Hell, I rejected Shelly's and my own feelings for weeks. Shoved her away after the kiss on the exhibition night. Subjected us both to suffering so *she* wouldn't hurt *me* the way I'd been hurt before.

I'd still hurt, but at least it was my own doing. At least I was in control.

But now, I need to be brave. I need to step up and ask for what I want. I need to stow my insecurities and be a little selfish. Not just with Shelly, but also in life.

I love her. I want her. And I shouldn't feel shame in that.

She makes my life better, brighter. Wraps me in her arms and warmth and heart. Gives me more love than imaginable. Soothes the pain of the past without effort and replaces it with hope and passion and conviction. Shelly gives me purpose. A reason to wake up and keep going.

"Thanks, Doc." I extend my hand and we shake. "See you in a few days."

"Take care, Devlyn."

I exit the office and head for my car. Unlocking it, I slip behind the wheel and press the ignition. For a beat, I sit idle in the lot. Stare out the window at nothing in particular. Let my eyes lose focus and my mind drift off with the clouds.

Shelly is not Kelsey. Shelly won't reject me. She won't throw me away.

I repeat this again and again. Let the words seep into my bones. Chant them like a mantra until I believe them into existence.

The past will not repeat itself. Shelly is not *Kelsey.*

Shelly's hesitation to move in is because we have dated such a short time. But Dr. Prince says no one person determines when to take the next step in a relationship. There is no handbook for love. No guide for relationships. We set the pace. We say what comes next.

Our relationship cannot be compared to anyone else's relationship. Sure, we may have similar circumstances, but our relationship otherwise is different. Because *we* are different.

Over dinner, I will ask again. Ask Shelly to move in. I just need to find the right words. Pregnancy or not, Shelly doesn't need additional stress or pressure. But I'd like to know if she has given the idea any merit.

I won't force an answer from her lips, but I would like to know if there's a chance she will say yes.

Now… time to butter her up. Thankfully, I know the way to her heart.

eleven

. . .

Shelly

I JUST LANDED IN HEAVEN.

The moment I walk through Devlyn's front door, the delicious scent of bulgogi hits my nose. Savory with a hint of spice. My mouth waters instantly. *Damn, that smells good. Thank god.*

After the cheese incident, I worried what else would turn up my nose and have me queasy. I'd cry if my favorites made me cringe. To date, cheese and cabbage are the only items on the naughty list. Everything else has been ten times better.

I toss my purse on the chair in the sitting room and toe off my shoes. Winding my way through the house, I slow my pace as I approach the living room. Rounding the corner, I spot Devlyn with his back to me. He removes boxes and tubs from a brown bag and sets them on the table. And for a moment, I stand silently in place and watch him move around the room. Watch him organize dinner and set up the room for a perfect date night in.

The bag crinkles as he flattens it. Then he spins around and spots me at the edge of the room. A small smile pushes up his cheeks and I melt at the sight.

"Didn't hear you come in." He saunters across the room, steps into my space, wraps his arms around my waist and crushes my lips with his.

Damn.

Every day should be this incredible. Every day *can* be this incredible. If I let it be.

When he breaks the kiss, I peer up at him. Stare at the darker shade of green rimming his glass-green irises. Swallow at the smolder in his gaze. At the love this man gives only to me.

Damn, I mentally repeat.

"Wasn't purposely quiet," I say. "Just saw you setting up dinner and didn't want to interrupt." I kiss the tip of his chin. "Smells so good."

He kisses the tip of my nose as he unravels his arms. "Sit. I was going for drinks." Before I offer to help, he steps around me and heads for the kitchen.

A few shifts on the floor pillow later, Devlyn walks back in with water and hot tea. Setting them on the table, he situates himself next to me between the couch and table on the floor. We tear open disposable chopsticks and break the sticks apart. And as Devlyn hits play on the remote, I dive into the bulgogi.

An unladylike moan exits my lips and Devlyn laughs.

"Good?"

"So damn good." I savor the bite. Let the umami roll over my tongue. "I'll admit, I was worried." His brows pinch at the middle. "That I wouldn't be able to enjoy it. After the whole cheese thing, I wondered what other foods would gross me out."

"And?"

I shrug. "Just the cheese." I clamp down on another piece of beef, then point my loaded chopsticks at him. "Actually, most of the dairy has made me queasy."

"At least you didn't eat or drink a lot before."

"True." I pop the beef in my mouth and close my eyes. *Thank you*, I say to the pregnancy gods. At least I still have this.

The rest of dinner goes by in quiet bliss as we watch *Dark*. This show really swirls my mind into a blur. But in a good way. Romance is my bread and butter, but this multilayered mystery is a close competitor.

When the boxes empty, we pause the show, take the trash to the kitchen, and grab dessert. Curled up on the couch, I lay my head on Devlyn's shoulder while I spoon ice cream into my mouth.

"Can I ask you something?" Devlyn asks as the end credits flit across the screen.

"You know you can." I wrap my hands around his bicep.

Three breaths pass before his voice fills the room again, so soft and quiet I almost don't hear him. "Is there a reason you haven't agreed to move in?"

Feels like a lifetime has passed since Devlyn asked me to move in with him. I'd told him I needed to think about it. He granted me the time and I have mulled it over, but I have yet to answer him. Is it too early to blame that on pregnancy brain?

I lift my head and rest my chin on his shoulder before kissing it and sitting up straighter. Glance into his glassy, soulful eyes. Eyes that question if I love him enough to want this. To be with him full time. To share the same space as him. To cohabitate.

And the uncertainty in his head and heart, that is on me. Too many days have passed since he asked. Too many days have passed without me answering. God, his mind must be in overdrive. Crazy with assumptions.

How unfair of me to make him wait, considering I decided not long after he asked. I assumed my actions made my answer evident. But Devlyn needs to hear the words. With all the hurt in his past, he needs to hear the answers. When it comes to Devlyn, I should never assume.

"It's not that I don't want to move in."

He shifts in his seat to face me more easily. Arm resting on the back of the couch, his fingers toy with the loose strands of my hair. Twirl and lightly tug. "Then what's holding you back?" His knuckles graze the angle of my jaw and I lean into his touch. Let my eyes fall shut and my body relax. "So beautiful," he whispers.

The backs of my eyes sting as I swallow down his words. God, I love this man. This beautifully broken man.

"I'm scared," I say, my eyes still closed. "I'm scared to give in." Slowly, I open my eyes. "Scared to fall harder and lose you."

His other hand cups my cheek, his thumb stroking

beneath my lashes. "You'll never lose me, Shelly. Never."

"How can you be so sure?" I fist the hem of my shirt and tug it over my swelling belly. "What if having the baby puts a wedge between us? What if I move in and things become too much? Right now, everything is new and happy. But what if that changes when the baby comes?"

Leaning forward, Devlyn kisses my forehead. His lips linger for three breaths before he resumes his previous position. Warmth spreads from the spot he kissed to my heart. I take a deep breath and hold his vibrant greens.

"I don't doubt things will change when the baby comes." His fingers go back to the loose strands of my hair. "But we control how they change. Yes, the baby will throw a glitch into the life we currently know, but we have the ability to shape how we want the future."

Since Devlyn started therapy, we haven't had many serious, in-depth conversations. I don't ask how his sessions go. I don't mention his mother or parents. Not from lack of curiosity, but more because I don't want to invade that area of his privacy. I don't want to rehash possibly upsetting moments. More than anything, I want to respect his boundaries.

With unparalleled patience, I wait for him to broach the heavy subjects. Wait for him to spark those weighted conversations. Because they aren't mine to bring up. They aren't my stories to tell when ready.

The strength in his words as we talk about our future tells me therapy has been beneficial. Has given him the opportunity to look at life through a new lens. With new perspective. With a positive outlook.

"I just don't want you to grow tired of me," I huff out. "Then we're both stuck in a crazy situation." I lift my hand to his jaw and trace my finger to his chin before letting it fall away. "Don't want you to feel pressured to keep me around if something changes."

"One… not going to happen." I open my mouth to rebut and he holds up a hand to stop me. "Yes, all couples experience the bad. Moments when they don't get along. It's inevitable." He takes my hand, brings it to his lips, and kisses each knuckle in turn. "But I'll never wish you away, Shelly Reed. All of my good days involve you."

He takes a deep breath and I don't interrupt. "Shelly, you are the only shining light in my life. My life preserver. The sunshine after the rain. The one person I can count on. No matter how shitty my day has been, no matter how poorly I behave, all the bad vanishes because I have you. And I realize how unhealthy and codependent that sounds. It's something I've been working on with Dr. Prince." He closes his eyes briefly. "But I also know those deep, deep feelings are genuine. They aren't misguided sentiments from a broken boy."

He presses the heel of his palm to the center of his chest. "You are here. Rooted so deep." His eyes glaze over. "I think you were here long before either of us knew. Because damn, I feel so much for you. So damn much. At times, I question my own sanity, my own mental health. But every time I do, I come up with the same result."

"What's that?" I whisper-ask.

His eyes roll closed for one, two, three beats. "That I've never loved anyone the way I love you. At times, the depth of that loves scares the shit out of me. Because I've only truly loved one other and that ended in devastation." He shakes his head as light laughter leaves his lips. "I fought this" —he gestures between us with his hand— "for so long. Tried to keep you in the friend zone. But fate knew better and I caved." He leans in and presses a chaste kiss to my lips. "Loving you was inevitable, Shelly Reed. And I will keep you forever, if you let me."

The backs of my eyes burn as tears blur my vision and emotion clogs my throat. I don't know what to say. How to react. What to do after Devlyn just spilled his whole heart at my feet.

Every truth that left his lips wrapped itself around my heart and hugged me fiercely. I will keep those truths tucked safely in my heart for the rest of my life. His sacred, vulnerable truths. His love. Him.

Concerned as I've been, I knew weeks ago I would say yes to him. I will always say yes. Not to please Devlyn, but because he will never intentionally put me in an uncomfortable situation. He will never intentionally hurt me.

More than any other person, I know Devlyn. Know his heart. Know his softness and the pieces he keeps hidden from the rest of the world. His softness is one of my favorite parts. A part he reserves only for me.

"Yes."

His eyes narrow as they study my expression, flit

over the angles of my nose and jaw, home in on my eyes and lips. "Yes?" A layer of uncertainty laces his voice.

"I'll move in," I whisper, the words floating softly from my lips to his ears.

The moment they hit, the moment they truly sink in, his whole body shifts. Lights up. Comes alive.

His hands frame my face, thumbs brush my cheeks. Inch by inch, he eviscerates the space between us. Vivid green irises hold my sparkly dark blues. His breath warm on my lips.

I fist the cotton of his shirt at the heart and tug him forward until our lips meet in the middle. Soft and warm, Devlyn kisses me with unprecedented tenderness. Once, twice, his lips sweep over mine reverently. Then his tongue paints my bottom lip and I gasp. Invite him in. Taste him on my tongue. Melt into him.

Crawling into his lap, we shift until his back presses against the cushions and I straddle his hips. His fingers curl at my waist as mine lace behind his neck. The kiss deepens as his hands shift and trail up my spine beneath my shirt. My fingers finding their way into his long, thick strands.

"Love you, Shelly." His lips kiss along my jaw, down the column of my neck, across my collarbone.

I curl my fingers in his hair, scrape my nails over his scalp. "Love you, Dev."

Over the next several hours, until the faint light of dawn filters through the windows, we love each other. With lips and fingers. Light touches and whispered words. Occasional scratches and bite marks. Skin on sweat-slicked skin. Linked and bonded through the most pivotal, base connection. The most real and raw and undeniable connection. His body and mine.

Until my heart no longer beats, until my lungs no longer fill with air, I will love this man. Will share my heart with him. Will let him hold it close to his own. Let him care for me—for us—in a way no one else ever will.

Because Devlyn isn't just a boyfriend. He isn't just the father of the baby growing in my womb. This man is my heart. This man is my soul. More than anything, this man is my life. Where I am meant to be. In his arms, every day of forever.

twelve

. . .

Devlyn

"Put that down," I shout across the living room of Shelly's apartment. She narrows her eyes. "Please," I say a bit softer. "You shouldn't be lifting anything that heavy."

Bending at the knees, Shelly sets the box on the floor and I breathe easier. "It's not even heavy." She rests fists on her hips. "Maybe ten pounds. Knickknacks from the kitchen junk drawer and the stuff I had on the fridge." Her eyes drop to said box. "Heck, it's probably not even five pounds."

Last week, Shelly had a checkup and the doctor said all looked great with the baby. We got our first baby picture with the ultrasound. Dr. Webster said the baby is roughly the size of a sweet potato, which I thought was odd as a visual reference but it works.

She asked if we wanted to know the gender of the baby. We declined, opting for the surprise.

During that same visit, Dr. Webster noted Shelly's

elevated blood pressure and ordered she take it easy. Rest as much as possible. Not strain herself or lift anything too heavy.

Packing up her apartment and moving her into the house have made this directive difficult.

Shelly spoke with her landlord at the start of the week and since she only has two months left on her lease, they agreed to let her break it. Granted, she won't get her deposit back, but the money doesn't concern me more than her well-being.

One step forward, then another, I hold her at arm's length. "This sucks, I get it. But you heard what Dr. Webster said. You need to take it easy. Pack up the boxes and I'll carry them."

Her eyes fall shut as she takes a deep breath and sighs. "Ugh. I hate this." She shakes her head. "Feels like I'm helpless. Incapable."

I wrap my arms around her waist and draw her close. Press my lips to her cheek. "You aren't and you know it. Pregnancy won't last forever. We're almost halfway there." I kiss her other cheek. "It's a big adjustment, but if it keeps you both safe, then it's what matters most."

Warm arms tighten their hold on my waist. "I know." She kisses my neck, then takes a step back. "I'll go work on filling the boxes in the bedroom."

Hours pass as Shelly and I fill boxes with clothes and books, dishes and small appliances. I carry them out, one by one, and load them in my car or hers. When not an inch of empty space is visible in either of our cars, we lock up the apartment and drive across town to the house.

We park in the driveway and I start unloading both our cars. Pile the boxes in the empty space near the sliding glass doors. Do my best to separate the box stacks by room to make the next step less stressful. When all the boxes are in the house, I help unpack, but let Shelly place her things where she'd like them.

"Is everyone getting together tomorrow?"

Weeks have passed since we last hung out with her friends. Not because we haven't wanted to; life has just been busy for us all.

"Yeah. Cora messaged earlier and asked if we'd be there."

I peel newspaper off a plate and hand it to her. "Did you answer?"

Shelly spent so much time with her friends before our relationship blossomed. Now, she sees them less often. Not because of our relationship and the pregnancy, thank goodness. I'd be upset if I were the reason. Between love and marriage and babies, everyone else's lives have changed too. Both Cora and Autumn have newborns. Cora and Gavin, as well as Micah and Peyton, are still in the honeymoon phase.

She nods. "Mm-hmm. Told her we'd bring potato salad." Her eyes find mine. "Hope that's okay."

I shrug. "Potato salad's fine. Kind of prefer macaroni salad, but it's cool."

She knocks my arm with her shoulder. "I meant me responding without checking with you, not the potato salad." A soft chuckle leaves her lips and I love hearing the gentle laughter.

Setting the dish in my hand down, I take her chin in my fingers and press a kiss to her lips. "More than okay. It'll be nice to see everyone."

Sunshine lights her face in the form of a smile and I question the last time I saw her so bright. It's been too long.

Right here, right now, I vow to make Shelly smile more often. Recent worries had stolen her smiles. Worry over herself, the baby, the move. I need to be better. Do better. Take some of that stress off her shoulders. Carry the burden and help her relax.

I flatten the empty boxes and take them to the recycling bin. Shelly and I cook dinner, then settle in front of the television to eat. When the episode ends, I carry our dishes to the kitchen and tidy up.

Back in the living room, Shelly sits curled in the corner of the couch with a book. I pad across the room, take her book, mark the page, and set it on the table. Slip my hand around hers, help her stand, then escort her up the stairs to my studio.

"What're you up to?" she asks, brow arched.

When we reach the landing, I spin around to face her and walk backward until we reach the middle of the room. I frame her face in my hands and crush my lips to hers. She fists my shirt at either hip and draws me in until no space exists between us. It is just her and me and our personal bubble of bliss.

Our tongues tangle. Hands skim arms and waists. I

graze the length of her spine as she kneads the sides of my neck. Fingers fist hair and tug. The kiss morphing from gentle to hungry in seconds. And when she tips her head back and gasps, I kiss my way down her neck and drag my tongue along her collarbone.

"I want to paint you," I say against the hollow of her throat. "But not like before."

Her fingers tighten in my hair and pull my lips from her skin. "How?"

I nip at her chin. "On canvas. Just you." I tug at the bottom hem of her shirt and lift up. My fingers skim down her sternum, over the center of her bra, over her belly that is slowly swelling with our child. "No barriers."

"Devlyn, I…"

"Abstract," I answer quickly. "Or not. I leave it up to you." My palm flattens on her lower abdomen and I splay my fingers. "So beautiful." I drop to my knees, my eyes peering up at Shelly as my lips press to the skin beneath her navel. "Please."

Gentle fingers comb through my unruly hair as she holds my gaze. Neither of us says a word for several heartbeats. And then her head slowly moves up and down.

"Okay," she whispers into our bubble. "You can paint me." She takes a deep breath. "However you're inspired to."

Once again, this woman astounds. Her love and bravery and confidence. Without much negotiation, she handed over an incomparable level of trust. Laid it in my hands, certain I would keep it, and her, safe. Something I will never abuse or take for granted.

I shift a few things around in the studio, run downstairs to grab several pillows and blankets, and set up a comfortable space for her to lie. As she disrobes, I prop a blank canvas on the easel and shift its position, grab my paints and brushes, and take a seat on my stool.

Shelly lies down on the pillows and shifts until she finds a comfortable position on her side.

"If you need a break," I say, "just tell me. It's late, so I promise not to keep us up here long."

Shelly folds a pillow in half and stuffs it between her head and arm. "How long will the painting take?"

My head teeters left and right. "Several hours." I lick my lips and swallow as my eyes trail over her curves. Take in her creamy, bare skin. "If we're up here daily, a couple hours each time, maybe two weeks. Or less." I trace a finger over my upper lip. "Also depends on how I paint you. The heavier the details, the longer it'll take."

She inhales deeply and swallows on the exhale. "Okay." Then she closes her eyes and her entire frame relaxes. Not a hint of resistance or timidity dons her expression.

Damn, she is beautiful. Too beautiful.

Over the next four hours, my eyes flit between Shelly and the canvas. The bristles of my brushes dip in various shades of pigment as I take in the bow of her lips, the slope of her nose, the swell of her breasts and arch of her hip. Blending. Shaping. Contouring. One stroke at a time, I bring this incredible woman to life on canvas in an unfamiliar way.

Abstract art has never been my style. I appreciate the style, but feel odd painting it. As if I'm misrepresenting the subject. Much of my art resembles the muse. Clean lines and sharp detail. When you study the piece, you see my muse.

With this, though…

Shelly bares herself to me fully, and not just her flesh. Just out of reach, she exposes every piece of herself and grants me permission to portray her beauty and vulnerability in my artwork. Allows me the opportunity to uncover an unseen layer of her charm and magnificence. Paint her nude heart and impassioned aura.

I have no plans for anyone else to see this painting. This piece is personal. The most intimate art I will create.

But accidents happen. And although I'd never intentionally betray Shelly or her trust, I can't take the risk.

So this piece will be as complex and stunning as the woman herself.

Splashes of color in a display unlike any other. Short, blotchy strokes of my brush on the canvas. Bursts of bright pigment to offset the occasional shadows.

And when she and I see it, we will know. We will see what no one else sees. We will remember the nights and hours we spent in this studio. The way her breaths evened out as she fell asleep. The way I bit the end of my brush as I looked from her to the canvas, then smiled.

We will remember, and that is all that matters.

Her love. My love. Us.

I set my brush down and open my mouth to call it a night, but snap it shut when I see her closed eyes. Her slightly parted lips. Hear her soft snores as her chest rises and falls steadily.

On and off during the session, her eyes drifted closed, but her body never fully relaxed. Not like it is now.

Quietly, I clean up what I need to. Then I tiptoe over to where she sleeps, wrap her body in the blanket, and scoop her up into my arms. Halfway down the stairs, her eyes flutter open and she curls into my chest.

"Sorry I fell asleep," she mumbles into my neck.

I press a kiss to her forehead and hug her closer. "Sleep, my Andromeda. Sleep."

In the bedroom, I lay her on the bed, but she gets up and shuffles toward the bathroom. After a moment to herself, she tugs one of my shirts over her head and slips on a pair of boy shorts. We crawl under the covers and I press my front to her back, slipping one arm under her pillow and laying the other over her belly.

"Love you," she whispers into the darkness as she scoots closer.

I kiss her hair. "Love you."

She drifts back to sleep within seconds. For hour-long minutes, I lie awake and listen to her soft snores. Stroke my fingers over her belly, over our baby, and I send a thank you to the universe.

Thank you for bringing this brave, strong woman into my

life. Thank you for gifting me with her heart. Thank you for giving me the chance to find love, real love, with her.

As long as there is breath in my lungs and blood in my veins, I will protect her, her heart and our baby. I will love them. Unconditionally and without fear. Always.

After one last kiss to her hair, I drift off to sleep. My entire world wrapped in my arms.

thirteen

. . .

Shelly

Something isn't right.

I take a deep breath. Then another. And another.

My heart pounds viciously in my chest. The beat hard and heavy. An uncomfortable throb beneath my sternum.

I close my eyes and try to calm the worry flooding my thoughts. Breathe deeply and picture my heart settling.

Deep breaths. Slow and steady. In through the nose. Out through the mouth.

Minutes pass and the bang, bang, banging of my heart settles a fraction. I kick my feet out from beneath the blanket and welcome the cool air. After a few more deep breaths, my throbbing heart calms further.

Devlyn shifts behind me, his fingers tracing small lines over my belly.

"Morning," he says with a rasp I've grown to love more each time I hear it.

"Morning."

His lips trail kisses down the side of my neck and along the ridge of my shoulder. His hand glides over my belly and up my body until he palms my breast. I arch my back and fill his hand further.

Rolling onto my back, I bring my lips to his. Weave my fingers in his dark, wayward strands. My heart beats a brutal rhythm, but it's nothing like the pounding from minutes ago. This rhythm is one I know, one I feel head to toe.

I peel my shirt off and strip out of my panties as Devlyn shoves his briefs down and tosses them to the floor. His lips dance over each collarbone, my sternum and breasts, down my midline until he lands beneath my navel. For a beat, he stares at my belly and caresses it with such delicacy. He kisses the slight swell, then lifts his gaze.

Tears brim his green eyes and it steals my breath. Freezes me on the spot. Thickens an emotional ball in my throat.

"Love you, Shell."

My eyes sting as I look down at him, as I stroke his cheek with my knuckles. "Love you, Dev."

His head dips beneath the sheet as his palms trail up the sides of my torso. His tongue paints the flesh between my thighs. Flicks my clit and licks up my center. Consumes me while his fingers toy with my nipples until I writhe beneath his talented tongue.

With my orgasm on his tongue and lips, he kisses his way up my body. Positions himself in the cradle of my hips. Crashes his lips to mine and kisses me fiercely.

Rocks his hips forward and fills me fully. Our shared gasps echo off the walls.

And then our eyes lock. For a beat, we simply breathe each other in. Connect in the most primal way. He kisses me once, twice, three times before sucking my bottom lip between his. The simmering fire in his green irises burns brighter. Hotter. Fire that ignites every inch of my soul. Fire that arouses and stokes my love for this man.

Our bodies move in a synchronized rhythm. An incomparable rhythm. A rhythm that is only ours.

My legs hug his waist, ankles lock at his lower back. As he thrusts forward, my heels dig into his muscled glutes and drive him deeper. Harder. With each rock of his hips, I climb back up that peak. With each stroke of his bare cock, I cry out for more.

His hand drifts down the curve of my breast, my waist, my hip, then dips between us. Slowly, his thumb paints small circles over my clit.

My jaw slackens as my breaths stutter from my lips. One delicious stroke after another, he summons my orgasm from somewhere deep. His tongue traces my lower lip. Teeth nip my chin and along my jaw. He sucks my earlobe between his lips. Kisses and nibbles down the column of my throat. Wraps his lips around the flesh at my shoulder and sucks. Bites. Ravages. Hard and fast and desperate.

And it's all too much.

A harsh growl spills from my lips as heat spreads up my chest, over my breasts and throat before hitting my cheeks. My legs shake as my body hugs Devlyn everywhere. And with one more rock of his hips, his orgasm fills me.

Sweat slicks our skin as our heavy breaths float through the room. His pulse pounds in his chest to the same beat as my own. My fingers trail up and down the sides of his spine before threading in his hair.

His lips kiss the spot on my shoulder where he sank his teeth in and imprinted my skin. One kiss at a time, he works his way to my lips. Our tongues twist and tangle and taste. Say I love you in ways our voices never will.

I will never get enough of his kisses. Never get enough of him.

He breaks the kiss and lifts slightly, bracketing me with his forearms. His fingers toy with strands of my hair as his greens lock onto my blues. One inhale after another, he breathes me in while I do the same.

I hadn't anticipated how emotional sex would be. How all-consuming the act would feel. Sure, I expected it to be more than just a physical act—hence why I waited—but I never imagined feeling so much, so deeply, all at once.

With Devlyn, sex isn't just something that happens with genitalia and lips and hands. It isn't just something we do to reach physical euphoria. We make love with our bodies and hearts and souls. Connect on a deeper, more profound level. Give in to our deepest desires and share a piece of ourselves no one else will have.

Until him, I never understood the bond Cora and Gavin shared. Couldn't grasp the devotion Jonas and

Autumn felt. Was confounded by Micah and Peyton's love after such a rocky history. And although I'd read countless romance novels, the concept of sex being more than a physical act left me baffled.

But I get it now. I understand.

Sex is more than a means to an end with Devlyn. I won't deny loving the bliss of orgasm. Surely, Devlyn wouldn't either. But it's more than that.

It's the way his fingers caress my body. The way his breath heats my skin. The way he whispers in my ear and tells me he loves me. More than that, it's how his eyes lock with mine as our bodies come together. How his gaze penetrates deeper and captures my soul. Pumps the fist-sized organ in my chest and floods my veins with unconditional love.

Devlyn owns my heart, is the protector of my soul, and I wouldn't want it any other way.

I comb my fingers through his damp strands and lift off the pillow to kiss him.

"Hungry?" he asks and I nod. "Take your time getting up. I'll make breakfast." He rocks back and I immediately miss the weight of him.

He kisses my forehead, then rises from the bed and grabs a pair of sweatpants. I stare after him without shame. Push up on my elbows and ogle his body as he slips on the pants. Watch his every movement as he pads across the room. Salivate as his muscles bunch and flex with each step. Clamp my thighs together as he ruffles his hair with his fingers. Lick and bite my bottom lip as a smile kicks up the corner of his lips.

He disappears into the bathroom to clean up and

brush his teeth. I fall back onto the mattress, close my eyes, and breathe in the moment. Breathe in the scent of him and sex and love.

After a beat, he reappears and presses another kiss to my forehead. "Any requests?"

Countless breakfast foods flit through my head, but one continues to circle back. "French toast, please."

"Powdered sugar?"

"Is that a serious question?"

He chuckles. "Powdered sugar it is. Bacon or sausage?"

"Bacon. Oh, and the leftover eggs from dipping the French toast, add extra cinnamon."

Walking out of the bedroom backward, he blows me a kiss. "Extra cinnamon. Check."

Pans and bowls clang outside the bedroom as I slowly slip out from under the covers. As I enter the bathroom, my pulse mimics the same turbulent beating from earlier. My heart feels bigger, heavier, almost painful. Every other beat, I gasp for air, but it doesn't fill my lungs. Not fully.

I plop down on the toilet, grip my knees, and close my eyes. Bend at the waist and drop my head. Inhale deeply and hold it until my lungs burn.

Several breaths pass before my pulse returns to normal and the pain in my chest subsides. Slowly, I sit up and open my eyes. Rub the center of my chest with the heel of my palm. The backs of my eyes sting as worry seeps in.

What is happening? Maybe this is a normal side effect of pregnancy. Should ask Cora and Autumn tonight.

After I use the toilet, brush my teeth, and untangle the bird's nest on top of my head, I tug on one of Devlyn's T-shirts and a pair of sleep pants.

The scent of maple and cinnamon and butter fills my nose as I head for the kitchen. The worry from minutes ago fades to the background. My stomach growls and I press a hand to the beast, muttering, "Almost time."

Before long, Devlyn piles two thick slices of French toast, scrambled eggs, several strips of bacon, and mixed fresh berries on plates. He dusts the French toast with powdered sugar, then fills glasses with orange juice. He delivers it all to the dining room table and waves me off when I try to help.

I pour a generous helping of real maple syrup—not that sugary brown goop—and dive in, moaning around my fork. Devlyn smiles in satisfaction as he lifts scrambled eggs to his lips.

"Maybe we should have breakfast for all the meals," he suggests.

Holding up a finger, I mumble around the bite. "I'd vote yes, but there're too many other good things to eat."

His smile widens. "True, but breakfast seems to be your favorite."

It is definitely a top contender. I point my fork at Devlyn. "Anything you make is my favorite."

A brow arches on his handsome face. "I'll have to remember that."

Why do I feel like I just walked myself into a corner? *Because you did*. Oh well, too late now.

~

We park at Jonas and Autumn's house just before seven. Two cars other than theirs are here—Gavin's SUV and Micah's truck. I scoop up the bag on the floorboard between my feet and Devlyn reaches for it.

"No." I hold it just out of reach. "I know I shouldn't be lifting anything heavy, but this is like three pounds max. It's freaking side salads."

"Shell..." Devlyn looks out the windshield and sighs. "Just trying to help," he mumbles.

My hand rests on his forearm as I wait for his eyes to meet mine. "I know you are and I love you for that." I take his hand in mine, lift it to my lips, and kiss the top. "But I'm not helpless. I can still do some things myself. Yes, I need to be cautious. But that doesn't mean I stop living." Holding up the bag, I say, "I got this." He nods as his lips fumble between his teeth. "And if I need help, I promise to ask."

"It's just..." He breathes heavily. "I worry."

I graze his cheek with my fingertips and his eyes close briefly. "Me too. But we're doing everything according to plan." I lean in and press my lips to his. Let the warmth of his touch and breath comfort me. "For now, let's try not to worry. Let's try to not stress ourselves over the what-ifs."

For a moment, we just stare at each other. Neither of us says a word. Then subtly, he nods. "I'll try."

We amble to the door, hand in hand, and are greeted by Clementine and Spartan first. Hugs are exchanged with everyone and it isn't long before I get pulled away by Cora and Autumn. Clementine watches over Clara and Ryker while we catch up for a few.

Two songs later, the house is bustling with all of our friends.

Laughter floats through the room and outside on the back patio. Hickory and the scent of grilled meats and shish kebabbed vegetables fill the air. Old-school rock plays from speakers mounted on the back of the house while fire lights tiki torches around the yard.

Devlyn chats with some of the guys while I sit with Cora and Autumn on the lounger.

The more Devlyn and I join everyone on Sundays, the more he steps out of his shell. The more he smiles and laughs and comes alive. Opens up a little more. This family… we balance in ways genetic families don't. We provide love and advice and comfort. We avoid judgment and hurt.

I love how easily Devlyn fits in our circle. How everyone accepted him without hesitation. He needed us as much as we needed him. And damn am I lucky that I get to call him mine.

Zoning out, I stare at the fire. Think back to this morning and the vicious pounding in my chest. Take a deep breath and blink away the fog. "Can I ask you guys something?" I ask Cora and Autumn.

"Always," Cora says as Autumn answers, "Of course."

"It's a pregnancy question." I toy with the bottom hem of my shirt. "I haven't said anything to Devlyn because I don't want him to freak out. Especially if it's a normal thing."

When I don't continue, Cora lays her hand over mine in my lap. "Shell, what is it?"

"A couple times now, I've had this heavy feeling in my chest." I press my palm to my heart. "Like a strange heartbeat. It doesn't *hurt*, per se, but it makes me breathless." I look to Cora then Autumn. "Did either of you have that?"

The twist in my belly sinks deep when both of them shake their head.

Not good.

"No two pregnancies are the same," Autumn says. "Clementine was a wild child in the womb and Ryker just chilled for the most part. But I never had chest pains." She winces. "Probably a good idea to talk with your doctor."

"I'll second that," Cora adds. "Clara was a little gymnast during the last trimester, and I had the occasional bout of heartburn, but nothing like what you're describing."

Great. This is what I feared. This is why I also haven't said anything to Devlyn yet.

As it is, he doesn't want me to do anything besides relax. Which, in theory, is nice, but spending every day on the couch with my feet up isn't realistic. I have a business to run, and eventually take over. There is so much to prepare for with the baby. Classes to attend. New mother skills to learn. Labor breathing and learning how to breastfeed.

The pounding in my chest kicks in and I press the heel of my palm to my sternum as I inhale deeply.

Cora leans closer and whispers in my ear, "Is it

happening now?" I nod. "What were you just thinking about? Right before it happened."

I close my eyes and pinch them tightly. Breathe through the pain in my chest. "Everything that's to come. With the pregnancy, motherhood." My eyes open and I glance up at my best friend. "The shop. How this baby changes everything I thought I knew. How it disrupts so many lives, not just mine."

Cora wraps an arm around my shoulders and pulls me into her side. Autumn scoots closer and leans her weight into my other side. On a sigh, I absorb their comfort. Let it fill the cracks of doubt. Let it ease my worry about the future and motherhood and new responsibilities.

"First of all, I felt everything you're feeling," Cora admits. "Gavin and I hadn't been back together long before we got pregnant." She shifts to look me square in the eye, her gaze never more serious. "I was scared, Shell. Scared we weren't ready. Scared I'd lose him again. Scared we wouldn't be *us* with a baby." The corners of her mouth tip up in a small, soft smile. "But my fear was for nothing. Just past pain haunting my present."

"How did you let go of the fear?"

She tips her head to the side. "It never fades. Not fully. But it lessens with each passing day. With each assurance that I'm not in this parenting gig alone." She looks across the patio. Her eyes land on Gavin, baby Clara cradled in his arms while he chats with a few of the guys. Jonas is there too, Ryker bundled in a blanket and snug against his chest. They talk and joke and laugh, all while doing the dad thing. "You aren't doing this alone, Shell."

"Not for a second," Autumn adds. "After everything with Clementine's father, I worried about Jonas's reaction to the pregnancy." She lays a hand on mine. "But then I reminded myself that Jonas is a different man. He walked through hell alongside me as I fought for Clementine, for our livelihood."

"Jonas has a heart of gold," I tell her.

Her eyes find his across the patio and his entire frame lights up. "That he does." Then she shifts in her seat to face me more. "What about Devlyn? How's his heart?"

God, what a loaded question. Not one I can answer simply. Not one I can answer fully without sharing secrets he isn't ready for the world to know.

"When it comes to me, to us, he has the biggest heart."

Cora's brows scrunch together. "Why do I feel like there's more to the story?"

Because there is. Because Devlyn has demons to face, to conquer, to let go. "There is more." I look to Cora, then to Autumn, before my eyes land on Devlyn, a brilliant, genuine smile on his lips. "But his story isn't mine to tell. All I will say is he came from a past none of us can comprehend. Not fully. But he's working on it. For me, for us, for the baby."

Cora rubs small circles on my shoulder. "It's silly, but I have to ask."

"What?"

"You're safe, right?" If I thought she looked serious

minutes ago, I was dead wrong. My best friend has never been more somber than she is now. "Please tell me you are."

I take her free hand and Autumn's in both of mine. My eyes darting between the two of them. "I swear to you, I am safe. And if that ever changes—for any of us—we tell each other." They both nod. "No matter what."

"No matter what," they say in unison.

After a squeeze of my hand, Cora releases mine from her grasp. "Enough of the heavy talk." Autumn nods in agreement. "Please call your doctor in the morning." She points a finger at me and narrows her eyes like a stern mother. "And tell Devlyn. I understand you not wanting to worry him, especially if it's nothing, but he deserves to know. This is his baby too."

I love and hate that she is right. But this is why I talk with my best friends. They look at my situation from a different angle, with a fresh perspective.

"I will. Promise."

The last hour at Jonas and Autumn's house goes by a bit lighter. Devlyn curls me into his side as we sit by the fire bowl and chat with our friends. By the time we exchange hugs and goodnights, I breathe easier.

Tomorrow, I will call Dr. Webster and set an appointment. Tomorrow, I will tell Devlyn what I felt earlier. Tell him about the pain in my chest. That is what partners in committed relationships do; we share everything. No matter the outcome.

fourteen

. . .

Devlyn

My phone rings on the drafting table, inches from where I'm sketching a new piece. A drawing requested by a new client. A portrait of the woman's grandchildren, their adorable smiles—one of which is missing a front tooth—glowing in the photo she sent.

I set my pencil down and swipe my phone off the table to see Shelly's name on the screen. I tap the green phone icon and smile as I say, "Hello."

"Hi," she replies, her voice a breath over a whisper. "Do you have a minute?"

My muscles tense up at her question. Why would she ask that? Of the two of us, my schedule is nothing but flexible. "Of course. What's wrong?"

"I, uh..." She goes quiet, but I still hear noises in the background. Then she exhales audibly. "I had to set a new doctor's appointment with Dr. Webster."

Metal scrapes wood as I rise from my stool. My vision blurs and stomach twists as my mind conjures up countless reasons why Shelly would need to see Dr.

Webster sooner than her next appointment. Unable to be still, I pace the length of the room. Take a deep breath and inhale the scents of the studio. Allow the earthy smells to ground me as I grow more frantic with each breath.

"Why?"

"I, uh…"

Shelly goes quiet again. I picture her fidgeting with her apron strings as she works up the nerve to answer. Why is she so hesitant? Did something happen to her? Is the baby okay? The longer she remains silent, the longer my list of worse-case scenarios gets.

After what feels like a week, she speaks again. "I've been having pains," she says a breath above a whisper.

As I reach the landing for the stairs, instead of spinning around to pace the room again, I take the stairs two at a time. Reach the bottom floor before the next words leave my lips. "What kind of pains? Is it the baby?"

I dash to the bedroom, put the phone on speaker and strip out of my clothes. I grab a clean pair of jeans and a fresh shirt, slipping them on as she talks.

"No. I don't know. I-I don't think so." Her voice stutters. "It's in my chest, near my heart."

My hands freeze as I slip on socks. *Her heart. No. No, no, no.* I take a deep breath and beg my mind to not travel down the road of misdiagnoses. Not to think of things such as heart failure or angina or embolisms. Shelly is too young for heart problems, isn't she? *Stay calm. You can't help her if you're freaking the fuck out.*

"When is your appointment?" My voice cracks at the end.

"Today at four."

"I'll pick you up."

"Dev, no." She huffs on the other end as I pick up the phone and take it off speaker. "My car is here. I'll meet you there."

My eyes close and I clamp them tightly. Let the discomfort distract me momentarily. Tell myself to take another breath and not force my insistence upon her. We don't know what the problem is. It could be something minor. Completely normal. I need to let her make decisions. I need to not steal her choices like my mother did for me.

Unless the doctor says otherwise.

"Okay, I'll be there." I wander out of the bedroom and into the kitchen. Stare blankly at the counters and cabinets and appliances, unsure what to do next. "Do you need anything until then?"

The clock on the stove reads just after two. I inhale deeply and twist the phone up on the exhale. Close my eyes and focus on what I *can* control. In less than two hours, I will see her. In less than two hours, we will figure out why she is having chest pains. *Shelly will be okay. The baby will be okay.*

"No, thank you," she says softly, a smile in her voice.

"Take it easy until you leave. Please." I don't care if I come across as desperate. I *am* desperate.

She chuckles. "I will. Elizabeth won't let me do

anything except arrange. Not even paperwork. She says it'll stress me out too much."

Light laughter spills from my lips, although I feel anything but weightless. *Thank you, Elizabeth.* "I need to send that woman a fruit basket or something. Gift her art for her birthday."

"She won't say no."

"I love you, Shell," I say, my tone more somber. "So much."

"Love you too, Dev. See you soon."

"Soon."

The call disconnects, but I don't lower the phone from my ear. My limbs remain frozen while my mind continually whirls from the news.

I don't know what is happening with Shelly, what has her heart in literal pain, but I swear to do whatever it takes to keep her safe. To keep the baby safe. She may not like what happens next, what treatment the doctor prescribes and how fragilely I tend to her every need, but I can't lose her. I *won't* lose her. Not now, not ever.

I *need* her. More than the air I breathe, more than the life force that keeps my heart beating, I need Shelly. And nothing will take her from me.

With each symptom Shelly tells Dr. Webster she experienced recently, I bite down harder on the inside of my cheek and curl my fingers tighter. Taste iron on my tongue as I break the skin. Feel the sting in my palms as my nails dig deeper.

These aren't minor issues. Chest pain that occasionally gets better with deep breathing, but not always. Tingling in the chest. Problems breathing and tightness in the chest. Profuse sweating and random dizziness. The more symptoms she rattles off, the more it sounds like signs of a heart attack.

Why didn't she tell me about this? I love her pride and independence, but this is different. This is serious. This not only affects Shelly, it also affects the baby.

You know why, my mind mocks. Because I would have rushed her to the emergency room. Would have begged her to stop working. Would have strongly encouraged her to sit on the couch all day and not lift a finger. All for something her regular doctor can easily help with.

Still… Shelly not speaking up and sharing this vital information makes me question her trust in me, in us. And that hurts the most.

Dr. Webster jots notes in Shelly's file, then looks up with a soft, but serious expression. "From everything you've shared, it sounds as if you're suffering from panic attacks. This isn't abnormal for new mothers or parents." She rolls herself closer to us on the stool. "But this is your body telling you that you need to relax more. Physically and mentally." She lays a hand on Shelly's forearm. "It's okay to let go of some control right now. It's okay to let others help."

Paper crinkles as Shelly drops her head back on the exam table. "Feels like I've already given up so much."

"And you may have. Just remind yourself why you're giving up these tasks. Temporarily." She scoots the stool back and stands. "When the little one arrives, life will slowly go back to normal. Well, the new normal." Dr. Webster shifts her gaze my way. "Let Dad help out. Anything heavy or stressful, let him carry some of the weight."

Pushing up on her elbows, Shelly moves to a seated position. "What about work?" She tugs her top back in position. "I need to work." Desperation licks her tone, pleading with Dr. Webster to not take work away from her.

"You're still at the florist shop?" Shelly nods. "Work is fine." Shelly sags in relief just as Dr. Webster points a finger. "But no picking up boxes or bending at the waist. Simpler tasks only. Desk work or flower arrangements. I don't foresee many disgruntled customers."

Except maybe another visit from my mother. *Please, no. No more visits from Karen Templar.*

"I know giving up some of your freedoms isn't easy, but it's not just about you anymore."

"You're right." Shelly sighs. "It's just... how will I know what's too strenuous until I do it?"

Dr. Webster chats with us a few more minutes before escorting us to the checkout desk. She mentions how panic attacks could elevate blood pressure. And uncontrolled blood pressure may equal bed rest, something Shelly definitely does not want. Before she walks off, she reminds Shelly one last time to go slow, to take her time. She suggests pregnancy yoga and meditation and more walks at the park.

We wander out the door and head for our cars. I hate that we are leaving in separate vehicles, especially after this visit, but thankfully the drive home is short. And then I will cater to Shelly while she relaxes.

The situation isn't what either of us expected or wanted, but we have to adjust accordingly. Remind ourselves this modification in our daily routine is temporary. Remind ourselves why this change is necessary.

Sidling up to Shelly at her car, I press my lips to her forehead. "See you at home."

She nods, her eyes glazed over slightly. "At home."

As she drives away, a weight forms in my stomach. A weight I cannot shake. A weight that tells me there is more to come. And honestly, I'm not sure how much more I can handle.

fifteen

. . .

Shelly

THE NEXT FOUR MONTHS ARE GOING TO BE THE DEATH of me.

Am I being a bit dramatic? Probably, but I don't care. I have earned the right to be a drama queen. When you have done everything on your own for decades, being told you can't sucks. Losing any semblance of your independence sucks. Feeling helpless sucks.

Not a minute passes where I regret this pregnancy. If anything, I consider myself lucky to have found Devlyn, to have fallen in love with him, to start the next phase of life with him.

But so much has changed in such a short period. In the process, part of me feels as if I have lost myself. Lost the woman I was before Devlyn and pregnancy. Lost the time I once had with friends and family.

Again, I have zero regrets about my relationship with Devlyn. I love him. More than I thought I could love another person. I don't regret the baby either. It's just... I wish our time line was different. I wish Devlyn and I would've had more time together first. To explore life and love, just the two of us, before going from zero to one-hundred in the blink of an eye.

All of it happened so quickly. Us evolving from *just friends* to boyfriend and girlfriend to living together with a baby on the way. In less than six months, we went from nothing to everything.

Much as I wanted a relationship like those in my romance novels, I didn't expect to get the whole shebang all at once. The guy, the house, the baby. Fingers crossed, I get the happily ever after too.

Two weeks ago, Dr. Webster said I'd suffered from panic attacks. The most unfathomable part of her diagnosis was that I'd never experienced anxiety prior to pregnancy. Not once. Perhaps it takes a momentous occasion to trigger anxiety or depression. Or maybe it's part of our genetic makeup and remains dormant in some until the match is struck.

Hopefully my lessened activity and new meditative regimen helps reduce the attacks. Hopefully they vanish altogether, otherwise there will be medication and the possibility of bed rest. I'd like to avoid both.

"That's stunning," Elizabeth says as she returns from lunch.

I eye the bouquet on the arrangement table, twisting the vase left then right as a smile plumps my cheeks. "Thank you."

The plethora of pink flowers is at the request of one of our regular customers. His wife adores pink—she obviously has good taste—and he ordered the arrangement for their twenty-fifth wedding anniversary. After a hefty payment, he gave us free rein to choose the flowers and greenery. His only request… *"It needs a lot of pink."*

"How many stems have you added?"

I lean back and look for any *empty* spots in the bouquet. "Thirty." I twist my lips in concentration. "I'd like to get a full three dozen."

Elizabeth pats my shoulder. "You will." A soft smile on her lips as she wanders off. "I'll be in the back unpacking the delivery. Holler if you need me."

"Will do."

I go back to the bouquet and zone out as I add the last remaining stems to the vase. Satisfied with the bouquet, I take it into the cooler where we stash orders waiting to be delivered. As I exit, I spot a man in the store near the meadow mural.

"Good afternoon," I greet him. "Is there anything I can help you with today?"

For two breaths, he doesn't acknowledge my presence. Doesn't speak a word. He simply stares at the painting on the wall.

Queasiness twists my stomach. Has me inching away from this stranger. My eyes fall shut as I inhale deeply and tell my body and mind to relax. Tell myself to not get worked up over nothing. He could simply be admiring the work, nothing more.

Cool and a bit more collected, my eyes open as I put on my best work smile. I open my mouth to tell the man I will leave him to browse and check back with him shortly, but he speaks up first.

"Beautiful piece," he states. The soft timbre of his

voice is vaguely familiar. Though I have never met this man, something about him screams recognition. My brows pinch together as I study him from the corner of my eye.

"Um, thank you." I wipe my hands on the apron at my waist. "A local artist painted the mural for the shop."

The man shoves his hands in the pockets of his dress slacks, rocks back on his heels once, then nods. "I'm familiar with his work."

Never said the artist was a man. The queasiness in my belly builds as bile climbs up my throat.

Who is this man? And why the hell does he make me uncomfortable?

Taking a step back, then another, I separate myself from the wobbly energy he exudes. "Well, if you need—"

"Are you Shelly?"

Every instinct in me screams to not answer him. Is he some kind of stalker? It wouldn't be the first time a customer obsessed over the way I arrange flowers. Odd as it is, it has happened. To both me and Elizabeth.

"Uh…"

The man twists to face me head on and extends a hand my way. "Sorry. James Templar."

For the love of all that is holy in this world. Someone, please rescue me from the never-ending surprises.

James Templar… for a beat, I take him in. Brown locks trimmed neat and close to his scalp. Familiar angular jawline. Same height. Same build. Same glass-green irises. Without question, this man is Devlyn's father.

But why is he here?

Reluctantly, I place my hand in his and shake. "Shelly. But you already knew that somehow." I quickly withdraw my hand.

His hand goes back to his pocket and he takes a step back, granting me room to breathe. Time ticks by and neither of us says a word. And in this momentary blip of time, I acknowledge that James Templar is nothing like his wife. Quite the opposite, actually. While she demands attention, he seems content with disappearing. She is the spotlight and he is the shadow. How odd.

So why is he married to her? Why does he allow her to verbally and emotionally abuse their only child?

"Is there something you needed?" I ask, my tone as neutral as possible. Although this man has not garnered my respect, my parents would berate me for weeks if I spoke to a stranger without courtesy.

"I, uh..." He glances back to the mural before meeting my eyes once more. "It's not my place or position to do so, but I came here to apologize."

My forehead tightens as my brows drop. "Apologize?"

The only person who should apologize is Karen Templar. She has inflicted one wound after another. This man, Devlyn's father, has not slighted me. As for Devlyn... I don't know their history or how often he speaks with his dad. I honestly can't recall a time when Devlyn mentioned his father.

He swallows, then nods. "Yes. For how Devlyn's mother has behaved recently."

Seriously?

Not sure what it is, but this man driving an hour to come apologize for his wife's actions pisses me off. Try as I might, calming my rising blood pressure proves challenging. But with each throb and whoosh of my pulse, I remind myself I need to find my zen. I need to relax. If not for me, for the baby.

But I swear, as soon as this baby is born, these people will hear my wrath.

"Why?"

He tilts his head and eyes me for a beat. "Why?" he asks and I nod. "Shelly, I don't know you. Don't know anything about you, but you seem like a nice person." He smiles and it instantly makes me think of Devlyn and the identical smile he doesn't grant many or often. "For Devlyn to be so taken by you…" His eyes avert to the mural for a breath. "With his past, it must mean you matter to him. Very much."

"So, you're apologizing because Devlyn and I are together and I seem like a nice person?"

What a strange reason.

First off, he shouldn't *have* to apologize for his wife. She should apologize. Not that I'd listen after her degradation. That woman believes she is the epitome of perfection, when in truth, she wouldn't know real courtesy if it slapped her in the face.

Second, and still, why? Why is he here? What has he heard in regard to our recent interactions with his wife?

Last, and probably most importantly, why does this

feel like a bandage over something that requires surgery to fix?

This whole interaction feels like one big clusterfuck of confusion. Maybe James Templar usually skirts around the truth. Maybe he is always the fixer-upper. The one that steps in after hurricane Karen wreaks havoc on whatever upsets her and rebuilds the broken structures.

I don't get it. Why he is here and what he hopes to resolve with this conversation. But if he doesn't get to the point soon, I may just ask him to leave and walk away.

On an audible exhale, he shakes his head. "Not just that." His head hangs forward, his eyes on his dress shoes. "I haven't spoken with Devlyn for months." Slowly, he lifts his head and our eyes meet. "Our relationship, mine with Devlyn, isn't the same as with his mother. Since he left for college, we talked less. That's just our personalities. But we always talked. At least every couple of weeks, if only for a few minutes over the phone." He works his jaw in a nervous jitter. His eyes crinkling at the corners slightly. "I haven't spoken with him since November. Not since the day before the art exhibition."

More than six months. Didn't he spend time with them during Christmas? Maybe his father wasn't there. Devlyn attended a holiday party his mother hosted, but perhaps it was more of a schmoozing event than actual time spent with family.

Did Devlyn cut his father off because of his mother? Because of me?

"I'm not sure what to say."

It's the truth. I have no clue what to tell this man. I don't make decisions for Devlyn. And from what he has told me about his parents, he didn't really make his own decisions until he left home. Even then, his mother still directed part of the narrative.

But I won't do that. Ever. Nor will I let his parents disrupt all the progress he has made with countless hours of therapy. Therapy no person should have to endure. Not for this.

"You don't need to say anything." He rocks back on his heels again and I realize this must be a nervous action for him. "I truly am sorry for how Devlyn's mother has behaved. Toward him and you."

"All due respect, Mr. Templar, you shouldn't be apologizing for her." I give him a tight, uncomfortable smile. "And I'm not sure if an apology will ever make up for the damage she has done."

An odd flutter erupts in my belly and, without thinking, I lay a hand on my lower abdomen. The second I do, his eyes drop and land on my hand. Immediately, I shift and tuck my hands in my back pockets.

But it is too late. The deed is done. I see it in the widening of his eyes. Hear it in his loud swallow.

His eyes lift to mine and I watch as they glass over. As recognition truly sets in. As this man realizes I am carrying his grandchild, someone he may never meet because of his wife.

"It's not your place, Shelly, but will you please ask Devlyn to call or text me?" He blinks back the tears rimming his eyes. "I won't say anything" —his eyes drift to my belly for a breath— "to his mother about…" *the baby*. I see the words in his eyes. A proclamation he won't voice, maybe to protect the baby and Devlyn.

"I will make mention, but not any promises." My eyes hold his. "Devlyn makes his own choices. If he wants to speak with you, that is his decision to make. His voice has been stolen from him for too many years. I won't do the same."

James nods as he rolls his lips between his teeth. "Thank you, Shelly." He takes a step back and removes his hands from his pockets. "For what it's worth, I hope to know you one day. From what I can tell, you're a good person. I'm happy my son has you."

Every cell in my body wants to thank this man for the kind sentiment, but I stop myself. Clamp my lips tight and refuse to grant him gratitude. Not when he has enabled his wife's cruelty toward Devlyn his entire life. Thanking this man wipes away all the harm he caused by not stepping up for his own child. Thanking this man would imply compliments and recognition diminish the pain his wife—and by proxy, him —inflicted.

I won't grant him such kindness. Not because I, too, am cruel. But because I love Devlyn. Unconditionally. I stand by him, through the hurt and happiness. Through the tears and laughter.

When it dawns on James I have nothing more to say, he nods, takes a step back, pivots away, and ambles toward the door. "Hope we meet again, Shelly." He glances one last time at my belly, gives me a pained smile, then leaves.

I wander to the door and stare out the glass to watch him drive away. He slips behind the wheel of a white BMW sedan, lifts a hand when he notices me watching, then backs out.

My hand goes to my ponytail, my fingers toying with the strands as I continue to look outside. Watching. Waiting. Praying for no more surprises. Although this one isn't half as bad as the previous surprises, it still unsettles me.

James Templar may be nothing like his wife, but he still hurt his son. Making up for all he and his wife have done will take a heck of a lot more than one conversation in Petal and Vine. It will take drastic measures. A larger-than-life change.

For Devlyn's sake, I hope he gets to keep at least one parent. Without the influence of his wife, James Templar may be a good man. A man worthy of being a grandfather to our child. A man Devlyn might look up to in the future.

sixteen

• • •

Devlyn

"Your dad stopped by the shop today."

My fork hovers between my plate and mouth as I process what Shelly just said. Slowly, I set my fork down and swallow. Let her words sink in.

My father was in Petal and Vine today.

Why?

"Are you okay?" I don't need my father stirring up my mother's wasp nest of activity and upsetting Shelly.

"Yeah," she says on a nod. "He was kind."

This doesn't come as a surprise. My father never had a mean bone in his body. He also lost his backbone standing beside my mother.

"What did he want?"

"To meet me, and to ask me to ask you if you'd call or text him."

Shelly says the words so casually. Not an ounce of concern in her tone. Which is a tremendous relief.

My father may not be barbaric like my mother, but he disregards her words and actions as if they mean nothing. As if they harm no one. Recently, I learned his behavior was unacceptable. I learned his actions were equally as damaging as saying and doing the acts themselves.

Shelly reaches across the table and lays her hand over mine. "He was kind," she repeats. "I made him no promises. That I'd tell you or that you'd follow through." Her shimmery blues lock with my greens. "Reaching out is your choice." She gives my hand a gentle squeeze. "Also…"

My eyes dart between hers as I wait for her to finish. "Also, what?"

"I think he surmised I'm pregnant." *Shit.* "I felt this flutter and my hand automatically went to my belly."

I don't curse Shelly for inadvertently letting my father know about the baby. I curse that he may say something to my mother. Which may trigger another visit. A visit we do not need.

"Devlyn, I don't know the first thing about your father, but he seems to genuinely miss you. Or at least the conversations you shared."

James Templar is a good man that has done countless good deeds for others. He never speaks ill of anyone, ever—including my mother, which is part of the problem. He may be a good man, but he doesn't know how to be strong—for himself or others.

If he has a good heart, is it possible to fix his broken pieces? Several hours per month, I work to mend my own broken parts. Perhaps he can do the same. I like to think it is possible, but as long as he stands beside my mother, I won't take unnecessary or foolish risks.

"I'll reach out to him." I pick my fork back up and lift the bite to my mouth. "How was the rest of your day?"

Over the rest of dinner, Shelly recants her day at work. Although she dislikes all the physical adjustments she's had to make, I see the impact. In the rosy blush on her cheeks and endless vibrant smile. In her twilight irises as they twinkle and shimmer. In the radiant light of her aura as she stands in my presence.

It is all I need. Her. Her smile. The peace she provides. The love she gives.

Just Shelly.

Bristles stroke the canvas as I paint Shelly in various swirls of pink. A splash of fiery rose. A sweep of delicate blush. A swish of addictive taffy.

Painting this piece without her here isn't the same. This interpretation is new. Poles apart from my usual pieces. An unrealistic portrayal of the woman I have come to love so profoundly.

I see her so clearly when I close my eyes. Her curvaceous breasts and hips. The hollow of her throat and contour of her collarbones. Wisps of hair on her cheek as she lies on the pillows and blankets. The parting of her lips and glimmer in her eyes as I leer around the canvas with the brush between my teeth.

The more pigment I add, the more abstract the painting becomes. As it evolves, I fall harder for my muse. *My Andromeda.*

More often than not, my art is realistic. I paint and draw objects and people as I see them with the naked eye. Maybe tweak the color or shading or position, but not much else.

This painting is unlike every other I have created. This painting is unrestrained passion.

Every tinge of red coats the canvas. From borderline black to muted pink. Because Shelly *is* the whole spectrum. She is red and pink and every tint and shade between. She is passion and love. Soft and pure. The gentlest caress and fiercest protector. She is the light to my dark. My North Star.

In my periphery, my phone lies on the table beside my easel. Taunting me. Provoking me. My hand freezes, the brush an inch from the canvas as I stare at the annoying piece of technology.

Computers and tablets and cell phones have existed in my life as long as I can remember. They were tools in school and distractions at home. Although I appreciate the ways technology has saved lives, I hate how some innovations have robbed people of their lives.

I may have grown up in the internet era, but I wish it didn't exist.

It sucks the joy from my soul and gifts anxiety in return. The pressure to always be available. Emails and text messages and calling you wherever and whenever. While people become addicted to apps and social media, I work harder to disconnect from it all. If a website wasn't essential for business, I would let it go.

My eyes shift to the table again and the urge to throw my cell phone in the garbage skyrockets. Only because my father wants to speak, wants me to call or text him.

"Should just get it over with," I mumble as I set down the paintbrush.

From everything Shelly told me three nights ago, my father was nothing but cordial and kind while he spoke with her in Petal and Vine. She said he'd even looked a bit sad.

Dad always had a forlorn look about him, but I never asked why. Was I the reason for his sadness? We hadn't spoken in so long, but it's not as if we had profound conversations. Or is it Mom who has made him unhappy?

As years passed, and I put more distance between myself and my parents, I often wondered if Dad was happy with Mom. On any level. She had always been equally wicked and degrading toward him. Criticizing him harshly and not strictly behind closed doors.

Why did he put up with it? Did he not think himself worthy of more? It boggles me how someone could be with a person who treated them as if they didn't matter, as if everything they did wasn't good enough. Even in love, a person should only tolerate so much. How did Dad love her, or even like her, when she treated him like garbage?

But asking myself these questions will get me nowhere. The only person that can answer them is him.

I need to call him. I need to talk with him. Both I have avoided, but can't put off any longer.

Swiping my phone from the table, I rise from the stool and step away from the painting. Regardless of the direction this call takes, I don't want negative energy tainting this piece. Not Shelly.

I trek down the stairs and head for the kitchen. With Shelly at work, the house is quiet. Too quiet. Months ago, the stillness of my house, my space, was something I craved. Solace in solitude. Peace among the chaos. An abrupt shift from my busy art mind.

Now, the silence makes my skin crawl. I don't like when Shelly leaves. Although her earthy floral scent lingers and I see her touch in every room, I miss her energy. Miss her sweet voice and soft words. The way she brightens a room without effort.

Her absence is why I seclude myself in the studio all day. When she works, so do I.

I fill a glass with water and reheat leftovers for lunch. As the microwave counts down to zero, I unlock my phone, press my father's contact in the list, and stare at the screen.

He isn't as bad as her, yet he is.

A shrill beep snaps my attention from my phone. I carry lunch to the dining room table and sit in my usual seat. At the heart of the table sits a small vase of peonies. Fresh flowers are a simple touch Shelly has added to almost every room in the house.

I ignore lunch to stare at the delicate pink petals for a beat. So soft, so elegant. Quintessential and very much Shelly. Even in her absence, she is here—her warmth and heart—swathing me in strength and support and love.

Unlocking my phone again, my finger hovers the phone icon as I pick at the pasta primavera.

Now or never. Just get it over with.

Before I lose the nerve, I press the icon and lift the phone to my ear. With it being the middle of the day, Dad should be at work and nowhere near Mom. The phone rings once, twice, then he answers.

"Devlyn?"

"Hey, Dad."

Silence stretches between us, but it doesn't unnerve me, not like with Mom. Dad and I have always had this unspoken language. A side effect of our reticent nature. Neither of us feels the need to fill every second with unnecessary speech. Sometimes, the most profound things come about in silence.

"How are you?" His question not abnormal, but his tone is hesitant. Unsure. Troubled.

I stab a piece of pasta and carrot. "Good. You?"

Shelly said Dad pieced together she was pregnant, but never stated as much before leaving the shop. Until he says or asks, I won't touch the topic. Until I know where Dad's head is, I will keep all things Shelly related in the background. To protect her and the baby.

"Could be better." His heavy sigh reaches me through the phone. Tugs at the sympathetic heartstrings I have for him. "Devlyn, I…" He goes silent for a moment, but I don't interject. Don't butt into the words he wants to say, but has difficulty vocalizing. While he thinks, I eat. "I have some news." The lack of inflection in his voice gives nothing away.

"Okay," I drawl out the word.

"I asked your mother for a divorce."

The bite in my mouth goes down the wrong pipe as

I go into a coughing fit. I pull the phone away from my ear, beat a fist to my sternum, and cough until the stray noodle dislodges.

When I bring the phone back to my ear, he asks, "Are you okay?" True concern laces his voice.

I cough again, then sip my water. "Fine," I croak out. "What brought this on? The divorce, I mean."

While Dad sits quiet on the other end, I drink more water. I push the food away with the intent to hear him out and not go into another choking fit. Who knows what other surprises he will hit me with.

"It's been a long time coming," he finally says, a hint of relief in his words. "When your mother and I met, life was different. *We* were different." He audibly exhales. "She changed after we said I do. I'd been so in love with her at the time that I didn't give attention to the little signs. When we found out she was pregnant, those little signs got bigger, but I blamed them on hormones. I blamed it on the worry that comes with impending parenthood." He goes silent and I picture him hanging his head. "But it wasn't that at all. As much as I wanted to leave then, I couldn't. I wouldn't abandon you and let you suffer alone."

Dad stayed married to Mom more than half his adult life… for me. Wow. Just… wow. I don't know whether to thank him or slap him.

Both of our lives could have been polar opposites of what they are today. It is quite possible neither of us would feel emotionally annihilated had he left sooner. Yes, most courts side with the mother in custody cases. But I question whether or not my mother would've wanted me without my father. Sure, she may have molded me more in her likeness had he not been around, but I can't picture her *wanting* me around. Period. Unless she had something to gain.

"Dad… why didn't you say something sooner?"

"Son, it's not your burden to bear." He takes a breath. "After the incident in the grocery store not long ago, which I cringed at when your mother told me, I knew it was time. Way past time. Since you moved out and we moved to Tampa, your mother has been on some kick. I thought it'd taper off, but it's only gotten worse."

Great. My mother losing her shit more often is not *what I need. Not what any of us needs.*

"When I asked why she'd been in the grocery store an hour from home, she struck me. Told me it was none of my business. That she was working." He audibly exhales. "But it was a lie. Her work never puts her near you. So, I started monitoring her closer. Tracking where she was and her phone activity." He laughs without humor. "Sounds creepy, but I was worried about you."

"You were?"

"Always, Devlyn. I took the brunt of your mother's attacks over the years… to protect you. As much as I could, anyway." He pauses a beat. "I learned your mother had been following you and your girlfriend. More often than I care to admit. When I called her out on it, she lost it. Said you were ruining your life." He sighs heavily and I picture him tracing his brows with his thumb and finger. "I don't want to rehash the horrible things she said, but in that moment, I no longer wanted to sit idle. No longer wanted either of us to be subject to her terror. So, I've spent weeks speaking with an attorney. A lot of things are tied to your mother's name, including parts of your life. I want both of us to come out as clean as possible when it ends."

White noise fizzles around me as I mull over this new information.

Dad is divorcing Mom.

He is leaving her.

For himself, but also for me.

Although I wish it would have happened earlier, I can't fault him for his decisions. James Templar is not brainless. For years, I questioned how he loved my mother. How he loved someone so manipulative and brutal and poisonous. But he'd hid what lay beneath the surface of his relationship with her. He buried his suffering to keep me close.

Much as I wish he'd made a change years ago, I understand his reasons for staying.

"What happens now?"

Not much of my mother is entwined in my life. Her name carried weight in the art community and opened doors for me in the past, but it no longer bears the same influence. Yes, the Templar name has significance in the area, but I tip the scales more than her now. My art speaks volumes and I no longer need the influence of Karen Templar.

The only thing I question now is my house. Mom insisted on helping out when purchasing the house after college. Seeing as I had minimal credit and was just building my savings, I didn't deny her.

When was the last time I looked at my mortgage statement? Months, perhaps. And how had the deed been titled when the sale of the house finalized? My name was on the deed, but it hadn't been the only name printed. Did half of my house belong to her? *Oh, god.* Bile rises in my throat at the idea of my safe space—the house I invited Shelly into, the place where our child will grow and learn and laugh—is possibly tainted and at risk.

Shit.

"I hear your mind spinning from here. Devlyn, everything will be fine."

"What about my house?" The words a squeaky whisper on my tongue.

If her name is on this house, I will move us out. Find us a new home, far from here. Last thing I or Shelly need is my mother's torment because her life is upside down. I won't put Shelly or the baby in harm's way. I won't allow my mother to ruin either of them the way she did me and Dad.

"Your house is yours, son."

"Isn't she—"

"No. She's not on the deed or the loan. I am, which I'll happily change, if you wish."

Thank the powers that be.

Dad and I talk another twenty minutes before he says goodbye. But before he hangs up, he asks to have dinner with me and Shelly sometime soon. That and he wants more calls or texts, even if there is nothing notable to talk about.

When the call disconnects, a tremendous weight lifts

from my shoulders. Not all of it is gone, but it feels more bearable. Manageable. Less pained and more healing.

It feels like my life is finally heading in a positive direction in every way. Something I need—not just for myself, but also for Shelly and our future.

For the first time in my adult life, I breathe and it hurts less.

seventeen

. . .

Shelly

I MIGHT DIE FROM THIS INCESSANT HEAT.

Far back as I remember, I have loved living the Florida life. Sunshine year round. Blue skies with the occasional fluffy cloud or two. Countless outdoor activities. Theme parks and festivals and concerts. The beach, the sand, the warmth.

But right now, in this paralyzing summer weather, my ankles are swollen. My fingers look more like small sausages than tools to write and eat and function. Sweat slicks my skin in the most awkward places. My clothes are itchy and tight and annoying. And this new ache formed in my lower back.

I am not okay with this. Not at all.

With each passing month, my body changes more and more. I get it. Really, I do. I am cooking a human.

Some of the changes aren't so bad. Nausea—gone. Me and all the cheeses are good friends again. Hallelujah. Body swelling… unacceptable. Wasting money on maternity clothes… unacceptable. Instead, I wear

Devlyn's T-shirts and loose shorts or lounge pants. Hell, I will wear a robe all day if need be. Back pain… also unacceptable.

Dr. Webster recommended pregnancy massage for the back pain. I jumped on that bandwagon immediately. She also said the swelling is perfectly normal, especially in the hotter months. She recommended less salt in my diet, more water, walking daily, and the usual rest and relaxation with my feet elevated.

I feel like an elephant. Maybe a hippo. No offense to the elephant or hippo population. But if I swell anymore, I will undoubtedly resemble Violet Beauregarde from *Willy Wonka and the Chocolate Factory* after she blows up—minus purple skin, of course.

"Why don't you relax while I start dinner," Devlyn suggests as we come in from a stroll around the neighborhood.

Tonight, Devlyn's dad is coming over for dinner. When Devlyn ran the idea past me weeks ago, my blood pressure spiked. So, he pushed it off. Told his father we needed more time.

In the last month, Devlyn has spoken with his dad at least three times a week. Gotten to know the man James really is versus the man he thought he knew. During those conversations, Devlyn found a new level of comfort with his father. A bond they should have had years ago. And when his father agreed two weeks ago to have joint therapy sessions with Devlyn, some of my own worry eased.

I want our baby to be surrounded by as much love as possible. Having at least one person from Devlyn's family present would be wonderful. Devlyn deserves love too. A love he wanted for years, but didn't realize how much he'd been deprived of until recently.

"I'd like to help," I say, toeing off my shoes.

We wander to the kitchen and Devlyn starts pulling food from the cabinets and fridge. I lean my hip against the counter and watch as he moves around the kitchen.

"Kick your feet up for a few. I'll do the tedious stuff, then come get you for the rest. Deal?"

I huff under my breath. *Really hate feeling like a useless child.* Not overexerting myself is good for me and the baby, deep down I know this. But when I am used to doing it all, sitting on my butt while others wait on me, hand and foot, makes me feel like a nuisance. Like I don't contribute in any way.

That stings the most.

Sticking out my pinkie, I wait for Devlyn to hook his with mine. Two steps in my direction, he latches our pinkies as his lips kick up in a half smile. "Promise."

Making my way to the living room, I plop down on the couch and scroll through the shows. I land on *The Vampire Diaries* and hit play. It's been a while since I binged this show.

Halfway through the episode, Devlyn wanders into the living room and parks next to me on the couch. He lays his head on my shoulder and stares at the screen. Minutes of the show carry on, neither of us speaking. And it is moments like this that calm every woe. Moments like this that make all the craziness—family and pregnancy and our fast-paced relationship —worthwhile.

For years, I wanted this. Someone to love me without effort. Someone that connected with me on an unprecedented level. Someone that will stick with me through the good and not so good.

The start of our love story may be muddled with indecision and chaos, but I wouldn't change it or us. Devlyn wouldn't be who he is today without his past, and neither would I. Our love wouldn't be what it is without it either.

"Ready to cook?" he whispers when the episode ends.

"Yes."

As if we have done it years, Devlyn and I move around the kitchen with ease as we prepare dinner. Minutes before the timer goes off for the oven, the doorbell chimes.

Here we go.

Devlyn sets the spoon on the rest. With his hand on my lower back, he kisses my temple. "Be right back."

"'Kay," I breathe out.

He pads off to answer the door and I stir the couscous with more gusto than necessary. Sweat dampens my skin as I hear the dead bolt disengage and the door open before mumbled hellos filter in.

This is it. I take a deep breath and check on the chicken in the oven. *Devlyn's father is* not *his mother. This dinner will end in smiles.*

A moment later, Devlyn reenters the kitchen with his father in tow. A loud beep fills the room as the timer on the range goes off. I turn it off, along with the burner for the couscous, top the pot with a lid and remove it from the heat.

Jitters flow through my limbs as I spin around to face Devlyn and James. Two breaths pass and my nerves settle a little as I stare at the two of them. Looking at James is like looking into the future. Devlyn is definitely his father's son. If James's appearance is any indication, Devlyn will age well.

The room is filled with awkward tension as the three of us stand there, unspeaking. After a beat, James breaks the silence. "Nice to see you again, Shelly." James offers his hand.

Devlyn's father is not his mother.

I take his hand and note how similar yet different his grip is from Devlyn's. Devlyn has soft hands with the occasional callous. His fingers are thin and long. His touch gentle yet strong. James harbors a different type of strength. One built from years of labor and life. The skin where his fingers meet his hand is rougher. Yet I still feel a gentleness in his touch.

"Nice to meet you officially," I say.

Our hands break apart and Devlyn offers his father a drink. The two men open a beer while I fill a glass with sparkling cider. While I fetch plates, Devlyn takes the chicken from the oven. We dish the meal onto plates and make our way into the dining room.

James's gaze drifts around the room as if seeing it with new eyes. *How long has it been since he has set foot in this house?* Until meeting James in Petal and Vine last month, I'd never seen him. It was always Devlyn's mother that made an appearance. And until last month, Devlyn hadn't spoken to James since late November.

I watch as his eyes take in all the new additions to the house. A short vase of flowers at the heart of the table. Art on two of the three dining room walls—Devlyn's art, of course. Large candles on either side of the vase that Devlyn lit when I wasn't looking. A soft rug beneath the table and chairs. And that is just this room.

Devlyn lived a monochromatic life filled with occasional color before we met. My life had been the opposite. Now we balance each other. Spark new life where things once faded away.

"I love the changes you've made," James says, eyes darting from me to Devlyn. "Feels more like a home."

"I'll give you an updated tour after dinner," Devlyn suggests.

Wrinkles form at the corners of James's mouth and eyes as an all too familiar smile dons his face. "I'd love that very much."

Thank goodness his genetics overpowered hers.

Dinner carries on with timid conversation. James asks Devlyn about his recent artwork and me about the flower shop. Neither of us dives in deep at first, but the more we chat, the more comfortable we all become. We have yet to discuss anything about the baby, but hiding my growing belly becomes harder with each passing day.

When our plates clear, I offer to do dishes so Devlyn can show his father around the house.

Not much of the house has changed from my

moving in. Not needing the furniture, I sold all but a few smaller items. The small space between the kitchen and doors to the patio had been empty prior to me moving in. Now, my small sofa, end and coffee table, and bookshelf fill the space and look out the sliding glass doors to the backyard. The small change doesn't overwhelm the nook, but makes it a cozy place to read a book or have additional seating if and when we have guests over.

As I load the last of the dishes into the washer, Devlyn and James enter the kitchen. Both wear matching smiles and carry a new sense of ease.

Devlyn needed this. They both did. The last several months have been a challenge for us both, but more for Devlyn. So much of his life has changed. He saw a new side to his mother, one he'd been willfully blind to for years, and disconnected her from his life. In doing so, pieces of his past flooded in and knocked the air from his lungs. Everything he thought he knew as a child and young man had been blanketed with falsehoods and manipulation. Although his parents, more so his mother, had twisted his mind, he has slowly found a way to unravel all the hurt and heartache and influence.

Now he has the chance at a new life with his father. One filled with love and compassion and trust—over time. And this small token warms my heart. That he gets to keep one parent. That he doesn't feel completely abandoned.

"So," James speaks up as we walk to the sitting room. "I don't know how to broach the subject..." Devlyn and I sit on the love seat as James sits in one of the chairs across from us. "Or if I should." He picks at the knee of his slacks.

"We won't know unless you do," Devlyn states with a chuckle.

I love how light and carefree he is at my side. How warm and comfortable he is as the evening progresses. Not that Devlyn has never displayed such qualities. Just wasn't sure what his reaction would be having his father nearby after a long absence.

A soft smile pushes up the corners of James's lips. "I'd like to talk about..." He pauses, his jaw working left and right, his lips clamped between his teeth. "About the baby," he says after a moment.

It wasn't a question of *if* the subject would come up before James left, it was a question of *when*. Honestly, it surprises me it didn't come up sooner.

Devlyn wraps an arm around my shoulders, tucks me into his side, and lays his free hand on my lap. If that doesn't scream his need to protect me and the baby, not much else would in this moment.

"Okay," Devlyn says, but doesn't expand further.

Tonight is more about Devlyn reconnecting with his dad than about me getting to know James. Devlyn needs this—they both do—but his instinct to shield me from the toxicity of his past far outweighs his need to connect.

Every word and action from James this evening has been nothing short of kind and caring. Not once has he been cruel. Nor has he belittled Devlyn. The entire evening felt *normal*. And we can use all the normal we can get.

That said, this man also spent more than two decades of his life with Karen Templar—a woman I will never trust.

Tension thickens the air in the room as we all wait for what happens next. Wait for what will be said or asked. As prescribed by Dr. Webster, I do my best to not let the stress of the moment consume my thoughts.

As if he senses my semifrazzled state, Devlyn's thumb draws small circles on my shoulder. I focus my attention on his light touch. Focus on the solace it provides. Count in my head with each circuit his thumb makes.

"It will take time for us to be in a better place, I know," James says with a subtle nod. "But I want to be part of my grandchild's life. In whatever way you feel is best."

"Dad, I…" Devlyn pauses and shifts his greens to my blues. "We will need to talk about it." His eyes go back to his father. "A lot has changed. With us all." Devlyn's grip on my shoulder tightens slightly. "But more will need to change before Shelly and I consider the possibility."

Across from us, James nods as he hangs his head a little. "I can't fault either of you in this. All I ask is that you give it consideration." James looks at Devlyn for a beat before his eyes find mine. "Whatever you need of me—joint therapy sessions, time, specific actions—I will do it. Just please, don't shut me out."

I feel for this man. Truly.

James, too, has been through hell. Stuck in a loveless

marriage for decades just so he knew his son was safe. To some degree, anyway.

"We will," I affirm. My eyes drop as my hand comes to my belly. "This baby will be loved like no other. I'd like them to be surrounded by as much as possible." I lift my gaze as a smile lights James's expression. "But… I don't know you. Not really." I flash him a sad smile. "Your wife made one heck of a first impression. Sorry to say, but it automatically made one for you too."

"I get it."

"All I ask for is time," I tell him. "Time for me to get to know you. And time with Devlyn." I look at the man holding me close, a small smile curving my lips. "In whichever way he needs it. If it's therapy, a night out together or space without you, you need to respect and grant it."

Devlyn hugs me closer and kisses my temple.

It isn't my intention to speak for Devlyn. In the eight months we have known each other, Devlyn isn't one to always speak his mind. Scared to hurt himself or the feelings of another, he shelters his emotions more often than not. I won't speak for him, but I will speak up for him. In his twenty-three years of life, not many have. Going forward, that will change.

"Promise, I will." James checks his watch. "I should get going."

James slips on his shoes. Devlyn and I walk him to his car and share hugs and goodbyes. A minute later, we wave him off as he backs out of the driveway and drives off.

Back in the house, we wander to the living room

hand in hand and plop down on the couch. Minutes of silence pass as we curl into each other and breathe through the tail end of our night.

"Was really nice seeing him again," Devlyn whispers against my shoulder. "He's so… different."

I rest my head on his. "How so?"

Devlyn traces his fingers over my own, then up my hand and forearm before drifting back down. I close my eyes and absorb his touch. Allow it to warm my skin.

"He's always been calm. Laid back. But now…" Devlyn sits up to look me in the eye. Tenderness softens his expression. "I can't remember the last time he smiled. Like a genuine smile. And tonight, he gave so many."

That he did. James's smiles varied from brilliant to subtle, but they were pleasant all the same.

"I hope he finds happiness," I say softly.

Devlyn lays his head back on my shoulder. "Me too. Although he hasn't made the best decisions, he deserves happiness. And the opportunity to change."

I wholeheartedly agree. My only hope is, after so many years under Karen's thumb, James is capable of change.

eighteen

. . .

Devlyn

Keeping secrets from Shelly is not my strong suit. But this secret must be kept.

Better to deal with only her wrath than the wrath of everyone else.

"Breakfast out was the best idea," she says as she wipes her mouth with a paper napkin. "And this café," —her eyes drift around the bustling restaurant— "how did I not know about this place?"

I shrug and give her a half smile. "Good ole Google found it for me, so..."

She waves me off. "Give yourself some of the credit. The thought crossed your mind. That's what matters most."

"Always finding the bright side." My smile widens.

An hour ago, we left the house under the guise of me not wanting to cook. Forty-five minutes ago, several of our friends pulled up to the house, went inside, and got to work. Decorations and food and whatever else happens at fun-filled adult birthday parties.

More than a week ago, Micah sent me a text message. He mentioned Shelly's upcoming birthday and how everyone wanted to throw her a party. He promised it wouldn't be much different from Sunday night get-togethers. The only difference will be decorations, cake and more time together.

I'd stared at the screen several minutes before responding. Too stunned because I didn't know Shelly's birth date, which is partially my fault. I hadn't offered mine three months ago. Had I asked hers, she'd have felt bad for missing mine.

I answered the message and soon learned it was a group text. My phone blew up for hours. One idea after another filled the gray bubbles. Party GIFs and a slew of emojis filled the screen. I'd been thankful it was the middle of the day and Shelly was at work. Half a day and an insane number of messages later, a plan was devised. A plan for a surprise party. At our house.

My responsibility for the day… don't mention birthdays or our friends and keep Shelly away from home until I get the all-clear message. Cora and Autumn estimated two hours for party setup.

So I planned breakfast out with Shelly. Although it is for her birthday, she thinks it's just because. When we leave the restaurant, the plan is to drive to a bookstore so we can walk around in air conditioning while she picks out a few new books.

She shrugs. "We should come here more. The eggs benedict was excellent, and I saw a dozen other things I'd like to try."

The server steps up and clears our plates from the

table. She asks if there is anything else she can get us—offering the restaurant's award-winning pie before ten in the morning—and Shelly's eyes light up. With a laugh, I gesture to the pie menu.

One slice of key lime and peanut butter pie later, I settle the bill and we leave. A mile up the road, I turn into the plaza with the bookstore and park the car.

Shelly unbuckles her belt and shifts to face me in her seat. Her eyes narrow as she studies me intently.

She knows that I know it's her birthday. Shit. Either that or she suspects I know. Play it cool.

"Why are we here?" she asks, a hint of suspicion in her tone.

She doesn't know. She can't. Play. It. Cool.

"You haven't gotten a new book recently. When we drove past on the way to breakfast, I thought maybe you might like to look at what's new." I shrug, hoping to come across as nonchalant. "Plus, I wanted to look at baby books for dads."

Her eyes soften around the edges. "Okay," she acquiesces without an ounce of fight.

The part about looking for a book for new dads isn't a fib. Sure, I could talk to Jonas or Gavin about first-time fatherhood and what to expect. But I'd also like a resource on hand, just in case something comes up neither of them has dealt with yet.

We wander the bookstore with no set path. Eventually, Shelly will make her way to the romance section, but she steers us toward the baby and parenting books first. I let her lead, but plan to keep us in the store until I get a thumbs-up text.

After discovering two great parenting books, Shelly leads us to her favorite part of the store. I sit on a chair randomly set up in the aisle while she peruses the titles. My phone vibrates in my pocket and, with as much discretion as possible, I remove it to look at the notification. A text from Micah with a thumbs-up and nothing more. I pocket my phone and wait until Shelly finishes browsing.

A hundred dollars later, we walk out of the bookstore and I drive us home.

"Did you find some good ones?" I ask.

Shelly nods. "Yeah. A few I'd heard other book friends online rave about and one by an author I read regularly."

"Good. Glad you found some pleasure reads. The baby books are nice, but you need books for you too."

"Do you pleasure read?" she asks as I turn into the neighborhood.

I shrug. "Not in years."

"What did you like reading when you did?"

"Mostly mysteries and thrillers." I glance over at her. "But I'll give anything a try."

As we approach the house, I note the absence of everyone's cars. Also part of the plan. To make everything look normal. Once everything was set up, all cars were to be moved a street over. The cars may not be out front, but everyone is inside. Once the surprise happens, the cars will be driven back to the house.

I fetch the bag from the back seat after parking in the driveway. Shelly and I slip out and walk leisurely to the door. She keys in her code, then swings the door wide.

From the foyer, the house looks the same. But I know the second we round the wall dividing the dining and living room from the kitchen and sitting room, a burst of surprise will echo around us.

We toe off our shoes and I set the bag of books down on the chair nearby.

"Want to binge that show you were watching the other day?" I ask, knowing it will lead us to where everyone waits.

She hooks my arm in hers. "Sounds great. Maybe I'll start one of my books after."

I lead her to the living room. Just as we breach the entrance to the space, a booming "Surprise!" fills the air. Shelly slaps a hand to her chest as everyone steps up to her and wraps her in a huge embrace. Individual hugs and happy birthday wishes are given. And when Shelly sidles up to me again, her eyes are rimmed in tears.

"Did you do this?" she whisper-asks as she takes in all of our friends.

"Not just me." Micah approaches us. "Your brother actually reached out."

"He did?" I nod and she swipes a hand over her cheeks. "Oh my god."

"Hey, sis." Micah pulls Shelly in for a hug. "Happy birthday. Hope this is okay."

She sniffles. "More than okay, big brother."

The remainder of the day goes by in good conversation, hearty laughter, great food—with cake, of course—and time well spent with people we care about. As the sun sets, we congregate outside and lounge in the back. Since Shelly moved in, we have slowly added more to the backyard. More seating and plants. A firepit and grill. A wooden fence around the perimeter for privacy. An array of colorful flowers near the swing under the large oak.

One day at a time, Shelly turns this house into a home. A place I want to share with her always. A place where our child will grow and laugh and wonder. Color with crayons and paper. Play hide-and-seek. Bring more definition to our lives.

"Have you picked a date for the baby shower yet?" Cora asks Shelly.

Shelly tucks her feet beneath her butt and leans into my side. "Not yet. Should I?"

"When are you due?"

"The date changes with every appointment." I *hear* Shelly's eyes roll and I bite my cheek to resist laughing. She isn't wrong, though. "Basically, anytime between September twenty-first and October eighth. Your guess is as good as mine."

Autumn chuckles. "Clementine's due date changed seven times. Inevitably, she arrived on the original date the doctor said." She smiles at Shelly, then me. "But they come out when they're ready." Autumn looks over at Jonas, who is chatting with Gavin and Micah. "Take advantage of your free time now. You'll wish for more after the baby is here." Autumn shifts her gaze to Cora. "Maybe we should plan the shower for her?"

"You don't have—"

Cora cuts me off. "Count me in." My best friend meets my gaze with softened eyes. "Let us do this for you, Shell." Her hands come together in prayer, inches from her lips. "Let us take this on. It'll be fun. And zero stress for you."

"We won't take no for an answer," Autumn adds.

Beside me, Shelly fidgets. But not so much anyone looking would take notice. I feel the slight tremble in her limbs, though.

I kiss her hair. "Your choice, but I think they would enjoy doing this for you."

Her frame relaxes into me more. "I swear I'm not a control freak." She laughs without humor. "But after giving up so much, it's hard to give up more."

"Wish I could relieve that burden for you. I would, if possible." I kiss her hair again. "A little more than three months. And then, once you're cleared, you can do everything and I'll sit back with the baby and relax."

"Ha ha." She shakes her head. "Fine," she huffs out like an annoyed teen. "You can plan the party." Cora and Autumn clap as giddy smiles stretch their cheeks. "But…" Shelly adds. "I want in on the plans too. I don't want it to be some big secret that I walk in on" —she waves her hand around us— "like today. If you promise to keep me in the loop, you have my permission."

"Done," Cora says at the same time Autumn says, "You got it."

Jonas comes up behind Autumn and rests his hands on her shoulders. "We should head out. Let Mom and Dad get home."

Babysitters. Another thing we should look into—although I am positive Shelly's mom will want every possible minute with the baby. With my flexible schedule, a babysitter will only be necessary when we want or need alone time.

If we are lucky, it won't just be Shelly's family and our friends who will watch the baby for an hour or two. Maybe, hopefully, my dad will be in the mix too. Only time will tell.

nineteen

. . .

Shelly

"READY FOR THE NEXT PHOTO SESSION, MOM AND DAD?"

I lie back on the exam table for my twenty-eight-week appointment. Inching my shirt up, I suck in a deep breath and prepare for the cold gel to hit my belly.

"Yes," Devlyn and I say simultaneously, then smile at each other.

Dr. Webster told us ultrasounds aren't done as frequently during normal pregnancies, but because of my blood pressure changes and increased anxiety, she added two more to the schedule. One today and another at week thirty-two. Either way, I get another snapshot of our little one to add to the album.

The gel hits my belly and I squeeze Devlyn's hand. He squeezes back. Then Dr. Webster presses the wand to my gel-coated skin and moves it around. Three sets of eyes fixate on the monitor as the blurry image becomes slightly sharper. Head, body, and four little limbs.

My vision blurs as tears flood my eyes. Devlyn

tightens his hold on my hand. The room utterly silent except for the fluttering sound of a rapid heartbeat through the ultrasound machine.

"Spine looks good." Dr. Webster traces her finger over the screen. "Everything looks on track." She presses a button on the machine and snaps the image. Her gaze meets mine, then Devlyn's. "Still don't want to know the sex."

I shake my head and Devlyn does the same.

"Okay." Her smile widens as if she has the answer on the tip of her tongue. "Just going to take a few measurements."

She shifts the wand over my round belly and pauses when she has a better view of the baby's head. She clicks a few buttons and moves on. All too soon, she removes the wand, cleans it and my belly, then makes notes in my chart before handing over our new photo.

"Everything looks great. Keep up with your vitamins and relaxation." She sets the chart on the counter and washes her hands. "Have you been experiencing any cramps, pain, nausea, shortness of breath?"

I shake my head as I tug my shirt back into place. "No."

Drying her hands, she resumes her spot on her stool. "Cramps and tightness are normal. How's the swelling been?"

"Better." Devlyn's been a trooper, making sure we walk each night, if only to the end of the street and back.

"And the baby's been as active or more?"

I rub a hand over my belly. "Yes." I peer up at Devlyn. "Our little water aerobics instructor."

Dr. Webster laughs. "That's a new one, but cute." She offers her hand and I take it. Devlyn places one on my back and helps ease me upright. "If you notice any changes that aren't normal or just feel off, call the office. But with everything we saw today, your little water aerobics instructor looks healthy and fit and right where they should be."

At the reception desk, I double-check the next appointment date and time. We exit the office, slip into the car, and buckle our belts. Devlyn cranks the engine, then looks at me over the console.

"I have an idea, if you're up for it."

I arch a brow at him. "Will there be food?"

He looks up, left then right, before meeting my eyes. "Kind of," he says on a laugh.

"Count me in."

twenty

Devlyn

Maybe this wasn't such a great idea.

I love color. I love seeing a wide palette of colors. But this… this is too much.

Every shade of pink—although I have a new appreciation for the color since Shelly—and blue, green and yellow, gray and khaki. Bolds and neutrals. Onesies and jumpers. Pajamas and long shirts. Pants with snaps from heel to crotch on both legs. Lace and frill. Sports logos and popular cartoon characters. Farm animals as well as sea creatures.

The baby and children's section in Target is bigger than any other section. Well, unless you go to toys. It has every possible thing you may need for a baby. Bibs and diapers. Clothing and bedding. Strollers and bouncy seats. Training potties and bathtubs. Bottles and nipples. Who knew there were so many types of nipples? *Jesus*.

And then I laugh. Shelly looks at me with pinched brows. "What's so funny?"

"Have you ever had the urge to scream *nipples* in the baby section? Like it's a eureka moment."

Shelly snorts, then stops and presses her legs together. "Stop it." She slaps my arm. "You'll make me pee."

"We wouldn't get in trouble. If a worker said anything, I'd act like we'd been looking for them and I found them before you."

"Devlyn," she says, laughing harder. "Seriously, stop."

"Fine," I huff out. "Party pooper."

I follow Shelly up and down the aisles. We stare at hundreds of baby products and read the packages of the ones we have no clue what their purpose is. Then I remember something Cora said.

"Hey, shouldn't we start a registry for the shower?"

Shelly pulls out her phone. "Oh, yeah." She pulls up the Target app and taps a few times until she reaches the registry she set up earlier. "All we need to do is scan things and add them to our wish list."

For whatever reason, I don't feel the need to add an overabundance of items. Just necessities. Then again, this is a wish list and what the hell do I know when it comes to babies. Maybe we will need the wipes warmer and double electric breast pump. Maybe we need the video baby monitor that connects to our phone and the ultrasonic humidifier. Hell if I know.

My vision grows hazy as Shelly wanders and scans items on the shelves. Bottles and nipples. Diapers and burp cloths. Tubs and toiletries. Toys and clothes. Once she has half the baby department logged on the registry, she stows her phone in her purse and hooks my arm with hers.

"I want to buy something for the baby." She rubs a hand over her belly as her sparkly blues meet my greens. "The baby will get a ton of gifts from other people, but I want them to have something just from us. Doesn't have to be big. A small toy or their first book."

Twisting to face Shelly, I frame her face with my hands and pull her in for a kiss. Not a juicy public display, but a sweet kiss that tells her I love the idea.

"Anything in mind?" I ask.

"No. Let's wander a little more. Maybe something will stand out."

We weave through the department again, but this time with new eyes. On the hunt for the perfect first gift for our upcoming little one. Hands laced, we wander with no destination. Shelly picks up a small puppy dog toy. Black and white and red. Parts of it soft while other parts crinkle or rattle. The tag says it is perfect for sensory stimulation.

"How about this?" she asks. "It's cute and functional."

"And is gender neutral, which is good for us."

We both smile and stare down at the bright and bold puppy toy. Awe hits me square in the chest. Obviously, I *know* we are having a baby. Purchasing our first baby item… it's a whole new level of reality. It has my stomach flipping and fluttering. Adds a new dose of thrill and eagerness.

I hope the baby has Shelly's dazzling eyes and cute

nose, as well as her kind heart and brilliance. More than anything, I just want our child to be healthy and happy.

Hand in hand, we wind our way out of the baby maze and make our way to the checkout. Shelly leans into me and I give her hand a light squeeze. As we round the end of the aisle near the registers, my feet stick to the floor and my legs lock in place.

Can life quit throwing curveballs?

I don't know what the hell I did, but I swear I will make up for it. Whatever *it* is.

Less than ten feet in front of us, Kelsey stands in the checkout line with a small basket in her hand. Maybe I can steer us right and she won't see me. But just as I shift us and point to a register with a shorter line, I hear my name.

"Devlyn? Is that you?"

Someone, anyone, send help.

Had she not spoken loud enough for Shelly to hear, I would have ignored her. But Shelly perked up at my name. I spin us slightly and meet the eyes of my first love. The girl who pulverized my heart five years ago. Someone I planned to never see again.

But the universe is intent on torturing me for some reason.

My hold on Shelly tightens as I say, "Hey, Kelsey."

Shelly jolts beside me. "*Kelsey,* Kelsey?" Shelly whisper-asks.

I give her hand a squeeze. A small assurance that everything will be fine. "Mm-hmm."

"How've you been?" Kelsey asks with too much excitement in her voice. "It's been what... five years?"

If my life could be summarized into one word this past year, it would be perplexing. Every sordid moment of my past has made some strange appearance. Like the universe is testing me on every level. Seeing if I am worthy and capable and strong enough to move forward. Not just on my own, but with Shelly and the baby.

Dear Universe, you can stop now. I swear, I'm good.

"Yep. Five years." I turn to look at Shelly and smile. "And life is incredible." For a moment, I lose myself in my Shelly bliss bubble. Stare at her shimmering twilight eyes and forget we are in the middle of Target and Kelsey is less than five feet away.

"Um, that's… I… that's great, Devlyn."

I kiss Shelly's temple before returning my attention to Kelsey. She shifts from foot to foot. Her eyes dart from me to Shelly and back. And for the first time in years, I don't open my mouth to try and appease someone else. Don't say anything to steer the awkward tension away from her. Because for too many years, I have always done things to make other people happy, but not myself. That time is over.

Except when it comes to Shelly. Her happiness is my happiness because she doesn't hold expectations over my head like a weapon. She loves me unconditionally.

"Well, we need to go," I say and start to turn us away.

"Was good seeing you, Devlyn."

I nod and lift a hand. "Bye, Kelsey."

Yes, I realize my response sounds cold and heartless, but I don't care. I owe that woman nothing. In another life, Kelsey meant everything to me. I would have done anything and everything for her. She took advantage of my selfless heart and broke it like I didn't matter. My curtness was me being nice, mature.

We go through the checkout and pay for the baby's first toy. Shelly and I wander to the exit, arms hooked at the elbows. If I were with any other person, I would have been bombarded with questions the second we stepped away from Kelsey.

But Shelly isn't like anyone else.

Inevitably, she will speak up. Curiosity will outweigh contemplation. But she will wait an appropriate amount of time to ask the most significant question. She won't drown me in an endless interrogation. Not Shelly. She will pick one question, just one, and ask without jealousy or guilt.

I crank the engine and let the air conditioning cool the cab before we back out. Shelly removes the toy from the bag and crinkles the floppy ears. Her eyes laser-focused on the little stuffed dog as she remains deep in thought.

I reach over the console and rest a hand on her thigh. In a flash, her eyes meet mine. And I see the question already forming on her lips.

"Are you okay?"

Of all the questions Shelly could have asked, of all the terse words she could have said, this was not what I expected. Not by a long shot.

Shelly has a big heart and a beautiful soul. The fact she is more worried about how I feel speaks volumes. She could have gone into a tizzy. Spewed words of jealousy or mistrust. Pushed away from me after dealing with yet another demon of my past.

But that isn't her style. Shelly has more class and is wise beyond her years.

"Yeah, I'm good." I shrug. "Honestly, I thought I'd feel different."

"How so?"

Months after our breakup, I often wondered what it would be like to see Kelsey again. Would it be tense and awkward or fueled by anger? Would I hate the sight of her or secretly wish to wrap her in my arms? With each passing year, the same unanswered questions lingered. Took up residence in my head.

Until Shelly.

In no time, everything I'd felt for Kelsey—the good and bad—vanished. For years, the sadness over losing one girl fueled a lot of my darker pieces. She'd blackened my young, impressionable heart.

The moment I saw Shelly, Kelsey became a ghost. I no longer saw or felt her. While the scars of what she'd done remained, her hold on me evaporated. Kelsey had been a placeholder until Shelly's path collided with mine.

"Long before you and I met, I pictured what it'd be like seeing Kelsey again. Considering her parents live in the area, the chances were likely. I'd always seen it as this big deal. Me being excited or angry when it finally happened."

"And how was it?"

My thumb strokes over her thigh and I watch the action for a beat. "Lackluster," I say on a laugh. "No anger, but there was a hint of happiness." Shelly tenses under my touch. "But not for the reason you think." My eyes lift to hers. "I'm happy because I've moved on. I'm happy because I have you." I suck in a deep breath. "Although what she did was horrible, although it sent me to a dark place for so long, had she not done it, I wouldn't be here with you."

Tears rim her eyes and add a new luster to the gold flecks.

"I love you, Shelly Reed. You." I lift my hand and rest it on her rounding belly. "I love everything about us. What we are and what we will become."

"I love you, Devlyn Templar." A tear falls down her cheek. "And I can't wait to see where we go from here." She holds up her pointer finger. "But first… can we stop bumping into the past?" she asks on a laugh.

I join in on her laughter. "Would be nice. I'm over this trip down memory lane."

Really, there is only one demon of my past left to conquer. Once that dragon is slayed, life will be as it should—happy and peaceful and full of love.

But I have a feeling that last demon won't go quietly. Let's hope I am wrong.

twenty-one

. . .

Shelly

THIS IS WHY I HAVEN'T BEEN HERE MORE OFTEN. THIS IS why I haven't answered my phone every time it rings. Nicole Reed may be the death of me. Not literally, but pretty damn close.

"Why don't you want to know the sex of the baby? How are we supposed to plan? How can you decorate the nursery without knowing?"

Jesus, take the wheel. I love my mother. I love my mother. I love my mother.

"And why haven't you been answering my calls? This is one of the biggest times in your life. A time when you need as much love and support as possible." Eyes that match my own lock me in place. "Family matters, Shelly."

Deep breaths. In and out.

Tell her how you feel. Best to do it now than drag it out.

"Mom, please." I pause and take another deep breath. "First of all, I'm a grown woman. I make my own decisions. Second, Dr. Webster put me on a strict health regimen. Low to no stress." My lips flatten into a straight line for two breaths. "And you stress me out." I shrug.

I will not apologize for giving myself air and room. I will not apologize for eliminating the stressors in my life, even if it is someone I love. It may not be what she wants to hear, but this isn't just about her. Not anymore.

"Shelly, I—"

My mother speechless is new. Is it wrong of me to be proud I put her in this state? If so, oh well.

How many times did Micah and I sit at the dining room table and listen to her drone on about how she wishes we'd find love and start a family? Far too many. And now that I have done both—not that the family part was planned—she complains I don't spend enough time with her. She complains I am not doing this parenting thing the "right" way, because it is not how she did it.

And I am done. Done.

My mother has good intentions, but there is more than one way to love and parent. Her method worked for her, but it doesn't make it the best way.

"Devlyn and I decided we don't want to know the gender because it doesn't matter." I rub a hand over my belly, which seems to have grown another few inches in the last two weeks. "We want to give our child everything they need, but most importantly, we want them to feel loved. They won't care what color the bedroom walls are painted. They won't care if they're wearing dresses or sports shirts. The only ones who care are the parents."

Her brows knit together. No matter how many times Micah and I have told Mom that our version of happy is not the same as hers, it hasn't clicked. And I think it may be slowly sinking in now. A little.

"I just…" Lines crinkle her forehead. "I don't get it." Her eyes hold mine. "But I'm trying. Promise."

"Thank you."

A gentle smile softens her features. "Do you have plans for the nursery?"

I wince on a shrug. "Yes and no. We're leaving the room the same gray color. And I liked the black and white animal theme Autumn and Jonas did, so we're going with a similar vibe. Except Devlyn is painting the animals and trees and whatnot on the walls."

"That sounds lovely."

"He's excited to start." I adjust my seat on her couch and reach for my glass of water. Each week, it gets harder to move like a nonpregnant woman. "We're waiting to buy furniture until after the shower."

Devlyn and I make zero assumptions about what will be gifted to us at the baby shower next weekend. The registry list has doubled since our trip to Target. Cora told me I could add things from the website that might not be available in the store. My fingers are calloused from the new additions and the registry is jam-packed with everything a baby, infant or toddler may need for the first two years of life.

We agreed to stash money and buy whatever necessities we don't get at the shower. Furniture being the most expensive, we saved enough for those big-ticket items.

"And you're having men at the shower too?"

Dear god, mother. Just quit with the gender nonsense.

"Yes," I say and purse my lips. "If you haven't figured it out yet, I'm a little over the whole traditional way of doing things." Mom opens her mouth, ready to cast her opinion on me, but I hold up a hand. "Devlyn and I have been through a lot. He has dealt with things you couldn't fathom. I won't make him or his father feel like outcasts because of some ridiculous, asinine tradition someone started long before I was born." I take a deep breath and settle my rising blood pressure. "Baby showers should be about celebrating new life… by everyone in that life's world. No matter what's between their legs."

"Shelly," Mom admonishes me as if I am a child.

"No," I say sternly. "No," I repeat for emphasis. "I get it. You want me and Micah to fit some mold that society created centuries ago." I shake my head. "But even when those ideals were created, people snuck around and did what felt natural and right for them." I look Mom square in the eyes. "Love isn't black and white, and neither is life. Both are full of color and wonder without borders. And I wish you'd see that."

The baby sticks a limb in my ribs and I suck in a breath.

Mom scoots closer, concern etched in the lines of her face. "Oh my goodness, Shelly. Are you alright?"

I sit on the edge of the couch, raise my arms, and take in a lungful of air and nod. "Yep." I lower a hand to rub my belly. "Just the baby giving a fist pump."

That's right. You tell grandma that Mommy is right.

With too much effort, I slowly rise from the couch. "I need to head home. Devlyn's father is coming over for dinner and I need to help prep."

Mom opens her mouth to say something, but snaps it shut.

It has been a monumental day. Nicole Reed speechless more than once is something worth noting. The shock on her face is priceless. If only Micah were here to see me standing tall. Well, as tall as a pregnant woman with a hot-air balloon belly can stand.

Mom walks me to the door and helps me with my shoes. I shoulder my purse and give her a hug.

"Love you, Mom. See you at the shower."

She nods with red-rimmed eyes. "I love you, Shelly. Your father and I wouldn't miss it for the world."

I walk to the car with a slight waddle and slowly lower myself into the driver's seat. Something else I will have to give up soon—driving. My belly is getting too big to reach the wheel and pedals comfortably. Plus, the stress of traffic is too much.

With one last look at my mother, I put the car in reverse, wave to her, and back out of the driveway feeling much lighter than when I arrived.

Today, I think it really hit her. Today, I think Mom finally realized that my life, and Micah's life, will be what we make it, not what she wants to shape it as. I don't doubt my brother still gets lectured on not having children. But maybe after today, maybe after the baby shower, Mom will learn to love how we live *our* lives. Maybe she will learn to love that we are happy like this.

twenty-two

. . .

Devlyn

Thank God we don't know the gender. I might have lost it if the house was a blue or pink vomitfest. Although Shelly has given me a new appreciation for pink, having it plastered in every nook and cranny would have been nauseating.

My eyes roam over the decorations strung up and laid out in every imaginable place. Banners and balloons. Confetti in the shape of bottles and pacifiers and diapers scattered on every available surface. *At least it's recycled paper and not plastic or glitter*. Stacks of paper plates and cups and napkins. A box of biodegradable cutlery. Food, lots and lots of food. And a cupcake tower with enough for triple the number of people attending.

I haven't seen the games yet, but I bet they are equally overwhelming.

Sitting on the couch, I watch as Cora, Autumn, and Elizabeth move around the house. They work in tandem as if able to read each others' minds and know what else needs to be done. Shelly loiters in the kitchen, picking at the trays of food and making space for the last few dishes expected as others arrive.

When Cora and Autumn set out to organize the shower, they asked if there'd been anything Shelly wasn't eating during pregnancy and what she'd been craving. The only enemy had been the cheese, but that phase passed. Now Shelly craves and loves her favorite foods more.

There is no shortage of variety on the shower menu. Had it been any other party, the crowd would question the assortment.

I wander into the kitchen, lean a hip on the counter next to Shelly and snag a chocolate-covered fruit skewer.

Excellent decision adding these to the menu.

"Nervous?" I ask before biting off a piece of pineapple.

She plucks a finger sandwich from the tray beside her—sliced banana, nut butter and chocolate peeking out from the slices. "Kind of." She takes a bite as her eyes scan the room and beyond. "I'm excited to celebrate the baby and get the room put together." She pops the last of the finger sandwich in her mouth and shifts her attention to me. "Don't really want to be fawned over, though."

My beautiful Shelly. The brightest star in the night sky, yet she doesn't want all the attention. Doesn't want all eyes on her. Soon, real soon, a lot of that attention will shift.

Shelly will always be my center, my point of gravity,

the person who brings balance to my world. But it won't be long before we both learn how to love each other and love someone new.

I lift my hand and cup her cheek. Slowly stroke her soft skin with my thumb. Stare into her starry eyes as her body relaxes. She leans into my touch, shuffles closer, and wraps her arms around my neck. Buries her face in the crook of my neck and breathes deeply.

Hugs are much different now. With her belly growing bigger every day, Shelly has learned new ways to do everyday activities. I won't say it aloud, but I love painting her toenails. I love massaging her feet every night before bed. And I love the way her eyes light up with both. It relaxes her and makes her smile. It also connects us in a new way. In a way more intimate than lips and tongues and sex.

Don't get me wrong, we still make out like lusty teenagers. Our sex life has never been more incredible. The hormonal changes have not only amplified her drive, but also cemented our emotional bond. Sex during pregnancy is… hot. Like *really* hot. And although we've had to learn new positions so Shelly is comfortable, it has also added a new level of spice to the bedroom.

"Won't be too long. Think of it like the normal Sunday gathering, plus some additional people and lots of baby gifts," I say.

"You're right." Her brows knit together as she clutches her belly. Before I open my mouth to ask if she is okay, she reaches for my hand and places it on the left side of her belly. "Wait for it." She shifts my hand a little lower and presses it more firmly into her belly. A second later, something jabs my hand. "Did you feel that?" she asks, eyes shimmering as they stare into mine.

"Yeah," I say in wonderment. "Is that a kick?"

She moves my hand again. "Or an elbow. Maybe a fist pump. Possibly a knee."

We laugh a moment, then fall silent as we wait for the next jab. Another two stretch her belly before the baby settles.

One hand on her belly, I cup her cheek with the other, lean forward and kiss her. The kiss is far from sweet as I haul her closer and trace the seam of her lips with my tongue. Public displays are not typical for us. Mini make-out sessions in front of people almost never happen.

But these aren't just *any people*. Every person here is family. With kindness and embraces and inclusion, these people have shown me more love than any person with my DNA. They accept me for who I am and not what I can do for them. They care for me because I care for Shelly and vice versa. And they will never say an unkind word to either of us. Doesn't mean they won't tease us later.

Slowly letting each of them into my life has been a gift I never expected. A gift I wouldn't have without this incredible woman in my arms.

"Our little water aerobics instructor," I say, pressing my forehead to hers. "Can't wait to meet them."

"Same. Won't be long."

~

The party is in full swing and it isn't as overwhelming as originally expected. It's like Sunday nights mixed with a birthday party. Kind of. If an actual itinerary for this shindig exists, I'd be shocked. So far, we have mingled and eaten food. I suspect gifts and games and cake will happen soon.

"Can I have everyone's attention," Cora yells over the chatter. She sidles up to Shelly and conversations quiet as all eyes turn her way. "Thank you." She smiles, then wraps an arm around Shelly's shoulders. "Today we're here to celebrate this awesome chicky." Cora presses a kiss to Shelly's cheek. "And her and Devlyn's impending arrival."

Hoots and hollers and applause fill the room. Shelly's cheeks pinken and I stare a little too hard at her heated skin. How long has it been since a blush stained her cheeks? Far too long. I'll need to remedy that in the near future.

Cora guides Shelly to a comfortable chair at the far end of the room that was decorated to mirror a throne. Once seated, Cora places a crown on Shelly's head decorated with mini plastic babies. I open the camera app on my phone and snap a picture.

"Gifts first," Cora says. "Then we'll do some corny games. And since the guys are here, us ladies should sit back and watch as they embarrass themselves." A chuckle leaves her lips.

Another chair is moved next to Shelly's and Cora gestures for me to sit.

Small boxes and big boxes. Jumbo bags and miniature bags. One by one, gifts are handed to Shelly to unwrap. After the first gift is revealed—an overflowing box of onesies and sleep shirts and jumpers—Shelly suggests we open everything together. That the day isn't really about her, but about us and the baby.

Wrapping paper tears and crumples. Tissue paper gets tossed to the side. The black trash bag at my right gets fuller with each unwrapped gift.

With each new present, shock and awe spread from my heart to my lips, tipping them up in an impossible smile. These people, our friends and family… they are the true gift. At this point, I don't think Shelly and I will need to buy much else. Their generosity is the biggest hug around my heart.

A bassinet with sheets and blankets. A crib that converts to a toddler bed and, one day, to a twin bed frame with more sheets. Clothes for home and outside the house for the next year. Bottles and nipples and cleaning kits. Baby bathtub and toiletries and cute hooded towels. Socks and mittens. Enough diapers and wipes to last us for several months—although, I hear you need more than you think—and so much more.

They thought of everything. Not just the items Shelly and I added to our registry list.

The backs of my eyes sting at their love and support and big, big hearts. Warmth floods my veins as tightness wraps my chest.

How many years have I wanted this? Love from others without conditions. Before Shelly, I thought I'd missed out on my chance at happiness and love. That my opportunity came and went after high school.

But I was wrong.

Shelly gifted me this. All of this. Love, life, a future.

Had I not been brave enough to take the leap, I don't think either of us would be here. I fought it for so long. Discounted my worth. Dismissed that love was possible again. Suppressed my feelings in fear of getting hurt.

Then, in a blink, I grew tired of fighting what my heart wanted. Grew tired of denying myself. And little by little, I opened up to her and to myself. I let myself feel, *really feel,* for the first time in years. And it was… sensational.

Shelly is sensational.

If not for this incredible woman, I wouldn't know happiness. I wouldn't know love. Wouldn't wake each day with a smile on my face and warmth wrapped around my heart. Damn, am I lucky. And I will never take Shelly or our love for granted.

I turn and see the tears ready to spill down her cheeks. Hormones aside, she would have cried at the level of love gifted today. Wrapping her hand in mine, I give a gentle squeeze. The tears brimming her eyes make the gold flecks sparkle brilliantly against her twilight irises and we stare wordlessly at each other. *I know*, I mouth.

The road of our relationship has been bumpy. Between my initial resistance and the sporadic roadblocks, it felt like we were driving the wrong way at every turn. That something bigger than us was intervening and steering us toward a dead end.

We didn't let them win, though. We never will. Our love is too strong.

"Alright, party people. Time for the good stuff," Cora shouts.

Autumn switches the music and an upbeat tempo fills the room. Gavin, Jonas and my father grab boxes and start hauling them to the nursery. I fill my arms and follow in their wake. By the time we have all the gifts moved, Autumn, Cora, Peyton and Penny are organizing something at the dining room table. Elizabeth and Nicole laugh at the display, and nervous energy floods my veins.

I don't know much about baby showers except for food and gifts. Shelly tried to warn me about the games. *"Some of them are just gross,"* she'd said. Time to pull up my big boy pants and do this. Enjoy the moment and suffer through the grossness with a smile on my face.

More than an hour later, we wrap up the last of the games. *Halle-freaking-lujah.*

Changing "dirty" diapers on baby dolls. Tootsie Rolls and soft fudge will never exist in my life again. Ever. Bobbing for pacifiers sounded like fun at first. Lies. All lies. Blindfolded while tasting baby food. This one wasn't as horrendous as I expected. I blame it on the organic jarred foods that were purchased.

Those were the more outlandish games. The rest I enjoyed.

Everyone was given a piece of stock paper along with pencils and crayons and asked to draw a picture for the baby. Didn't need to be pretty. Just something to look back on years later and smile over.

Next, we were all given two index cards. On one, we were asked to write names for a girl and on the other, names for a boy. Shelly and I had briefly scoured the internet for baby names, but nothing had stuck yet. This game was the perfect way to come up with fresh ideas.

The last game—although not really a game—everyone was given a small card, blank on the inside. We were tasked with writing a note or letter to the baby. Nothing specific. Whatever was in our heart.

And when I put pen to paper and slowly wrote a letter to my unborn child, I couldn't hold back the tears. I didn't sob, but the tears came and I let them flow freely as I wrote. One drop, then another, splattered on the card, but I didn't wipe them away. I left them right where they were. Exactly where they belonged.

"We'll help clean up and get out of your hair," Gavin tells me and Shelly.

"You don't need to," Shelly offers. "We can clean up."

Cora sidles up the Gavin. "Uh, no you won't. You just sit there and watch. Tell me what leftovers you want and which we should divvy."

"Fine," Shelly grumbles.

When Dr. Webster first put Shelly on light activities only, she protested with every breath she took. But as her health became more of a risk to the baby, she conceded. Although she grumbles still, I know she doesn't mind the help.

With each passing day, the circles beneath her eyes grow a touch darker. Her belly more round and body more uncomfortable. Her willingness to give up tasks she once argued to do on her own has grown tenfold. Her grumbles are more for show now.

We wave everyone off as they leave and go back inside to a quieter yet fuller house. But not as full as it will be in the next eight to ten weeks. Before long, our house will be filled with more love than imaginable. It will be chaotic in the beginning, but beautiful chaos. The thought thrills and terrifies me equally.

My inner pessimist says it is too good to be true. My inner pessimist says nothing this wonderful ever lasts.

I do my damnedest to shove that negative beast down. To smother it with all the good. To suffocate it with love. To extinguish its existence.

Maybe it is time to up my visits with Dr. Prince. Maybe it is time I ask Shelly to come with me.

twenty-three

. . .

Shelly

I STARE AT THE BEIGE WALLS, LIGHTLY DECORATED WITH colorful framed art prints, and wonder how many secrets have bled into the drywall.

Spilling my past or how I feel doesn't make me uncomfortable. I have nothing to hide.

Guess I wonder how a person can listen to other people's problems all day, every day, and not feel overwhelmed or ready to crawl out of their skin. How do they sleep at night after digesting all the trauma or heartache?

They are saviors. True miracle workers.

On the couch beside me, Devlyn bounces his knee uncontrollably. His fingers pick at the exposed threads in the distressed part of his jeans. Every few seconds, his eyes land on the edge of my profile.

His nervous energy is palpable, comprehensible. Although we are honest with each other, tonight, in this place, sharing himself with me is different. A new level of vulnerability for us both. Devlyn is familiar with Dr.

Prince. Has shared countless secrets with him. More than likely, secrets he has yet to share with me. That fact doesn't hurt. My hope is that after today—and future sessions—Devlyn won't feel uncomfortable sharing painful parts of the past with me. That I gain a new level of trust with Devlyn. Strong enough for him to consider me his safe space in all matters.

Arm extended across the table, Dr. Prince offers me his hand. "Nice to finally meet you, Shelly." His smile is kind, warm, sincere. His expression gentle and soothing as he waits for me to take his hand.

Placing my hand in his, we shake. His grip is firm yet soft. Solid yet gentle. "You as well. Devlyn speaks highly of you."

We sit back in our seats. I rest a hand on Devlyn's leg and he takes my hand in his, lacing our fingers as his bouncing knee settles. Dr. Prince takes a sip of water, then picks up a notepad and a pen. He scribbles on the paper for a moment, his eyes occasionally peeking up at us. Observing us. Making note of Devlyn's reaction to me and mine with him.

His observation doesn't unsettle me. This is part of his job, not just to listen but to also survey. I will say his perception of us has me curious.

"How've things been since our last appointment, Devlyn?"

I turn my head slightly, enough to get a better view of him but not look at him directly. He nibbles at his lips as he mulls over his answer.

"Good." He shrugs. "The baby shower was this past

weekend." He looks at me briefly and gives my hand a squeeze. "Was nice, but overwhelming."

"Overwhelming how?"

His knee starts to bounce again. I stroke my thumb in a slow rhythm over his hand and, after a beat, his leg calms. Dr. Prince jots something on the notepad then meets my eyes, smiles, and returns his attention to Devlyn.

Devlyn laughs under his breath. "Not like I didn't know the baby was coming, but after the party, it just felt more real. Y'know?" His fingers toy with mine. "Plus, we got so many gifts for the baby." Green irises meet mine for a breath. A nervous smile on his lips. "I didn't expect that much… love."

I watch as Devlyn's brows pinch together, his eyes narrowing as he drops them to stare at his lap.

In this very moment, I see so much, but one thing stands out the most. Devlyn feels undeserving of this level of love. He feels unworthy of affection from other people.

And it pisses me off.

As if sensing my irritation, Dr. Prince directs his focus my way. "Shelly, tell me what you're thinking right now."

Spotlight, party of one.

My eyes linger on Devlyn's profile a moment before I turn to look across the table. I lick my lips, swallow past the anxiety ball in my throat, and tighten my hold on Devlyn. "I hate that she did this to him."

Dr. Prince tilts his head. "His mother?" I nod. "Take

a deep breath and let the anger pass. Then, when you're ready, I want you to expand on that."

I do as he suggests and take a deep breath. Then another. And another. One breath at a time, I feel my pulse settle and the pang in my chest dissipate. "When it comes to Karen Templar, I can't seem to keep my emotions at bay. I apologize."

"No need to apologize. There is no judgment here."

With one last deep breath, I continue. "Devlyn and I became friends in October. We'd met in passing a year earlier through work, but it wasn't until this past October that we spoke and interacted." I grab my water bottle, twist the lid off and take a sip. "It took time and effort for Devlyn to open himself up. To let me in. Partly due to a past relationship gone sour." I turn to lock on Devlyn's soft green eyes. "But another piece was because he'd never really been shown love. Not real love." I return my gaze to Dr. Prince and press the heel of my hand to my chest. "And that hurts on so many levels."

The backs of my eyes sting as the words leave my lips. But I bite them back. I don't know if my body is overreacting because my hormones are out of whack or if I'd feel the urge to cry normally. Right now, all my body wants is to release. Heartache. Pain. Love. All for the man at my side that holds my hand like a life preserver.

"Shelly, your feelings toward Devlyn's mother are natural and reasonable." Dr. Prince shifts his attention to Devlyn, but continues to speak to me. "I don't know how much Devlyn has told you about his mother, but we have been working through the harder parts of his past." His gentle eyes meet mine again. "It will take time, but I hope the both of you are able to heal from this. That one day, you'll be able to not give so much of your energy to someone undeserving."

For the remainder of the hour, we discuss how the healing process is going with Devlyn and his father, and what my feelings are in relation to James. With each new interaction, I grow fonder of James. He hasn't told me his entire story, but from what he has shared and what Devlyn has told me, he felt trapped for years. Not because of Devlyn, but because he didn't trust his wife to raise Devlyn without him present. He wanted to escape with Devlyn, but didn't know how to safely.

But James smiles more now. The gentleness in Devlyn is equally visible in James. Excitement vibrates off James as each day passes and we get closer to the arrival of his first grandchild.

I trust the Templar men will slowly heal and become whole again. Put the harsh years of the past behind them and move forward. Both have so much love in their hearts and it'd be a shame for them not to share it with others.

Minutes before the session ends, Dr. Prince gives us homework. Before the next appointment, which I have been asked to attend, Devlyn and I are to spend time in the nursery. Whether it is unpackaging gifts and finding them a new home or building the crib or just sitting in the room. We are to spend time in the room and just feel. Fill the room with love. Talk to the baby while in the room. Get used to the idea of having more than just the two of us in the house.

After handshakes and goodbyes, Devlyn and I leave the office. And it isn't until we are in the car and driving down the road that I feel it. A newfound level of relief. A comfort that had been missing. I didn't know it was something I needed, but now that I have it, I am grateful.

twenty-four

. . .

Devlyn

Is it weird for me to be turned on right now?

Having Shelly at my appointment was beyond therapeutic. A buzz coursed through my veins. Perspiration dampened my skin. And the pain of the past was slowly released from my bones. For the first time in years, it feels as if I can draw in a full, deep breath.

And damn, it feels spectacular.

I don't keep secrets from Shelly—well, unless you count surprise parties—but I haven't unpacked all of my past with her. Not yet. Not because I don't want to, not because I don't trust her, but more because it is a lot to take on and I have no idea where to begin.

Insert Dr. Prince.

This man has been a godsend. He doesn't look at me like I have two heads. He doesn't call me crazy or judge how I feel about my mother. No, he listens, digests, then helps me look at each point in time from a different angle. One memory at a time, he guides me down the road to resolution. Shows me how to let go of the bad and find ways to forgive the guilt I feel. Teaches me how to move forward and love myself first without fear of repercussion.

When the holidays roll around this year, I plan to get Dr. Prince something to show my appreciation. He will decline and tell me gifts are unnecessary, but I beg to differ. Without his counsel, my life would still be a mess.

I park in the driveway and dash to the passenger door to help Shelly out. Early in the pregnancy, she'd wave me off. Tell me she was capable of getting out on her own. But as her belly rounds more, she waits for my hand. Allows me to take on more of the load. Smiles or kisses my cheek when I suggest she rest.

With Shelly less than ten weeks from delivering, Elizabeth insists on her working less hours. Instead of forty to forty-five, she now works closer to twenty. In a few weeks, depending on how she feels, Shelly plans to start maternity leave. Originally, she wanted to work until her water broke. With her belly rounding faster, her ankles and fingers swelling more, plus the general discomfort of being on her feet all day, she conceded on the idea. Confessing she will likely start leave a week or two before the baby arrives. Which is right around the corner.

To say I am relieved would be an understatement.

"Should we start on our homework assignment now?" she asks, humor lacing her voice as we toe off our shoes near the door.

I remember the first homework assignment from Dr. Prince. How ridiculous it felt to have *homework*. But I followed through. Completed each task without argument. And now, I have grown to like the assignments. Grown more comfortable with the familiar activities that aid my peace.

"Yes and no."

"Yes and no?"

I nod. "Mm-hmm." I lace my fingers with hers, spin to face her, and walk us down the hall. She starts to pull us toward the nursery, but I tug us in the opposite direction. Toward the bedroom. Our bedroom.

"Want to change?" she asks as her brows knit together.

I shake my head as my legs bump the foot of the bed. I lift my free hand to her cheek and stroke her soft skin with my thumb. Leaning forward, I press my lips to hers. Brush her lips with mine slowly. Paint the seam of her lips with my tongue until they part and let me in.

In two rapid heartbeats, the kiss evolves from sweet to hungry.

Her fingers curl into fists and cling to the cotton of my shirt. She tugs me closer. Drags her hands up my torso and along my shoulders before wrapping them around my neck. The kiss turns frantic as our tongues tangle and hands grope.

I break the kiss, reach back for the collar of my shirt and yank the cotton over my head before tossing it to the floor. Shelly fumbles to tug her shirt free. "Let me," I say as I reach for the hem and slowly pull it up and off her body.

Not a breath passes before I drop to my knees. Inches from my face, her belly button pokes out. Pink and brown marks highlight her belly. Marks she isn't fond of, but I find sexy as hell. Those marks are evidence my baby—our baby—grows in her womb. Can't think of anything more beautiful.

"Gorgeous," I whisper as I lean in and press my lips to her belly. I lift one hand and rest it on her belly, then the other. Tipping my head back, my eyes trail up her midline until I reach her starry blues. "The most beautiful, remarkable, astonishing woman I know."

Pink floods her cheeks as she combs her fingers through my hair. "Make love to me," she says with fierce boldness.

The further into pregnancy Shelly is, the more challenging sex becomes. It took several nights to find the most comfortable position for her, but neither of us complained.

Her shorts and mine land in the same pile as our shirts, followed by her bra and panties. I help her onto the bed, add a second pillow beneath her head, then crawl up beside her. Plant my hands on either side of her. Feather kisses over her skin. Along her jaw and neck. The curve of her shoulder and length of her collarbone. Over one breast, sucking her nipple between my lips before trailing over to the other. Inch by inch, I kiss my way down her belly, whispering words of love—for her and our baby. Then I dip lower. Drop between her thighs and lick up her seam.

She gasps and reaches for me, clutching my hair in her fist. "So good."

Her moans fill the room while I feast on her body. Her fingers in my hair tug harder. Nails digging into my scalp as her thighs tremble and tighten around my head. On the brink of her orgasm, I insert two fingers and pump at the slow rhythm she begs for every time. With one last flick and pump, her body constricts around my fingers as a guttural moan spills from her lips.

Before she comes down from her high, I crawl up the bed and kiss her deeply. Her hands roam from my face to neck and down my upper back. Moving to her side, she shifts the second pillow to the side and rolls onto hers. I brush her blonde locks aside and kiss the back of her neck and over her spine between her shoulder blades. She lays a hand over mine on her hip, lacing our fingers and encouraging me to paint her skin with my touch.

Shelly hasn't stated as much, but I get the impression she feels less attractive as her belly grows. The dramatic changes to her body have darkened her mood some days. Stolen her sunshine. And on those days, I hold her more. Closer. Tighter. Longer.

Each day of this journey… I have loved them all. The light and dark. The highs and lows. They give me perspective. Allow me to appreciate life and love and us in unimaginable ways.

She may not enjoy the changes to her body, but I love her more because of them. Love what those changes represent. Our connection. Our love. Strength and bravery and hope. The future.

Tracing my hand along the curves and dips of her torso, she releases my fingers when I reach her breast. I palm one in my hand. Massage and pinch and tease. A moan floats through the air as she grinds her butt against my erection.

I want to be inside her, desperately, but I take my time. Tease her body with lips and fingers and insatiable hunger. Make her comfortable. Make her feel good. Make her as equally desperate for me as I am her. Let her know that I love her and her body at every stage of life.

Sex with Shelly isn't just about getting off—both of us could do that easily. Sex with Shelly is uninhibited intimacy. Deep and pure and indestructible. A physical act to show her just how much I want her, need her, can't be without her. A way to show her she is still who I want, always. That when I look at her, heat floods my veins, my heart, every cell in my body.

"Devlyn," she whisper-moans as I pinch her nipple harder. She pushes her breast into my touch. "Please," she begs as moisture coats the tip of my erection.

I release her nipple and trail my fingers down her body, over the curve of her ass, and dip down between her thighs. Two fingers trace her seam and she shivers. Up and down. Up and down. I slick my fingers in her juices before pushing them inside.

Her gasp fills the air as I slowly pump two fingers inside her, over and over. She grips my forearm, her nails biting my flesh. This pain is one I have come to love, one I look forward to feeling, receiving.

My fingers pump faster, harder as her breaths come in quick, shallow pants. She rocks her hips harder against my touch, grinding, and I know she is close. I slip my fingers out and circle her clit once, twice, three times before dipping back inside. Pin her back to my front with my other arm. Circle her clit again and close my eyes as her body catapults once more.

She rides out her high with my fingers still inside her. As her body comes down, I pull my slick fingers out and paint her orgasm on my cock. Positioning my tip at her entrance and hand on her hip, I kiss her shoulder. "Love you, Andromeda."

She brings a hand to my hair and fists the locks, pinning me to the crook of her neck. "Love you, too."

With a slow rock of my hips, I fill her fully. We moan in unison. Her grip on my hair tightens as she grinds back against me. Inch by thick inch, I pull out to the tip before plunging forward. The first few rocks of my hips are slow, methodical, premeditated. I bask in every little whimper that leaves her lips. Relish every move her body makes as she silently begs for more.

And then, we are anything but slow and steady.

In a blink, the beast inside me claws its way to the surface and growls. My hips piston faster as my touch digs and bruises her hip and breast. I strengthen my hold on her frame and pump a vicious, hungry, punishing rhythm with my cock.

Her sweet cries of pleasure fill my ears. Her sweat slicks my skin and hers. And it isn't long before her body lets go and she moans my name. I bite the curve of her neck as I come undone inside her, my hold on her never more fierce.

Nothing compares to this. Shelly in my arms. Our bodies connected in every possible way. Both of us in a state of euphoria. Our connection isn't purely sexual, but the sex is explosive.

Shelly and I were lucky. We connected as friends before becoming lovers. Formed a bond I never thought possible. Discovered love slowly and together. Constructed an unbreakable connection.

In less than a year, Shelly and I have experienced so much together. Good and bad. Had we not faced the hardships and heartache, our love may not be what it is today. In our small blip of time together, we have been through a lot. Although there was hurt, I wouldn't change any of it. Although I almost lost her, and myself, we found our way back to each other.

My arms band around her body—one above her belly, one below—and hug her closer. I pepper her skin with kisses from her neck to the edge of her shoulder. Breathe her in and bask in the taste and touch and scent of her.

"Love you so much, Shell," I whisper against the back of her neck. "So much." My hands shift and embrace her expanding belly. Our baby.

She lays her arms over mine and squeezes me to her. "Love you more, Dev."

Not possible. Not by a long shot.

A chuckle slips from her lips as her body shakes. "Should we do our homework now?"

I join her light laughter. "Yeah. In a minute. Just want to lie here a little longer." And never let go.

twenty-five

. . .

Shelly

I wake drenched in sweat, the covers tossed from my body hours ago. The ceiling fan whirs above as the air conditioning blows cool air from the vent. Yet, I look like I just stepped out of the shower.

Looking to Devlyn's side of the bed, I find it empty. The cotton sheets cool.

Pushing up on my elbows, I peer around the darkened room, Devlyn nowhere to be found. I inch up to a sitting position, scoot to the edge of the mattress and let the cool air chill my heated skin. Easing off the bed, I peel my top over my head and toss it in the hamper before grabbing a dry shirt.

I tiptoe out of the room, the house alight with the rising sun coming in through the windows on the back of the house. Wandering down the hall, I listen for any indication as to where Devlyn might be. But I hear nothing. No clanking utensils in pans or food sizzling on the stove. No muted sounds from the television. Nothing.

Just as I consider climbing the stairs to his studio, I stop between the kitchen and living room.

In my periphery, I spy Devlyn out back on the patio. A canvas on his easel, paint palette on one hand while a brush rests in the other and paints in varying shades of pink and red on the canvas.

As if he might hear me, I tiptoe toward the sliding glass doors and loiter just out of view. But not far enough that I can't watch him while he works.

In seconds, I realize the painting on the easel is the nude of me he started before my belly was so round. The full canvas isn't visible from my vantage point, but I see the length of my legs and curve of my hip. Scattered in the image are various flowers and a winding length of green vines. Looking at the canvas, I *know* the image is me. But from an outsider's perspective, someone who isn't familiar with me or us, no one would know who the woman is in the flowers.

The sun slowly rises in the eastern sky, but the pergola covering the patio keeps some of the sunbeams out of Devlyn's line of sight. Leaning on the frame, I watch him a little longer. Absorb the serenity he bleeds as he puts paint on the canvas. Breathe deeper as I watch the muscles of his back flex as he paints a new likeness of his favorite person—his words, not mine. Rub my swollen belly as I stare at the man I love.

My stomach grumbles and I decide to leave Devlyn to his solitude while I make us breakfast.

The buzzer for the turkey bacon sounds as Devlyn pads into the kitchen and leans against the counter.

Sliding on a hot mitt, I open the oven and take out the pan, setting it on a trivet.

"I would've made breakfast had I known you were up," he says as I add shredded cheese to scrambled eggs on the stovetop.

Setting the package next to him, I stir the cheesy eggs and turn off the burner.

"Didn't want to disturb you." My lips curve up slightly. "You looked so peaceful and in your element."

He fetches plates as I start toasting slices of bread. "Still too hot to be outside after the early hours. I try not to wake you when I'm up at dark thirty."

Plates piled high with cheesy eggs, turkey bacon, fresh fruit and toast, Devlyn carries them to the dining room. I park myself in the chair as he wanders back to the kitchen.

"Tea, water, juice, chocolate milk?"

On the last one, the baby gives me a swift kick to the lungs. I gasp, then settle my breath. "Junior wants chocolate milk," I say on a laugh.

"Oh yeah?"

"Yep. Soon as you said it, they kicked."

"Chocolate milk it is."

The first several bites go by in relative silence. After I down half the glass of chocolaty goodness, I point my fork over my shoulder. "How's the painting coming along?"

Devlyn finishes his bite. "Almost done." He pushes around a slice of watermelon with his fork. "Maybe a few more sessions on the stool."

Next week, I officially start maternity leave from

Petal and Vine. Although I am not due for another month, minimum, standing and walking all day is becoming more difficult and uncomfortable. It isn't that I *can't* do it. More like it exhausts me to be on my feet more than an hour.

Weeks ago, Elizabeth made me sit down every so often. *"I've been there, sweetheart. You will thank me later for the stool," she'd said.* And she was right, of course. Parking my butt on the stool helped some with the swelling, but so did walking. If I was arranging flowers, my instructions were to be on that stool.

And I definitely didn't want to be in trouble with Momma Davies.

Working less hours had been a big adjustment. So was learning to give up my independence. Not that I gave it up fully. Some tasks I still manage on my own just fine. But driving and setting up the nursery are not on the "Shelly is allowed to do these alone" list.

With me home full time soon, part of me feels as if I am stealing Devlyn's time from him.

For years, he was used to his solitude. He was used to climbing those stairs and getting lost for hours or days in his art. And now, it feels as if I rob him of it all.

"Why don't you spend more time on it today," I suggest as he eats his last bite of toast.

Cocking his head to the side, he narrows his eyes. "Thought we were finishing up the nursery today. Or trying to, at least. I need to put the final touches on the mural."

I swallow down the last of my chocolate milk. "But if you want to paint more of something else, you can. I can unbox the diapers then fold the washed baby clothes and put them away."

The nursery is practically finished. Some bigger items still needed to be assembled, but the crib and bassinet are done. The baby swing and items the baby won't use right away are still in the box. They don't concern me, though I know Devlyn will assemble them sooner rather than later.

"Maybe for a little bit," he concedes.

A tension I didn't realize was in my shoulders relaxes. Parenthood is a big change for us both, but I don't want either of us to forget who we are and what we love. Devlyn should still get to spend time in his studio. Although I may need him to watch over me for a short time around the birth, I don't want him to feel trapped or bogged down.

"Good, because I want to see the finished product. Please and thank you."

Wood scrapes wood as he scoots his chair back, rises from his chair and laughs. "Yes, ma'am." He picks up my empty plate and his. "I'll get the dishes since you cooked. You do what you need to do and I'll meet you in the nursery in a bit."

I brace my hands on the chair and table and push up. Following him to the kitchen, I kiss his cheek. "Take your time."

I sway back and forth in the rocking chair near the window. My eyes on the tree just outside the baby's bedroom on the side of the house, watching the wind rustle the leaves as birds flit to and fro. My hand rubs small circles over my swollen belly as I talk to the baby.

"Mommy and Daddy should put a bird feeder in the tree. Maybe treats for the squirrels too. Then we can watch them while we rock in the chair together." My eyes fall to my belly. "Definitely need to add some more color. A flowering shrub, so you always have something beautiful to look at. What do you think?"

A knee or elbow or foot protrudes to the left of my navel as the baby stretches. I consider it an agreement to my idea. "Glad you think so too."

Laying my head against the back of the chair, I close my eyes and continue to sway. Minutes pass before I hear Devlyn pad into the room. He doesn't say a word, but I sense him close by.

Slowly, I open my eyes and scan the room. Just out of reach, he leans against the wall, arms crossed in front of him. His expression soft as he regards me in the rocking chair. The corners of his mouth tip up.

"Didn't mean to disturb you."

"You didn't." My eyes drop to his bare chest where random streaks of paint stain his skin. Heat floods my cheeks as the memory of us painting each other comes to the forefront. "Was just relaxing after putting things away."

In two long strides, he reaches the front of the rocker and squats down. His hands come to my knees and slowly drift up my thighs. "What were you just thinking?"

"What?"

His thumbs draw small circles on either leg. "Just now, you looked at me and blushed. What were you thinking?"

Will I ever not blush around Devlyn?

Devlyn is the only man to stir up such desirous feelings and thoughts. Enough to heat every cell in my body and pink my skin. In the beginning, I was embarrassed by my reaction. Now, I embrace the way my body responds to his proximity, his words, him.

Licking my lips, I swallow and point to his chest. "Saw the paint on you and thought about the morning when we… uh… painted each other." Heat floods my cheeks anew.

His hands trail from my thighs to my round belly, his thumbs and fingers lightly massaging the stretched skin. And damn, does that feel good. So good.

"Definitely need to do that again," he says as he leans in and presses a kiss to my belly. "Maybe before you arrive into the world, little one," he whispers to my belly. Then he lifts his gaze, his eyes a shade darker. "Maybe now."

Heat spreads throughout my body for a wholly new reason. Hunger and love rise to the surface. My relaxed state from moments ago morphs into something new, something primal. Although my body wants to rest, my mind and heart scream to get out of this chair and follow Devlyn up the stairs to his studio. To squeeze colored pigment from tubes and paint him with my own abstract passion.

"Yes," I whisper. "Now."

Not needing reassurances, Devlyn rises to his full

height and offers me his hand. My warm fingers slip into his hand as I stand from the rocker. Without a word, we weave our way through the house and climb the stairs to his studio. He parks me on the stool near his easel. While he sets everything up, I stare at the painting of me he has worked diligently on.

I have no words.

The piece so different from his others. A mess of pinks and reds layer the canvas. Some spots thicker with paint and in harsh yet soft lines. My face is almost absent of detail… except for my eyes. My nose is a simple streak and change in color. My unshapely lips a deep, rich red. But my eyes… I should expect nothing less from Devlyn. They pop on the canvas. Dark blue with gold flecks, naturally. Strands of hair fan over my cheek and down my shoulder to my breast.

My eyes drift along the canvas and take in the curves of my breasts, the dark pink of my nipples. The brush strokes on my body softer. Smoother. Gentle. He painted my belly—our baby—with even more tenderness. My hand splayed beneath my navel, and his hand added in and next to mine, forming a cradle.

The backs of my eyes burn with unshed tears.

The depth of this man's heart is unparalleled. He loves me in a way no one ever has. In a way no one ever will. He brought a new gentleness into my life and I showed him what real love looks and feels like. Our love is pure and breathtaking and everything I wanted in my life.

A sudden rush of images flash before my eyes. Mental snapshots of our past. Assumed depictions of our future. And it is so odd, the clarity of those pictures. Especially those yet to come. But I see it all.

Devlyn with our little one bundled in his arms. His eyes glassy with unshed tears as he stares down at them. And the way he holds my gaze when he looks up at me in pure awe. Delight. Brilliance.

Then the images flash forward to years from now. Devlyn and I swinging our mini between us as we walk down the beach along the surf. A sweet voice begging us to swing them higher. Soft giggles and shrieks of joy.

Tears spill down my cheeks without effort as my mind comes back to the present. The beautiful painting a blurry mess of reds and pinks as I swipe my cheeks and eyes. Devlyn catches the movement out of the corner of his eye and spins to face me.

"What's wrong?" A whack fills the air as he drops the supplies from his hands and strides across the room. He cradles my face in his hands and brushes away the wetness with his thumbs. "Tell me. Please," he whispers.

I lick my lips and swallow as I point a finger at the canvas. "This is the first time I've really seen the painting. It's just…" My blues dart between his greens. "It's so beautiful." I shrug. "Guess it overwhelmed me." I shake my head on a chuckle. "Damn hormones."

Devlyn leans in, kissing each tear trail on my cheeks before pressing his lips to mine. The kiss is sweet and gentle, and ends far too soon.

"You're beautiful." His thumbs stroke my cheeks again. "The most beautiful creature I know."

"For now," I mutter as my eyes fall between us.

"Hey." One hand drifts to my chin and tips it up so I look him in the eye. "No." He shakes his head. "No, Shelly," he repeats.

One of my creeping insecurities rises to the surface. Maybe because I am overwhelmed with seeing the painting. Maybe because there isn't a lot of time of just me and Devlyn left. Whatever the reason, my secret spills from my lips with too much ease.

"When the baby comes, things will change." My vision blurs for a new reason. "They'll easily be more beautiful."

"Not possible." I open my mouth to rebut his words and he shakes his head. "Not. Possible." He presses another kiss to my lips. "Yes, we will love this baby. So much." His hand falls to my belly and rubs the outer swell. "But that won't change how I love you. Ever."

"You don't know that," I whisper-choke.

"I do." Soft, warm lips press mine. "Shelly, I will never love anyone the way I love you. Will I love our baby with unmatched affection? Absolutely. But my love for them will be new. A love neither of us will understand until it hits."

As his words sink in, as they resonate in my bones, I believe them more. The love for our child will be phenomenal. Otherworldly. Surreal. But loving them will be different than loving Devlyn.

I nod. "I love you."

His fingers twirl a strand of my hair as he drops his forehead to mine. "Love you, Shell." After another chaste kiss, Devlyn straightens to his full height. "Come." He offers his hand. "Time to paint."

The corners of my mouth tip up as I take his hand. "As you wish."

Hours pass without care as I paint every line, curve and valley on Devlyn's body. And he paints mine as if it is the most precious thing his hands have touched.

twenty-six

. . .

Devlyn

Shelly shifts on the bed for the umpteenth time. I curl into her frame, my front to her back, and try to calm her.

But she isn't sleeping.

Her hand takes mine and squeezes. Just as I open my mouth to ask if she is okay, her body tightens. Her breathing pauses a beat before she grunts softly.

"What's wrong?" I whisper-ask and kiss her shoulder.

I feel her head shake in the dark. "Can't get comfortable. And my stomach…"

When she doesn't elaborate, I prop myself up on my elbow and look at her profile. "Your stomach what?"

"It's just tight. Like painfully tight."

Without a word, I whip the covers off my body and slip out of bed. Circling the bed, I stand in front of Shelly. "Close your eyes. I'm turning on the lamp." I give her a moment, then flip the switch. We squint into the lit room until our eyes adjust. I hold out my hand. "Let's try to walk a minute. See if that helps."

She takes my hand without argument. I help her off the bed and guide her out of the bedroom. We take slow steps through the house. To the kitchen, then the living room before sliding the glass doors open and stepping outside.

Minutes pass as we wander through the yard barefoot. Shelly appears more relaxed than when we left the bed. Just as we turn to head back for the house, she stops. I take in her profile and see her brows knitted together.

Something's wrong.

Is it time?

It can't be time. The due date isn't for a few more weeks. Early October. Right?

My brain scrambles back to all the doctor's appointments, trying to recall the dozen different dates Dr. Webster told us. And then it hits. A couple months back, when the number of appointments increased and we visited every other week, then every week. At one of those appointments, Dr. Webster said the baby may come sooner. That it wasn't abnormal. But as long as Shelly was in the last four weeks, it was safe.

Is that what this is? Shelly going into labor.

We hadn't attended classes like most normal new parents. With all the mothers surrounding us—Elizabeth, Nicole, Cora, and Autumn—we'd been coached on all things birth and baby related. Shelly had found several Lamaze breathing videos online and opted to do those instead of in-person classes. They made her more comfortable and we did them on our schedule.

What did those videos say? For the life of me, I can't seem to remember a damn thing about the breathing right now.

And what about the books I'd read? They talked about what happens when labor starts. But it also stated no two labors are alike. So what good is that information?

Damnit.

"Talk to me," I tell Shelly. "Do you think it's time?"

Her free hand goes to her belly and rubs circles. Over and over. Again and again. From the expression on her face, she doesn't appear to be in pain. But maybe it isn't *pain*. Maybe she is super uncomfortable. Neither of us knows what to expect with labor, least of all me.

"It just feels tight." She looks up at me, unable to straighten to her full height. "Like my skin is being stretched." Her brows pinch at the middle. "Shit."

"What?"

"Need to pee. Now."

Quickly as possible, I guide us inside and to the bathroom. I stand outside the open door while Shelly does her business. I do my best not to stare or appear overbearing, but I worry. Maybe we should hop in the car and drive to the hospital. I glance across the bedroom to the alarm clock and note the time: 3:55.

The doctor's office doesn't open for another three and a half hours.

Do we wait? Give it time and see if it passes?

I should make her something to drink. Something soothing. A mug of hot cocoa.

Shelly flushes the toilet and washes her hands. "God, it feels like I need to pee constantly, but barely anything came out."

I take her hand and walk us toward the kitchen. "How about some tea or cocoa? Maybe it'll settle whatever this is." And while she drinks, I will search the internet and the stack of baby books for answers.

A smile tips up her lips as she curls into my side. "Cocoa would be great."

With measured steps, Shelly paces the kitchen while I heat the oat milk. I scoop two spoonfuls of her favorite cocoa mix into her favorite mug and add the warmed milk.

Guiding us out of the kitchen, I park us on her old couch in our reading area. While she sips her cocoa, I Google what labor pains feel like. Thousands of results fill the screen and overwhelm me with all the possibilities.

Some articles indicate true labor starts when the water breaks. Others say labor begins when contractions start, that sometimes the water doesn't break on its own. Either way, Shelly's water hasn't broken yet. So I move on to another article. This one talks about painful contractions and the need to push. Shelly hasn't mentioned the desire to push, just the need to pee. Again, I move forward.

The next article has me blinking, again and again.

The article states some labor starts with a general pressure, low in the belly. The mother may feel like her skin is stretched to extremes—very tight. The need to use the bathroom often may be present, without much of a release. I continue reading down the page. The more I read, the more I am convinced it is time.

But the article also points out it may be false labor. That the baby may be shifting and moving into position for the big day. The article goes on and says to time how long the sensations last and how far apart they are.

Not wanting to alarm Shelly, I speak in mellow tones and relay what I just read. Surprisingly, she appears quite calm when I finish.

"I wondered as much," she says. "Right now, it isn't so bad. Like a barely noticeable ache." Her hand paints small circles over her belly while she sips her drink. "This has helped."

"Then I guess we wait." I shrug. "If it starts back up, we time it and make note." I lay my hand over hers on her belly. Lace our fingers together and help soothe her discomfort. "Until then, maybe we just take it easy. Sit on the couch, under the blanket, and watch a movie in the dark." I kiss her cheek. "In a few hours, I'll make breakfast. Sound good?"

"Perfect."

I add eggs to each of our plates already filled with sausage, hash browns, and toast. Setting forks on each plate, I carry them to the living room and hand one to Shelly, who has made a makeshift table with a throw pillow on her belly.

We dive into our breakfast while a Passionflix movie plays on the television.

When Shelly added the Passionflix app to the Apple TV, I asked what the channel was all about. She'd said, *"It's all my favorite romance books coming to life."*

I have yet to read any of the countless romance books on her shelf, but perhaps I should check them out. See what all the fuss is about. The movies have been interesting and lovely, but the book is always better.

Over the last few hours, nothing new has happened. No more tightness. No urgent need for the bathroom. So, we have taken it easy. Rested in each other's arms and occasionally drifted off. Perhaps it was false labor. Books state false labor—Braxton-Hicks contractions—is one way the body prepares for the big day. Kind of like a delivery practice drill.

Whatever it is, I hope it passes until the real time occurs. Last thing we need is a scare after things have been so good.

When our plates empty, I take them to the kitchen and clean up. Just as I place the last pan into the dishwasher, Shelly wanders in. I open my mouth to tell her I was on my way back. That she could have waited and I would have gotten whatever she needs.

But I don't say a word. Not when I scan her head to toe and take all of her in.

One hand braces the edge of the kitchen counter while the other rubs back and forth in rapid strokes on her belly. Her lips trapped between her teeth as her jaw works back and forth. The space between her brows wrinkled and tight.

And I know this is it.

Earlier was a drill. Like a like tremor before an earthquake. Like the warning winds and rain before the hurricane makes landfall.

But this is no longer a drill. It's go time.

"Talk to me, Shell."

"It's like before." She closes her eyes for a breath then holds my greens captive. "But stronger. Tighter. More intense."

"Did it just start?"

She nods. "A minute after you walked out of the room."

"Okay," I say, calmer than I feel. "Let's get the hospital bag and leave."

In the bedroom, Shelly puts on a pair of pajama pants before grabbing her phone from the charger. I trade my sweats for jeans and tug a shirt over my head. I grab us each socks from the dresser. We slip on socks and shoes at the door. Shelly fetches her purse from the hook while I shoulder the hospital bag.

Slowly, we make our way to the car. A minute later, I pull out of the neighborhood and aim the car west toward the hospital. Traffic isn't too bad yet, but may pick up the longer we're on the road.

At a red light, I turn to face Shelly. Her eyes forward as she takes slow, measured breaths. Her hands massage her belly from back to front, occasionally switching positions.

"Doing okay?" I ask, feeling like a fool the moment

the words hit the air. *What a stupid question.* Of course, she isn't okay. The baby is trying to evacuate the womb. No way she isn't in some kind of pain. I sure as hell would be.

"Okay," she says between breaths. "But it's becoming more intense."

Sweat licks my temples as she says the words. I did this. I put her in this position. It is me who is responsible for her pain. Me, not her.

Give her pain to me.

If only it were so simple.

The city passes in a blur of fast-driving cars and a blend of residential and commercial buildings. Now isn't the time to take in scenery. Now isn't the time to observe sights and smells and places to visit in the future.

I flip on the blinker and zip into a turn lane. Tap the steering wheel as I wait for the light to turn green. An older man strolls leisurely in the crosswalk in front of us. Bass thumps from a car nearby. Sirens wail in the distance. But all of it vanishes as the light turns green.

And Shelly's water breaks.

"Oh god," she whispers. "Oh god."

Fuck. I smash the pedal to the floorboard and whip down the road. *We're almost there.*

twenty-seven

Shelly

PAIN. EXCRUCIATING, INEXPLICABLE PAIN. IT IS ALL I FEEL. All I hear. All I see. Pain… it is everywhere. Everything.

I clutch my belly and bend slightly in the seat. "Ow. Ow, ow, ow!"

The car picks up speed as Devlyn takes the next right. I fist the handle above the window and hug my belly tighter.

"Sorry," he mutters. "Just trying to get us there."

"I…" Another stab of pain tears through my belly. I suck in a deep breath, hold it and count to three, then exhale. "I know. Just be careful."

Not a minute later, Devlyn whips into the hospital parking lot. He drives to the drop-off spot near the doors, jumps out and jogs to my side of the car. Flinging my door open, he helps me step out, kisses my forehead, and tells me he will be right back. From my spot near the entrance, I watch as he finds the closest parking spot to the entrance before bolting from the vehicle and running to me, hospital bag slung over his shoulder.

From there, everything but the pain is a blur.

Arm around my waist, Devlyn holds on to me as if my knees will buckle. Which is smart, because I may give up any minute.

Elevator doors whoosh open and the familiar view of the labor and delivery floor comes into view. Today, I won't be twiddling my thumbs in a hard chair in the waiting area. For the first time, I will be in the hospital bed, cursing out people left and right as I push our baby into the world.

As we reach the nurses' station, Devlyn explains the past few hours and my water breaking in the car. As the words leave his lips, another contraction rips through my lower abdomen.

"Argh!" I bite out, bending slightly and clutching my belly.

Before the contraction ends, warm hands guide me to sit in a wheelchair. A nurse steers me down the hall like she drag races cars for pleasure. Three deep breaths later, the wheelchair is parked next to a hospital bed and I am ushered onto the mattress.

"We'll need you to change," the nurse says, offering me a sympathetic smile and a hospital gown. "Or, if you'd prefer, just strip down and slip under the sheet. If you choose to wear the gown, leave the front open." Then, she steps out of the room.

"Do you want the gown?" Devlyn pulls back the top sheet on the bed.

I shake my head. "Just want to ditch the wet clothes."

Devlyn helps with my bottoms and underwear. As I lift my shirt over my head, another contraction hits. While I clutch my belly and breathe through the pain, Devlyn wiggles off my top. He situates me on the bed and covers me with the sheet.

"What can I do?"

I hold up my hand. "Just be here."

He laces his fingers with mine, leans in and kisses my forehead. "Nowhere else I want to be."

The contraction settles and realization strikes. "We didn't call anyone." Our family and friends will lose their shit if we don't let them know I am in labor.

Devlyn releases my hand, pulls his phone from his back pocket, and taps on the screen. A moment later, he locks the device and stows it once more. From my spot on the bed, I hear the repeated vibration of responses, but Devlyn doesn't answer any of them. Instead, he takes my hand again and kisses my knuckles in turn.

It isn't long before nurses flood the room. A thick band gets strapped around my belly and the nurses adjust my position in the bed. Ice chips, water, and a cup are brought in and set up on the rolling table behind Devlyn. Dr. Webster walks in decked out in scrubs with a bright smile on her face. A nurse holds a glove open for her and she slips her hand in one, then another.

She steps closer to the foot of the bed, between my feet in the stirrups. "How you doing, Mom? Dad?" Her smile intensifies. "I hear this little cutie is ready to meet everyone?"

Devlyn remains a quiet beacon of strength at my side as I relay how I feel. The pressure from earlier, the cramping, and then the pain once my water broke in the car.

"Everything sounds on track and normal. Let's have a look and check your dilation."

Once upon a time, I reddened with embarrassment even thinking about my appointments at the lady doctor. Now, I don't care. All the people in this room are trained medical professionals. They have probably delivered hundreds, if not thousands, of babies. Nudity doesn't shock them. No doubt, they have seen it all. And in this moment, I honestly don't give a damn who sees what.

Just get this damn baby out of my body.

Dr. Webster recovers my knees and removes the gloves from her hands as she stands from the stool. Tossing the gloves in the biohazard trash bin, she turns on the faucet and washes her hands.

"Dilated to seven. Shouldn't be long now." Her glowing smile makes another appearance. "I'll be back to check on you soon. In the meantime, keep breathing and resting as much as you can." Her eyes go to Devlyn. "Dad, you're in charge of keeping her as calm as possible. Water and ice chips may help. But not too much."

All but one nurse leaves the room. He pulls things out of cabinets and sets up items on counters and trays and carts. I close my eyes and listen to the machine as it registers my heartbeat, the baby's heartbeat, and contractions. I let it soothe me as I rest against pillows softer than I imagined for the hospital.

Devlyn traces my fingers and hand with his. And right now, everything is calm and normal.

But that all vanishes a second later as another contraction stretches and pulls and rips at my abdomen. Devlyn kisses my temple and encourages me to take deep breaths. I squeeze his hand hard enough to detach it from his arm, but he doesn't complain.

When the pain eases, Devlyn offers me ice chips and pours water in a cup with a straw.

Not a minute later, another contraction hits. This one like a knife to my insides. Stabbing. Painful. Burning. Before I get the chance to voice my pain, the monitor off to the side wails loudly. Too loudly.

In an instant, the room overflows with medical personnel. One silences the machine, while Dr. Webster gloves up. Her smile from earlier gone. Her demeanor and body language more serious as she reads the numbers on the monitor.

She lifts the sheet away and exposes me fully. "Shelly, are you in pain?" She surveys between my thighs. "More than the previous contractions," she clarifies.

"Yes. What's wrong?"

She feels around my lower abdomen, near my pelvic bone, and presses hard in a few spots. "Does this hurt?" I suck in a sharp breath and nod. Her eyes drift to a nurse in light-blue scrubs and she gives a subtle nod. The nurse blurs out of sight and starts grabbing more items from cabinets and drawers. "I don't want to alarm you, but it seems as if this little one isn't getting enough oxygen. Your body isn't ready to push yet, so we need to do an emergency C-section."

Tears rim my eyes, blur my vision and spill down my cheeks. "Oh god."

"This isn't abnormal, Shelly. But we can't wait."

A nurse comes to Devlyn's side, hands him a pile of green scrubs, and tells him he needs to change before the surgery starts.

He kisses my forehead. "Be right back." And then he dashes into the en suite bathroom.

I cry harder the second he steps away. Dr. Webster continues to assure me everything will be fine, but I tune out her voice. I tune out every sound in the room. Because this just feels like another snapped tree in the road. Another major obstacle to challenge me. To challenge us.

And damn it. I am so fucking tired of this. So tired of having to fight. So tired.

twenty-eight

• • •

Devlyn

Once I have the scrubs on and the booties over my shoes, I exit the bathroom. The room is abuzz, and not in a good way. When I look to Shelly, I notice her eyes are closed. My initial thought is she is relaxing between contractions.

As everyone moves rapidly around the room, a curtain is erected to hide the lower half of her body from sight. I go back to my position next to Shelly and scoop up her hand, lacing my fingers in hers. But she doesn't curl her fingers.

In fact, her arm is deadweight.

"Something's wrong," I say, but no one pays me attention. So, I repeat myself, louder this time. "Something is wrong." Dr. Webster peers around the curtain, mask covering her face. "She's limp," I choke out.

If I thought the room was chaos moments ago, I was dead wrong.

Dr. Webster shouts orders, but none of them makes

sense to me. Then a nurse is at my side, taking my arm and guiding me out of the room.

"Everything will be fine, Devlyn. Just let us work and we'll be out to get you in a minute," Dr. Webster says, calmer than she lets on.

"What's wrong with her? Is Shelly okay? The baby?"

"A nurse will be out to speak with you in a moment."

And then, the door is closed.

I have no idea what is happening, but it can't be good. At all.

First the baby is in distress. Then Shelly passes out. This isn't normal. Not by a long shot. Worst of all, I have no idea what is happening on the other side of the door. No idea if I am losing Shelly. Or if we are losing the baby.

Or both.

I fall to my knees. The linoleum smacks my bones hard, but I welcome the pain. I welcome every ounce. Because it is nothing compared to what is happening to my heart.

I can't lose Shelly. Or the baby.

Losing either of them isn't an option. Not even close.

twenty-nine

. . .

Shelly

EVERYTHING IS FOGGY. THE AIR, MY THOUGHTS. IT FEELS AS if I am floating. Lingering. Not really here or there.

What the hell is happening?

My eyes feel puffy and weighted. Heavy. Unable to open.

My throat is swollen and scratchy. Abrasive like sandpaper. My lungs dry and burning. I will myself to swallow to moisten my throat. But nothing happens. No relief comes. I try to take a deep breath, but my lungs won't fill fully.

Again, I try to open my eyes and take in my surroundings. Open my mouth and say something. Anything. Again, I fail.

What the hell is going on?

And where is Devlyn?

I don't sense him nearby. Not the smell of his addictive, earthy scent. Not his warm, charismatic energy. Not his whispered words of reassurance or the weight of his hand in mine.

Where is he?

My brain tells my muscles to move, tells my mouth to open and my voice to work, but nothing happens. I want to scream for help. Want to ask what is wrong with me. Want to ask if the baby is okay.

But none of it happens. Nothing works.

The thick fog returns. Clouds around me and pull me down, down, down. Without effort, I drift further into the darkness.

In the darkness, life feels peaceful.

In the darkness, everything feels safe.

In the darkness, the weight of the past falls away.

And now I understand. I get it. Why Devlyn liked the darkness for so long. It's like a warm hug after a long day. A welcome home when you have been away for days or weeks.

In the darkness, there is no pain. Just relief. And I welcome the repose.

thirty

. . .

Devlyn

The past ten hours have aged me ten years.

Shelly lies in the hospital bed. Still. Silent. Except for the beat of her heart through the monitor. The room dimly lit by a lamp off to the side. The baby in the hospital nursery being monitored by nurses and the doctor.

And me… I stand on the edge of a cliff, head tipped back as I scream at the heavens.

This doesn't feel like another test. Another measure of my strength. No, this feels like the end. The end of a long obstacle course. One I didn't choose, but one I can't seem to escape.

Dr. Webster says Shelly will wake up soon. That her body is exhausted and needs the rest. Her vitals are perfect. It's just a matter of the anesthesia leaving her system and her mind waking up. Dr. Webster says there is no need to worry.

But worrying is all I can do. It is all I know.

With Shelly's hand sandwiched between mine, I

give her a gentle squeeze. Paint lines my fingertips over each finger, each knuckle. I press my lips to the top of her hand on either side of the IV line.

"I need you to wake up, Andromeda," I whisper against her skin. The backs of my eyes sting as tears surface and well. I don't fight the tears. Don't try to shove them down. No, I let them spill. Let them paint my cheeks. Let them fall from my chin to her hand. "I need you, Shell. Forever. Please," I choke out.

I close my eyes and lay my head on her fingers. Pray to whatever force, whatever deity is willing to listen. Beg them to help her wake. Open her eyes. Squeeze my hand. Whisper my name. Something. *Anything.*

Whispering voices in the room startle me from sleep. But I don't lift my head and greet them. Without seeing, I know it is Nicole and George Reed. They have been in the room almost as much as I since Dr. Webster allowed us. More than once, they suggested I get food or a drink or take a walk down the hall. That they would be here with Shelly and let me know if anything changed.

But I refuse to leave her side. Not for a minute. Food and drinks and walks can wait.

Shelly needs me more than I need anything else right now. Leaving her isn't an option. I fear what may happen if I leave this room. One step out, one minute away, and everything could change.

"We need to do something, George," Nicole whispers to her husband. Her voice scratchy and tired. "I can't stand this. The waiting." She sniffles. "What kind of doctor tells a mother to be patient while her only daughter lies in a coma? Does the woman *have* children? Does she have an inkling of what this feels like?" With each word she speaks, her voice escalates in volume.

George shushes her. "Everything will be fine, Nicole."

"You don't know that," she rebuts with a sharp edge to her words. "You can't be positive."

He audibly exhales. "You're right, I don't know what will happen. But I choose to believe she will wake up any minute. I choose to believe everything will be okay. Is it easy? No." At this, I twist my head and peek at the two of them on the couch in the room. George points a finger toward the bed and Shelly, but his eyes remain on his wife. "But I won't give an ounce of my energy to negative thoughts. Not when it comes to our children. Or our grandchild." He lowers his hand. "She will wake up." Rising from the couch, he stares down at Nicole for a beat. "I'm going to stretch my legs and get something for us all from the cafeteria."

Then he storms to the door and leaves without another word.

Although my mind drifts so easily into the dark, I side with Mr. Reed and silently vow to Shelly I will only think positive thoughts. I won't give in to the darkness that has come to me with such ease in the past.

Shelly will wake up. She will. She has to.

I lift my head and shift in the chair that now has a permanent mold of my body. Nicole catches the movement and swipes at her cheeks.

"Sorry if we woke you."

"Don't apologize," I tell her. "We're all on edge right now."

She rises from the couch and shoulders her purse. "I'll go update whoever is still here. Maybe walk the halls for a bit. Clear my head."

I nod. "Okay."

The door quietly clicks shut and it's just me and Shelly and silence. On a normal day, I love the silence we share. It isn't awkward or uncomfortable. Many of my favorite moments with Shelly didn't involve a single word spoken.

But this silence… I never want this type of silence again.

I kiss the back of her hand and stand from the chair. Twisting left and right, forward and backward, I stretch my stiff muscles. I lift my arms over my head and roll my neck. Shake my legs and wiggle my toes. Work my body from head to toe and get my blood flowing.

While her parents are away, I step into the en suite bathroom, leaving the door wide open, and relieve my bladder. Hands soaped up, I run them under the water and rinse away the suds. As I fetch a paper towel from the holder, my ears perk up.

The monitor beeps a different rhythm. Faster. Seemingly louder.

I drop the paper towels in the direction of the bin and dash out of the bathroom. Sidling up to the bed, I take Shelly's hand in mine and lean over her.

"Shell? Can you hear me?"

Her eyelids tighten briefly. Her fingers twitch in my hold.

Leaning in closer, I press my lips to her forehead. Then drop them to her ear and whisper, "I'm here, Shell."

Her fingers curl and wrap around my own. A low groan echoes from her throat.

Hovering inches from her face, I wait for her eyes to open. Wait for her sparkling blues to meet my faded greens. It hasn't been a full day, but I miss the hell out of those eyes.

Slowly, her lids lift. She blinks and blinks and blinks. Her tongue darts out to wet her lips and she groans. She lifts her free hand and taps her throat.

"I'll get you water." I kiss her forehead before untwining my fingers from hers. I pour water from a pitcher into a cup with a straw on the rolling table. Bringing it to her, I bend the straw and press it to her lips. "Small, slow sips."

She takes one, then another. Licks her lips. Swallows. Parts her lips in a silent request for more. After a few more sips, she releases the straw and nods. I set the cup down and take her hand in mine once more.

"How do you feel?" I whisper-ask as I brush stray hairs from her face. My knuckles graze her cheek and her eyes roll shut as she leans into my touch, a low hum in her throat.

Her eyes open and lock on mine. "Tired," she says, her voice raw. "Pain." She inhales deeply before her face morphs. Deep lines mar her forehead. The skin between her brows bunches and tightens. "Where…" Her eyes dart around the room, then circle back to mine. "The baby?"

And for the first time in what feels like forever, I smile. "She's in the nursery." My thumb strokes her cheekbone. "Healthy and perfect." I press the button on the bed and call for the nurse. "When you're ready, they'll bring her in."

Tears rim Shelly's lower lids before they spill down her cheeks. "She?" I nod and wipe the tears away. "A little girl," she whispers.

Nurse Tracy wanders into the room. "Did you—" Her eyes dart to Shelly and she smiles. "Glad to see you're awake, Ms. Reed." She steps up to the bed and looks over the monitor. "How are you feeling?"

"Tired." She swallows. "Some pain."

Nurse Tracy checks the saline bag and IV line. "That's to be expected." A soft smile lifts the corners of her lips. "Your body went through a lot today. Let's raise you up." She presses a button on the arm of the bed and the bed slowly scoots up. When Shelly is sitting up, but still leaning back slightly, she stops. "Let's adjust those pillows and get you water."

Once Shelly is a touch more comfortable and a little more hydrated, Nurse Tracy gives us each a smile, tells us she will page Dr. Webster, and then be back with our baby girl.

I sit on the edge of the bed near Shelly's legs and retrieve my phone from my back pocket. "Everyone's been on edge, waiting for you to wake up." I unlock my phone and open the group chat.

Shelly lays her hand on my thigh as her eyes roll shut for a beat. "They're probably all freaking out," she chokes out.

There is no sugarcoating the situation. When I was kicked out of the room as they performed emergency surgery, I sat in front of the door for quite some time. Eventually, I ambled down to the waiting room and spoke with everyone. The shock was evident on each family member and friend's face, but no one lost it more than Micah.

I'd never seen a man so distraught, but I knew exactly how he felt in the moment. Frightened beyond words. Terrified of what might happen. Helpless because it was out of our hands.

I won't stress Shelly with all of that right now, but I will tell her. When she has her strength back. When we are home and she has a moment to rest and feel more at ease.

"Yes, they are, but they'll feel a million times better knowing you're awake and okay now." Her hand tightens on my thigh as I type out a text.

Devlyn: Shelly is awake. Waiting for the doctor to arrive. More details soon.

And as suspected before I hit send, my phone blows up with one text after another.

Micah: Thank fuck.
Cora: Give her our love until we see her.
Autumn: Oh, thank goodness.
Nicole: On our way back.

One after another, the texts keep coming. I hold up

my phone and Shelly stares at the screen, a small smile forming on her lips. I ignore the messages, lock my phone, and stow it back in my pocket.

And for the next few minutes, while we have alone time, I press my forehead to hers. Breathe her in. Feel her breath on my lips. Feel the weight and heat of her fingers and hand on my leg. I press a gentle kiss to her lips. Then another. Tears blur my vision as I hold her gaze. Emotion clogs my throat.

"I love you, Shelly Reed." My lips press hers again. "And I never want a day without you."

Tears roll down her cheeks as she tips her head and kisses me with desperation. "I love you, Devlyn Templar. Always."

And until Nurse Tracy reenters the room with our baby girl, we don't move an inch. Don't take our eyes off each other.

thirty-one

. . .

Shelly

Desirée Rose.

God, she is beautiful. The most perfect thing I have seen in my life. Her plump little cheeks. A full head of brown hair. Eyes a hint lighter than my own, although Dr. Webster says both her hair and eyes may change color. Either way, she is flawless. A little piece of me and Devlyn in the sweetest package.

I stare down at our little girl as she suckles my breast and lays her hand on my skin. Soft sounds vibrate from her lips to my skin. Devlyn sits beside me on the hospital bed, his head on my shoulder as he watches her, watches us. Every few seconds, he twists to kiss my shoulder.

"God, how is it possible to love her so much already?" he whispers.

His question resonates deep in my bones because I wonder the same. How it is possible to love someone you just met. And not just love… no, it is much more complex than that. Not something I know how to define. Incomprehensible love.

"Not sure." I tilt my head and rest it on Devlyn's. "But I feel it too."

After four days in the hospital, we finally get to go home today. Of course, we will have a caravan. Since not everyone had the opportunity to come see us in the hospital, and because my labor circumstances were not what anyone expected, we will have visitors at the house on and off for the next few days. Mom already stated she will be at the house more often than not.

For once, I don't mind. I look forward to having her help. May even ask her to stay the night once or twice. While I feel less mentally foggy, my body still needs more time to recover. Until I heal fully, I can't lift anything more than one to two pounds, including the baby. Which means, to nurse her, I have to get situated before someone hands her to me.

Dr. Webster assures me I should be better in the next two weeks, then reminds me that everyone heals at different speeds.

Desirée falls asleep with her lips wrapped around my nipple. Slowly, I lower her and Devlyn fixes my gown. Then he drapes a cloth over his shoulder, scoops her up from my arms, rests her against his chest, and bops her up and down as he lightly pats her little back.

I love every side of Devlyn. The quiet and reserved. The passionate and hungry. The gentle and sweet. But seeing this side, watching him hold our daughter, care for her with such tenderness… renders me breathless.

After a soft burp leaves her lips, he carries her to the

plastic bassinet and lays her down. He tightens the blanket around her tiny frame before leaning down and kissing her forehead. He whispers something to her, his voice too soft for me to hear, and I don't ask what. It's something for just the two of them. A shared moment.

Devlyn helps me up from the bed and leads me to the bathroom. Peeling away the gown and my underwear, he helps me bathe with a small tub of warm water, a cloth and soap that smells sterile like the hospital. He dries me off and helps me into my clothes. Then he brushes my hair and secures it with a hair band. After I brush my teeth, we exit the bathroom and I slip on shoes.

Dr. Webster makes one last stop in the room and reviews our appointments over the next few weeks—for me and the baby. She gives us each a hug and walks out with us after Devlyn secures Desirée in the stroller. The moment we exit the hospital, I stop and take a deep breath.

"You okay?" Devlyn takes my hand in his.

"Yes," I say on a nod. "Just happy to leave." Out of nowhere, tears flood my eyes and stream down my face.

Devlyn steers us toward a bench, lowers us to sit, and parks the stroller in front of us. His hands cup my cheeks in an instant. His eyes lock with mine as he searches for the reason for my tears.

"I've got you." His thumbs stroke my cheeks. Scooting closer, he leans in and kisses me chastely. A breath later, he cocoons me in his arms and hugs me tight to his chest. "Always."

My fingers curl around the cotton of his shirt and ball into tight fists. "I was so scared," I admit, whispering into the crook of his neck. "It was so dark. At first, I enjoyed the peace that came with the darkness. But after a while…" I shake my head over and over. "I felt empty. Lost." I sob into the collar of his shirt. "I-I couldn't find you." My arms squeeze him impossibly tighter to my frame. "Couldn't see or hear or smell you."

"Shh, shh, shh." One arm tugs me closer. Squishes me to his chest. His other hand strokes my hair, my neck, my back in an effort to soothe the fear in my veins. "It's over now. You're here. I've got you." I don't miss his hushed sniffles and tears on my shoulder. "I was scared too. So scared," he confesses in a whisper. "Never been more scared in my life." He leans back and frames my face. His eyes red and veiny and laced with unspoken pain. "If I lost you…" His eyes fall shut as he shakes his head. I wait for him to finish, but he doesn't.

I press my lips to his. Taste his salty tears on my lips. Breathe in his faded, earthy scent as our lips part. Loosen my hold on him and take a deep breath. I trace the line of his jaw with shaky fingers. The scruff on his jawline the longest I have seen it. The dark half-moons below his eyes less prominent today, but still noticeable.

"Let's go home," I whisper.

It isn't only me that needs to escape the memories of this place over the last few days. I may need to heal physically, but Devlyn needs to heal too. Needs to know I am safe. That Desirée is safe.

And home… home is safe.

~

Much as I want time alone with Devlyn and Desirée, I have never been more appreciative of having so many wonderful people in my life.

For the last week, Mom has been a constant presence in the house. Dad practically shoved her through the front door and dropped her bag in the foyer. It didn't really happen that way, but he didn't hang out long on the first night.

Part of me thinks Dad is as exhausted as us. Sleep hasn't been easy to come by since I went into labor. But another part of me thinks Dad just needed time to himself. Time to mull over everything that happened in the hospital. Between Mom and Dad, he is the more sensitive and reserved person. Less likely to share his feelings. And seeing me in the hospital bed, completely out of it, probably took its toll on him.

With time, he will be okay.

Aside from Mom helping me with Desirée, she has also been a saint with housework and cooking. Taking on the tasks we sometimes take for granted. Not having to wash dishes every time we eat or drink has been a relief. Not having to worry over cooking or grocery shopping or general errands has been a tremendous help.

Occasionally, Devlyn goes into his studio and works. For the most part, though, he sits with me and the baby. On the couch while a movie plays softly in the background. On the back patio, when the sun begins to set and the heat is milder. We just sit together and hold Desirée and bond more.

"How's she doing?" Mom whispers as she enters the living room.

I peer down my chest and see a sleeping Desirée. My fingers gently stroke her hair. "Fast asleep."

"Want me to put her down?"

Since I still have at least another week—hopefully not more—before I am allowed to carry her on my own, Mom has helped with putting Desirée down in her crib or bassinet while Devlyn works.

"That'd be great. Thank you."

As Mom reaches for Desirée, Devlyn pads down the stairs and enters the room. He sidles up to Mom, leans in and presses a kiss to Desirée's crown. Devlyn drops on the couch beside me as Mom walks off. But the second Mom is out of sight, the doorbell rings.

"I'll get it," Devlyn says loud enough for Mom to hear, but not loud enough to wake the baby.

Devlyn starts for the door. Scooting to the edge of the couch, I gingerly stand and follow. With our friends on a daily rotation of stopping by to check on us and the baby, Devlyn doesn't think twice before unlocking the dead bolt. He doesn't hesitate before twisting the knob. He doesn't consider, not for a second, to check the peephole or peer out through the blinds.

But I wish he would have.

The door swings open and I freeze on the opposite side of the sitting room, near the kitchen. Because standing at the door, with a wicked grin on her lips, is

Karen Templar. And something about her expression twists a knife in my already tender womb.

Why won't this woman just leave us be? Why won't this woman leave Devlyn alone?

Let him be happy. Without you.

Because if she isn't happy, she has to bring everyone else down. And people like Karen Templar will never be happy. Not until the entire ship sinks.

thirty-two

. . .

Devlyn

"I hear congratulations are in order," my mother says with disgust on her tongue. "You can imagine how upset I was to have heard I am a grandmother through a gossip circle." She curls her lip as her head tilts. "Don't be rude. Invite your mother inside."

I peer over my shoulder at Shelly and give her what I hope is an apologetic smile. "Be back in a second." Her eyes widen. "I'll be okay. Just stay in the house. Please."

She nods and walks toward the hallway. Toward her mother and the nursery.

I step out the front door and close it, but don't take another step. Crossing my arms over my chest and widening my stance, I form a barricade in front of the door. A barrier. A way to shield my home from this woman and the negativity she carries like a handbag.

"What do you want, Mother?"

She straightens her spine and rests her hands on her hips. "Has that girl drained you of intelligence and manners?" She shakes her head, her lips flattening for a beat. "I came to see my grandchild," she states, talking to me like an insolent child.

I take a deep breath and prepare myself for battle. I knew this day was inevitable, but hoped I wouldn't have to fight so soon. Dr. Prince's voice rings in my head as if he were here.

"You will never be able to move forward until you deal with your past. Don't let your past set the tone for your future. Sharing genetics doesn't give someone power over you. It doesn't give them the right to harm you—physically, mentally or emotionally. It is one-hundred-percent acceptable to sever ties with relatives so you may live a happy, healthy life."

"You don't have a grandchild," I say with more strength than I feel. But I refuse to back down. I refuse to give in. I refuse to let her hurt me or Shelly or our daughter. Not now. Not any day moving forward.

She rears back as if I slapped her. Disdain oozing from her every pore as she stares me in the eye. With a shift of her weight, her head tilts the opposite direction.

"What was that? I swear I misheard you."

"You didn't mishear a word." I harden my gaze. Inhale deeply and dig for the courage and strength Shelly has given me over time. Straighten my spine and square my shoulders as I speak with a firmer voice. "*You* are not a grandparent. My child is not some trophy you can parade around to get attention." I crack my neck left then right and roll my shoulders. "And I am not your son. Not anymore. You lost that privilege."

Loud laughter rips from her lips as she tips her head

back. The sound and her action remind me of every on-screen villain. Heartless and maniacal. It sends a shiver down my spine and makes me nauseous. But I refuse to give in to her. Refuse to back down. Refuse to let this vicious woman squash me with her thumb. Never again.

"You can't just get *rid* of your parents, Devlyn. It doesn't work that way."

I smirk. "Parent," I correct. "Just you."

Her lip curls as her eyes narrow. "This is your father. Feeding you bullshit stories and pegging you against me."

"No," I shout. Her eyes widen, but I don't care. I am sick and tired of this woman trying to use and abuse me for her own benefit. Sick. And. Tired. "You need to leave. Now." She opens her mouth to speak, but I cut her off. "Do not return. Ever. Stay away from me and Shelly and our family. Do not look for or follow us. No calls or texts or letters. Nothing. Not one single thing." I take a breath. "I will not be your punching bag. I will not be your scapegoat." I point a finger toward her. "And if I ever see you again or if you do anything to bother us, I will file a restraining order. I will take legal action." Taking a step toward her, I extend my finger farther. "Now get the hell off my property before I call the police."

Anger flames her cheeks and burns hot in her eyes. But I don't give a damn. I am done. More than done. And I will not subject my daughter to this woman. Not for a single second.

She storms down the walkway and gets in her car. A

minute later, she drives away and I breathe deeply for the first time in minutes.

Please let this be the end of her. Please.

I walk inside and see Shelly lingering at the edge of the hallway. No doubt she heard everything. Which is good because I don't really want to repeat any of it.

In three strides, she closes the space between us, wraps me in her arms and hugs me with her fierce love.

It is in this moment that I feel a shift. Like the closing of a long and horrible chapter. Like the start of a new chapter—perhaps a new story.

The story of Shelly and Devlyn. The story of our life. The story where we both learned how to love.

thirty-three

. . .

Shelly

Life has been peaceful. More peaceful than I imagined it could be.

Baby Desirée has been sleeping through the night more often than not. According to Mom, this is a miracle at ten weeks. Unsure if she was pulling my leg, I thumbed through several of the baby books and scoured the web. In black and white, each source verified her truth. Supposedly, most babies don't sleep through the night for several months.

Devlyn also appears to be sleeping better. Since the blowup with his mother, a new version of calm has washed over him. An incomparable tranquility he has needed for years. Before the verbal altercation with his mother, Devlyn had been pretty chill. Mostly. I'd only seen him upset or angry a few times—two of those three occasions involved his mother.

Now, Devlyn is the ultimate definition of relaxed. Zen master extraordinaire.

"Who's my little princess?" Devlyn says sweetly to

Desirée as she drinks from the bottle in his hand. Swaddled in the crook of his arm, he rocks her side to side. His eyes on hers as she stares up at him and curls her little fingers in his shirt.

Each time he speaks to her, a small smile tips up the corners of her mouth and she makes a bubbly sound around the nipple. Ovary. Explosion.

When she finishes the last of the bottle, Devlyn sets it on the table before lifting her to his shoulder and gently patting her back. It isn't long before a ferocious belch echoes through the living room.

"Good push, princess." Devlyn sets Desirée in her bassinet before twisting to face me. "Want to finish shopping today?"

Last year, Christmas was a bust. Leading up to the holiday, things had been weird between me and Devlyn after our first kiss at the end of November. And until things started to mend, my mood had been sour. Christmas didn't feel merry or bright.

But this year… bring on all the holiday cheer.

For the first time in my adult life, I get to *really* decorate. Not just a measly little tree in the house with a few candles and decorative pieces. I get to pull out all the stops and decorate without limits. And Devlyn gets his first dose of Festive Shelly.

I close my eyes and picture all the merriment.

Outside lights strung along the roofline, around the windows, and on the trees. A blow-up tree for the front yard and an artificial tree for the back patio. Reindeer figurines for the lawn. I wanted the animated deer, but Devlyn mentioned the likelihood of them breaking easier. So I found a beautiful set of lifelike deer figures.

Today, since Devlyn offered, I'd like to get more holiday items for inside the house. Last time we browsed Target, I spied a whole section of holiday decor that called my name. Soft colors with a vintage feel. Classic.

"Are you trying to butter me up, Mr. Templar?" I tease.

His lips tip up on one side. "Maybe."

I'd meant it as a joke, but now I'm curious. What is up Devlyn's sleeve?

I narrow my eyes at him. "What're you up to?"

Leaning in, he presses his lips to mine and kisses me breathless. All too soon, he breaks the kiss. He rises from the couch, swipes the empty bottle from the table and takes a step away. Peering over his shoulder, he taps his temple then leaves the room.

I love this side of him. Happy and optimistic and flirty. Much as I want to pry the plans from his lips, I won't ask what he has in store. Something about the surprise has me jittery, in all the right ways.

While I lock Desirée's carrier in the car seat cradle, Devlyn loads our purchases in the back of the car. Warm air floats from the vents and replaces the cooler December air. Jolly holiday music echoes from the speakers at a low volume. The sky a little more gray than blue as the sun hides behind puffy clouds.

Once he has everything stowed, Devlyn hops in the driver's seat and holds his hands in front of the vents.

A minute passes. Then another. Devlyn has yet to put a hand on the steering wheel or gear shifter. *Is he really that cold?* I note the outside temperature on the dash display. Fifty-seven. Chilly, but not cold.

"Everything okay?" I ask as he rubs his hands together.

Green eyes flick in my direction. I study the lines of his face that are a hint deeper. The corners of his lips and eyes turned up a touch. And I swear I see his eyes twinkle a second before he blinks.

"Fine. Just trying to feel my hands again." He makes a fist with each hand, then flattens them out again.

"It's not *that* cold," I tease as I reach for his hands and sandwich them between my own. Immediately, I note how warm his hands feel. Not warm. Hot. I loosen my grip on him.

A soft chuckle spills from his lips. "They *were* cold. Now I'm just trying to feel them again." He jerks his chin toward the back of the car. "My fingers went numb after store number two."

Heat crawls up my neck and floods my cheeks. While I pushed the stroller through the mall and ogled all the festive decorations, Devlyn walked beside me and carried all the bags from our purchases. We visited ten stores over the last two hours, easily. Which means Devlyn grinned and trudged through the numbing pain for more than half that.

"Why didn't you say something?"

He waves a hand. "It's no big shake."

"I could've put bags in the stroller basket or carried one."

"Shelly…" He cups my cheeks, leans in and kisses me softly. "I didn't mind." His words are calm and barely above a whisper. "I'll carry twice that to see your smile again."

My eyes dart between his and look for things left unsaid. As he stares back, all I see is his truth, out in the open.

"Okay." I press my lips to his. "Now take me home," I demand, sitting back in my seat and buckling my seat belt. "Time to decorate."

He blinds me with a bright smile before he buckles up and drives us home.

thirty-four

. . .

Devlyn

I'm going to be sick.

The blinker ticks at a deafening volume as I wait to turn into the neighborhood. *Ticktock. Ticktock.* I blink a few times in an attempt to clear the fog coming in from all sides. Swallow past the building lump in my throat. Breathe slow and steady as I tell myself everything will be okay.

It will be, won't it?

With a break in the traffic, I steer the car into the neighborhood. If I drive slow enough, I can stretch the minute and a half to two minutes without Shelly asking questions.

Everything will go according to plan.

Shelly sings to the Christmas song on the radio, a slight bop in her shoulders on every other line. I mentally soak up her joy. This time last year, we were finding our way back to each other after my freak-out. The weeks leading up to Christmas were a little less cheery as we tiptoed around our relationship.

But everything worked out. Slowly, steadily, we fell in love.

Now, I am about to stir things up.

"Eeee!" Shelly squeals as I park in the driveway.

Twisting to face her, I can't help but match the bright smile on her lips. Her happiness is my happiness. Period.

"Will we see you at all today?" I tease. "Or should I take little miss up to the studio while you decorate?"

Shelly play slaps my arm. "It won't be that bad." Her eyes veer up then left and right as her lips shift side to side. "Maybe a little. But only because I've never had so much space to decorate. Plus, I get to decorate, *really decorate,* outside for the first time."

I lean across the console and press my lips to her cheek. "Decorate whatever you want." And I mean it.

When we exit the car, she retrieves Desirée's carrier from the back seat while I fetch all the goodies from the back. With each step closer to the front door, my stomach twists in a new knot. I stay a pace or two behind Shelly so she doesn't notice the shift in my expression.

It. Will. Be. Fine.

Inside the house, Shelly goes about unbuckling Desirée and getting her a bottle. I take all the bags to the reading nook near the sliding glass doors. It's the most centralized room in the house and should make it easier for Shelly to go room to room and add splashes of holiday cheer.

I stop at the entrance of the living room and watch my girls for a beat. Desirée stares up at Shelly as she drinks her bottle. One of her little hands grips Shelly's finger while the other hand plays with the ends of her hair. I snap a mental picture of the sight and make note to bring the image to life with pencil on stock paper.

"Be right back," I say just above a whisper. Shelly tilts her head enough to flash me a soft smile.

Taking the steps two at a time, I dart up the stairs to my studio. My eyes roam the room from the landing. Nothing is out of place, not that I expected otherwise. Shelly only comes up here when we are together or I am working in the studio.

In three long strides, I reach the entrance to the closet. Tucked away behind new tubes of paint is one of the biggest gifts I will ever give Shelly. Well, besides our sweet baby girl. I pick up the smallest, heaviest gift on the planet and stow it in my pocket.

I park on the stool at the drafting table and zone out. Minutes tick by as I breathe deeply and mentally work to unravel the knots beneath my diaphragm. Calm as I can be, I rise from the stool and make my way back downstairs.

Now. Do it now.

At the base of the stairs, I peer into the living room. No sign of Shelly or Desirée. The house is quiet as I pad past the kitchen, sitting room and down the hallway toward the bedrooms. Just outside the nursery, I hear Shelly whisper to Desirée.

"Nap time, little angel. When you wake up, the house will sparkle. Lights and snow people and a beautiful tree. Blue and silver and white. It'll be the best first Christmas ever."

The door slowly opens and Shelly startles and slaps a hand to her chest when she spots me just past the frame.

"Sorry. Didn't want to disturb while you got her settled."

She drops her hand. "It's okay. Just didn't expect you there."

Without a word, I take her hand in mine and walk us down the hallway. She doesn't ask where we are going as I guide her through the house. She doesn't ask what I am doing when I park us on the couch in the living room. I wrap an arm around her shoulders and tuck her into my side. Just like every other time, she melts into my side. Becomes an extension of me, of us.

"Love you," I whisper against her hair.

"Love you too."

I kiss her crown and give her shoulder a squeeze before straightening in my seat. She tips her head back enough to peek up. To steal my every breath with her shimmering twilight eyes.

The weight in my pocket digs at my thigh.

Everything will be fine. Do it. Now.

"Shell, I…"

She sits up straighter. Her hands come to my cheeks as her eyes scan every inch of my expression. "What is it?" A crease forms between her brows as horizontal lines mar her forehead.

My eyes drift shut for one deep breath. When they open and all I see is my Andromeda, every nerve in my body calms. Every doubt in my mind gets washed away.

This is Shelly. My Shelly. My Andromeda. Goddess and ruler of my heart.

Leaning into her, I press my lips to hers. Let her warmth blanket me. Let her vibrance and zeal soothe every ounce of skepticism. Let her love consume every molecule in my body.

Reluctantly, I break the kiss. Brush the hair from her cheek and tuck it behind her ear. Hold her blues with my greens. Then, I lay my heart in her hands.

"Shelly, will you marry me?"

thirty-five

. . .

Shelly

I'M SORRY, WHAT?

Every muscle in my body, head to toe, locks up. I stare back at Devlyn, unable to breathe or think or form words. I blink to moisten my dry eyes. Then do it more.

Marriage is not something I am opposed to, but it isn't something I foresaw in the near future. I love Devlyn, but this seems... sudden. Unlike him. Questionable. Our relationship time line has flown by, one momentous occasion after another.

Is this because of Desirée?

I don't want Devlyn to feel obligated to marry me because we have a child. That shouldn't be why he proposes. God, please don't let it be the reason he is proposing.

I love this man more than imaginable. His heart is limitless. He gives without second thought. And in the past fourteen months, I've felt and experienced so much with him. A love to rival all others. A love I never thought I'd have in my life. He has gifted me so much.

That said, I pray the reason for his proposal is love and not obligation.

"Uh..." I tap my toes on the floor. Pin my lips between my teeth as I study the seriousness in his gaze. Tightness forms between my brows as my eyes narrow.

Why does this feel so weird? Me wanting to ask him the reason why he asked me to marry him. Prepregnancy Shelly wouldn't think such preposterous things. Prepregnancy Shelly would have been in his lap already, hands on his cheeks as she kisses him senseless.

So why isn't that me now? Why am I sitting here like he asked me to solve a quantum physics equation?

With each passing second, I watch the shimmer in his green irises fade. I witness the upward turn of his lips fall into a frown of despair.

Shit.

His eyes drop at the same time as his hands. Then his head begins to shake slowly. "I shouldn't have..." He scoots an inch away. "What was I thinking?" he mutters, moving back farther. "Idiot," he whispers.

Before he retreats farther, I wrap my fingers around his wrist and stop him. "No." His eyes shoot to mine, glassy. Agony pours off him in waves. I shake my head. "Not no to the question. No, as in don't pull away."

Tears brim his eyes that have reddened in less than a minute. "It's too soon." He shakes his head. "Me asking you was impulsive. Sorry for putting you on the spot. I just thought—"

"Devlyn, stop." I inch closer to him and press my lips to his. "It's not that I don't want to marry you. And proposals always put someone on the spot," I say on a laugh. "But we've never discussed marriage and I..." I pause as I try to gather the right words.

"You can be honest with me, Shell. Always."

I lift a hand to his cheek and he leans into my touch. His eyes fall shut as he takes a deep breath. Then another. And it is in this singular moment that I have my answer without even asking the question. Not like I didn't know the answer to begin with.

How could I ever think Devlyn would propose out of obligation? Nothing about us has ever been like that. Hell, he fought our relationship so hard in the beginning. Fought the inevitable with every breath we took.

"What I was going to say was I don't want you to feel obligated to marry me because we have a child together." I half shrug and work my lips between my teeth. "Before the words formed on my tongue, the thought tasted sour. Foolish. And I'm sorry it crossed my mind." I shake my head and laugh. "I swear... little Desirée sucked all my sensibility away while in the womb."

Devlyn takes my hands in his. A glimpse of a smile appears on his lips and disappears just as fast. He stares down at our hands as his fingers caress each of mine before cradling them in his. Left then right, he rocks his head on his shoulders as he sorts through what to say next.

"Desirée is not the reason I asked," he says as his head lifts. His greens lock onto my blues and all I see is vulnerability and love and hope. "Honestly, I didn't know if I'd have the courage to ask." My brows pinch together as I wait for him to elaborate. "After the way my parents' marriage played out, I didn't want that to happen to us." His eyes widen. "Not that we are anything like them."

I nod and squeeze his hands. "Agreed."

"I've never loved anyone the way I love you, Shelly. It scares me while my heart begs for more. Before you, I avoided things that scared me. With you, though… I'll gladly walk through hell. Because I know you'll be on the other side, waiting with arms wide open."

Tears sting the backs of my eyes. Emotion clogs my throat as I try to swallow the excess saliva flooding my mouth. The urge to wrap Devlyn in my arms and hug the breath from his lungs surges in my veins.

What did I do to deserve this man?

Why did I question his reasons?

Things between us have never been simple. From the start, we toed the line. Devlyn fought the undeniable love he had for me. At that point, it may not have been *love*. Perhaps, extreme like. As for me, I only sheltered my feelings because he was reluctant. Without a doubt, I knew he felt something stronger than friendship between us.

Friends.

God… Devlyn made that word my least favorite. I hated it more than *moist*. Only because I knew, deep in my bones, he wanted more than friendship. His resistance to see us beyond more than friends didn't hurt. He had been broken. Thrown away. Used until no longer necessary. Had that happened to anyone else, their trust and willingness to love would be shattered too. Hence why I didn't blame him.

But all that changed.

The night he gave in to what he felt for me, the night he kissed me, everything changed.

At first, not for the better.

We suffered on our own for several days. And when I finally found a way to breathe again, I opted to let go. To move on. To say goodbye.

That single text led us to where we are today. Lovers. Parents. Connected in a way I never thought possible with another person.

So why did I hesitate? Why did I question the path that led us to this moment?

Devlyn proposed and I doubted his reasons for asking. It was foolish and absurd. I love him, plain and simple. I love Devlyn more than I have loved another person.

"Ask me again," I whisper.

He scoots the table away from the couch, then drops down to one knee. One hand digs in his pocket while the other takes my left hand. Tears burn the backs of my eyes once more. Clasped tightly between Devlyn's thumb and forefinger is a ring with more diamonds than my eyes can count with one glance. At the heart of the ring… an oval-shaped dark-blue stone with the occasional sparkle.

His eyes lock with mine and I stop breathing. His thumb draws small circles over my ring finger as he worries his lips between his teeth.

"Shelly Nicole Reed," he says just above a whisper. "I have loved you longer than I was willing to admit. Maybe from the first moment I saw you more than two years ago." A small smile tips up the corners of his mouth. "But there's no use in denying it another minute. Shelly, you make me whole. Make life worth living. Your light and warmth and kind heart are what I was missing. Your love and passion and gaiety. *You.*" He takes a deep breath and swallows. "Before you, I merely existed. With you, I see every color. Every facet. Every angle. Light and beauty and brilliance. With you, because of you, I know love. Real love. True love." His thumb trails my ring finger from knuckle to tip. "Will you marry me, Shelly?"

Tears spill down my cheeks in parallel lines. Though Devlyn is a blur, I refuse to wipe the tears away. I swallow past the thick ball of emotion in my throat and slowly nod.

"Yes," I croak out. Swallowing again, I repeat myself with more gusto. "Yes, Devlyn." My lips roll between my teeth. "I will marry you."

The biggest smile brightens his face. I get lost in the sight as he slides the ring into place on my finger. As he lifts my hand to his lips and kisses my ring finger. As he wiggles his way between my legs on both knees, frames my face in his hands, and kisses me senseless.

In a matter of seconds, our clothes are peeled away and we are connected in every way possible. Mentally, emotionally and physically. We make love on the couch, in the middle of the day, without a worry in the world.

It is simply him and me and a love to rival all others.

epilogue

. . .

Devlyn

June 30th—the following year

If someone told me two years ago I would fall in love, welcome the most precious little girl into the world, and marry my best friend, I'd have laughed in their face. Because two years ago, love felt like an impossibility.

Until Shelly.

The love of my life. My fiancée. The woman who I get to call wife in… I look down at my watch. In thirteen minutes, Shelly will be my wife.

God, just thinking the word seems surreal.

Wife. Shelly will be my wife. Mine. Forever.

A knock sounds at the door. "It's Micah."

Not seeing my bride since yesterday afternoon is the only "tradition" Shelly enacted today. Last night, she stayed with Cora, Autumn, Penny and Erin at Cora and Gavin's house. All the guys crashed with me at my house. And all us parents got a night free of children, courtesy of our parents.

To say it has been odd to not have my girls close by for the past twenty-four hours would be an understatement. Though it was nice to get a night off from dad duties, sleep evaded me for hours. Wouldn't put it past one of the ladies to offer to hide the dark circles I noticed in the mirror as I buttoned my dress shirt.

I'd let them put makeup on my face or style my hair, so long as Shelly and I exchange vows this evening.

"Come in."

The door swings open and in steps my brother, Micah. It's an odd feeling to have a sibling after being alone the past twenty-four years. Odd in all the right ways.

The Saturday after I proposed, we invited her family and Dad to the house for dinner. Considering we were weeks from Christmas, they assumed it was us wanting a small gathering before the main event. They weren't wrong, but they didn't know the extent.

That night felt weeks long. My knee had never bounced so much beneath the dinner table. I'd scooted food around my plate more than a child avoiding Brussel sprouts on his plate. And when Shelly finally flashed her ring to the group and announced our engagement, I'd never sweated so profusely in my life.

Thank god for dark-colored shirts.

Nervous as I was, each member of the Reed family welcomed me with open arms. Micah pulled me in for an unexpected warm hug. Not the *slap-a-shoulder, one-armed* kind. A true, genuine, constricting hug.

"Congratulations," he'd said. *"My sister is lucky to have such a wonderful man love her. Welcome to the family."*

Not only does Shelly make me whole with her love, but so does her family. *My family.* A family I never saw coming and will never take for granted. These people—Nicole and George, Micah and Peyton—fill in all the gaps and holes my mother created years ago. These people make me feel like I belong. They give me purpose and strength.

Loving Shelly had been but the beginning. Receiving more love than I knew possible in return has been the greatest gift.

"You ready?" Micah shuts the door behind him. "Only a few minutes until showtime."

I have never been more ready for anything. "Was ready the second she said yes."

A brilliant smile lights Micah's face. His eyes shimmering with excitement.

Though Micah and Shelly shared the same eyes as their mother, the three sets sparkled in a different way. At first, seeing the three of them together was strange. I'd never seen such unique irises. But with each visit together, I began to notice the differences.

Nicole's blues were a hint lighter than her children's. The luster more noticeable when she was happy or excited.

Micah's irises were the darkest. Borderline black. And the first time I heard his wife, Peyton, call him starlight, I knew the reason why. The sparkle in his dark irises was visible, but faint in comparison to Shelly's.

I may be biased, but it is my opinion that Shelly got

the prettiest version of their constellation eyes. *My Andromeda.* The blue of her irises is darker than her mother's, but lighter than her brother's eyes. A rich blue. Like royalty. A queen. A goddess. My goddess. And the golden flecks that formed my favorite constellation, I knew all the ways to make them glow. With my hands and lips and words.

It took a while to see the difference between the three sets of matching eyes, but Shelly's sparkling blues are the ones that hold my heart captive and steal my breath.

And then there is my sweet little Desirée. Eyes as ravishing as her mother's, but with a thin ring of tea green around her pupil. The addition of my eye color gives hers an almost ethereal look.

"Whenever you're ready, let's get in position," he states, coming in for a hug. "Not every day my baby sister gets married and I get a kick-ass brother." He releases me from his grip. In two lengthy strides, he reaches the door and twists the knob.

Inhaling deeply, I take one last look in the full-length mirror and exit the dressing room. My fingers brush over large leaves and grassy bushes as Micah leads us through the gardens to the north lawn. White chairs sit in lush green grass on either side of a brick aisle. Thousands of red, pink and white rose petals line either side of the aisle and add a pop of color. A color that will always be my Shelly.

Pink.

At the end of the aisle, the bricks extend left and right to accommodate the wedding party. An arch of greenery and flowers and brilliant colors showcase where the ordained minister will perform the ceremony.

Micah leads me down the brick aisle. The rows of white chairs filled with family and friends. As I pass each, I hear words of congratulations, but don't stop to chat. Because any minute, music will float through the air. Bridesmaids will walk the aisle in soft-pink dresses. And behind them, my bride will make her way toward me.

When I reach the front, I give each of the guys a hug. Dressed in sharp gray suits to match my own is Micah, Jonas, Gavin and Chet. White button-downs beneath suit jackets, accented with a black-gray-and-pink bow tie. Each congratulates me on the big day.

I open my mouth to thank them, but get cut off by the change in music.

We shuffle into position and my eyes lock on the start of the brick path where Shelly will enter. To my left, Gavin mutters, "No better feeling than watching the woman you love walk to you in a breathtaking dress." I simply nod, not daring to look away from the entrance.

In a pale-pink dress that brushes the brick as she moves, Clementine steps out from the lush gardens and into the north lawn first. In one hand, she carries a small wooden pail adorned with white and blush roses, moss, and vines that trail up the handle on either side. On the front of the pail is a white heart that reads *Here comes the bride.*

With each step she takes toward us, she reaches into

the pail, grabs a fistful of blush rose petals, and tosses them along the brick path.

This is happening. Shelly and I are getting married.

When Clementine reaches the back row of chairs, the first bridesmaid comes into view. Erin. Her blush dress sweeps the ground with each step. Her hair in some fancy loose braid and secured at the nape of her neck. A small bouquet of pink and white calla lilies and roses gripped in her hands.

Three breaths pass before the next bridesmaid appears. Autumn. Her appearance the same as Erin before her, with an additional splash of color from her tattoos.

Jonas sucks in a sharp breath. "Gorgeous," he whispers. "Absolutely gorgeous."

Today is my and Shelly's day, but hearing these men, my brothers, revel over their wives… it makes my heart hammer harder beneath my rib cage. Makes my breath come in short bursts. Because in less than a minute, it will be my turn. My only prayer is that my knees don't buckle.

Seconds later, Peyton comes into view. Her eyes flit to Micah as a glowing smile lights her expression before she winks at her husband.

"Goddamn, I am a lucky man," Micah says loud enough to garner a few laughs from the crowd.

Only one more bridesmaid left. The maid of honor. Cora. The second she steps into view, Gavin leans toward her without taking a step. He doesn't say a word, but I *feel* the love radiating off him as he watches his wife. Feel the connection they share. A connection that rivals what I share with Shelly.

When all the ladies are lined up on the opposite side, the music in the garden shifts.

Without warning, my palms sweat. An electric vibration hums through my veins. I lean to the right and try to peek through the thicket of greenery blocking Shelly from view, but it is no use.

My eyes laser-focused, I catch movement through the thinnest part of the plants. An hour-long second passes as I hold my breath and wait.

Then, she steps into view. Everyone rises from their seats, but I still see her. The queen of my heart. Goddess of my soul. *My Andromeda.*

My eyes trail down the length of her body as I memorize her in this moment. Breathtaking in desert-pink tulle. Wide straps across her shoulders that come to a point at the base of her sternum. A thin band of satin around her middle. The skirt layered and in waves. Small white flowers and pearls decorate the bust and trail down half the skirt. A lush bouquet of white, blush, and dark-pink roses, pink calla lilies, baby's breath and greenery clutched tightly in her hands.

Speechless, I remind myself to breathe. My vision blurs and I blink a few times, not wanting to miss a second of this moment. George rubs a hand over her forearm as they step closer, but I don't dare shift my gaze from Shelly.

Although we have forever, no day will replace this one. The day Shelly says she will be mine in every way. Always.

Shelly

My pace slows as I catch sight of Devlyn.

Damn, he's handsome.

I grip Dad's arm tighter with my bent elbow. He brushes his hand over my forearm ever so gently in silent reassurance.

"Got you, Shelly Bear." His hold on me tightens. "Promise."

The backs of my eyes sting. A thick ball of emotion rests dead center in my throat. Every nerve in my body comes alive with excitement, becomes overwhelmed with joy. I blink a few times. Tip my head back slightly. Tell the tears rimming my eyes they need to wait a little longer. I swallow. Then swallow again.

"Thanks, Daddy," I whisper.

The aisle straightens as we reach the back row of chairs and I pause for a beat. Rake my eyes over Devlyn in a smart gray suit, white dress shirt, and charcoal-and-pink bow tie. On the breast of his jacket, a dark-pink calla lily and blush rose makes up his boutonniere. His floppy brown locks, a little lighter from time in the sun, parted off-center and styled to look messy on purpose. Hands clasped at his waist, I take in the slight bounce in his stance. As if he can't contain the energy flowing through him.

Faster than imaginable, we reach Devlyn and the minister. Dad kisses my cheek and I close my eyes for one rapid heartbeat. Then he places my hand in Devlyn's and takes a seat in the front row.

"You're stunning," Devlyn whispers, his hand squeezing mine.

"Pretty handsome yourself."

I pass my bouquet to Cora, then Devlyn and I turn slightly toward the minister. The next few minutes pass by in a haze of watery eyes and white noise. The minister reads the wedding script he has undoubtedly read hundreds of times prior. Every now and again, I catch a word or two, but otherwise drown out his voice.

Instead, I focus on Devlyn.

My husband.

Technically, we are already married. Hours ago, the minister went to each of our dressing rooms and had us sign the marriage license. During and after the ceremony, many things get lost in translation or forgotten. When we hired him, he told us of the few times couples forgot to sign, too swept up in the moment.

Devlyn's fingers weave and stroke and warm my own as he holds my gaze. His green irises bright and glassy under the setting sun. A burnt-orange glow highlighting his skin.

The minister quiets. Devlyn releases one of my hands, digs in the inside breast pocket of his jacket, and retrieves a slip of paper.

His vows.

He breathes deeply and swallows before my favorite smile dons his lips. And as his lips part to speak, I block out everyone but him.

"Shelly… my Andromeda." His smile brightens

infinitesimally. "A warm October day, more than two years ago, was the first time I saw you. The dazzling blonde who peeked through the windows of a flower shop. For days, I denied myself the sight of you. But it wasn't long before I caved. You'd seen me and I you, but we'd never spoken a word." He takes another breath and licks his lips. "And then I saw you again. In a bar, yelling your love for Karaoke Grandpa."

At this, the majority of the wedding party, including myself, bursts out in laughter. Several seated guests appear bewildered, but most smile or shake their head.

"Bars have never been my scene, but a friend was in town and we went out to catch up." Devlyn briefly glances over his shoulder to Chet. "Had I not seen you that night, I may not have had the urge to call Elizabeth. To insist on touching up the mural I'd painted the previous year." Devlyn looks up from his paper, a small half smile softening his expression. "You see, you'd already been my muse. The woman in the window." Subtly, he shakes his head. "I didn't know your name, but I knew *you*." He presses the heel of his palm to the center of his chest. "Here. And as much as I tried to fight it, I needed to know you more. Even if I was just a friend."

I roll my eyes and Devlyn laughs.

"Shelly, you were never just a friend. Not one second. From the very start, you've always been more. It was me who needed time to learn this." Paper still in his hand, Devlyn takes hold of my free hand once more. "Thank you for loving me. Thank you for putting up with my stubbornness early on. For giving me another chance." His eyes dart to my parents and his dad in the front row, Desirée drooling in Mom's lap. "And thank you for giving me something I never thought I'd have… a family. I love you, Shelly Nicole Reed. And I will love you every day of forever."

Over my shoulder, Cora hands me a tissue. I tip my head back and blot my eyes.

Cora and Autumn warned me about this moment. Listening to the person you love as they confess the biggest reasons for loving you. Sounds simple when said aloud, but hearing it while loved ones watch and listen… cue the messy, happy tears.

Once my tears seem to be under control, I stow the tissue in my dress and retrieve my own piece of paper. I stare down at the scribbled words and question the vows I'd written days ago. Compared to Devlyn's confession, my vows seem small.

I close my eyes and fill my lungs fully, opening my eyes on the exhale. Devlyn's thumb paints small circles on my hand. His eyes locked with my own. It is him and me and no one else in this moment.

"Devlyn… the *artist*." Behind me, Cora snorts. "If you asked my closest friend, she'd tell you, without hesitation, how I rambled on about *the artist* after you painted the first mural. She'd tell you how I talked about you for weeks. The guy I couldn't stop sneaking a peek at. God, the front of the shop had never been so pristine." At this, Elizabeth chuckles in the crowd. "That display window got so much love that week." I pause and hold his green irises for three quiet breaths. "Because I just knew… I didn't know who you were, didn't ask for your name, didn't say one word to you, but I knew."

Plucking the tissue from my dress, I blot my eyes again.

"And then you reappeared a year later. Your warm smile and addictive eyes. The way you looked at me… I couldn't breathe. Couldn't form intelligible speech, which is miraculous for anyone who knows me well." Chuckles float around us. "But more than anything, I couldn't stay away."

At this, Devlyn squeezes my hand. His silent way of reciprocating the feeling.

"Devlyn, my life was monotonous before you. I had love, but nothing compared to the love you give. I had family, but not like the family we created together." I inch closer to him and tighten my hold on his hand. "Loving you is effortless. The most natural thing I have ever done. Life and love didn't make sense before you. I'd read about love, the type that steals every thought and breath and moment, but I'd never felt it firsthand. And I wholeheartedly believe it was because I'd been waiting for you." The backs of my eyes sting as my vision blurs. "I love you, Devlyn James Templar, more than I have loved anyone. And as long as there is air in my lungs and a heartbeat in my chest, I will love you. Always."

The paper in my hand falls to the ground as I step forward, ritual be damned, and press my lips to his. Devlyn frames my face with his hands and kisses me back with equal fervor. The minister says something and cheers erupt around us. But neither of us moves to break the kiss. Lost in each other, we kiss until we are breathless.

And when we break apart, the world finally levels out. Colors are brighter, bolder, more vibrant. Life is warmer, fuller, more passionate. And love… it isn't just something I read about anymore. Love is this living, breathing force. Powerful and daring. Strong and profound. Abstract and impassioned.

Mom walks to us and hands over a wiggly Desirée. She kisses my cheek and congratulates us.

And there, in front of the most important people in my life, I feel whole. Fortunate. Loved.

bonus content

one

. . .

Devlyn

June—Three years later

This is my life. Love and laughter and joy.

I never imagined myself in this position. With so many wonderful people in my circle. Family and friends I can't picture a day without. Nor would I want to.

Our Sunday get-togethers still happen every week. Since the first I attended with Shelly, they have become much grander. Not the party, per se, but the number of guests in attendance. When Penny's husband, Jameson, bought the tattoo shop a month after Shelly and I married, he hired more staff—artists, piercers, and front desk personnel. It was an adjustment to welcome in the new faces, but it wasn't long before they were just as much family as the rest.

Today, everyone will be here. To enjoy our regular Sunday gathering, but also to celebrate Shelly and my third wedding anniversary, Independence Day, and baby Garrett's first birthday.

I peer out the kitchen window facing the backyard. Watch Shelly and Desirée as they decorate tables with small vases full of colorful flowers. Place wicker mats at each place setting and add a plate and utensils. Add candles and poppers to the center. String holiday lights around the pillars of the pergola and check the tiki torches for fuel.

Desirée skips over to Shelly and says something. Shelly surveys the tables where she had Desirée add forks and spoons to the place settings. After a kiss to our daughter's forehead, Shelly says something else and Desirée skips off to her outdoor playset-slash-mansion.

Best. Investment. Ever.

Shelly strolls inside and sidles up to me in the kitchen. "Need help with anything?"

I twist and press my lips to hers. "No. Just cleaning up and waiting for everyone to show." Glancing back at Desirée, I watch as she climbs up the ladder, runs through the wooden fort and slides down the green slide. "Can't believe she'll be four in a few months."

Shelly rests her head on my shoulder and stares at our daughter. "Me, either." A heavy sigh leaves her lips. "Think she'll be excited?"

Today is a big day. Three celebrations everyone knows about… and one they don't, but will before long.

My head tips to the side and rests on Shelly's. "Yeah, she'll be the most excited." I lift my head and kiss

Shelly's crown. "Go out back and relax for a bit. I got the rest of the cleanup."

"You sure?"

Another kiss to her head. "I'm sure."

I finish cleanup in the house while Shelly sits on a lounger out back and watches Desirée play. Just as I start the dishwasher, the doorbell rings. One by one, our friends and family arrive. Additional food items are deposited on the kitchen counters. Jonas holds up a cooler and tells us if anyone needs him, he will be at the grill.

In no time, our house booms with music, conversation and laughter.

Clementine, Clara and Ryker join Desirée in the play fortress. Soon followed by Ashton, Avery and Lex when they arrive.

Again… best investment ever.

It isn't long before Jonas removes cooked burgers, brats and chicken from the grill, putting the meatless options on a separate dish. The parents plate up food for the kids first then sit them at the kiddy tables. Clementine is the oldest of the kids, and Jonas and Autumn have offered her a spot at the grown-up table several times. She declines each time and tells them she loves sitting with her brother and cousins.

Over dinner, we regale the past week's events. School and work and all the projects in between. And when the table quiets, Shelly looks to me and nods.

It's time is what that single nod says.

Pushing my chair back, I rise and look around the

table. Without a word, all conversation ceases and all eyes swing in my direction.

"Shelly and I have news." All forks hit the table. All chewing stops. And suddenly, I am more nervous than excited to share.

Sensing the shift, Shelly rises and hooks her arm in mine. "We're pregnant."

For a beat, white noise fills my ears. Then it vanishes, replaced with louder-than-life roars and hoots and hollers. Behind us, I hear Clementine say to Desirée, "You're going to be a big sister." Then she gives her a high five.

And it is moments like this that overwhelm me with gratitude.

Had I not found this incredible woman, who refused to give up on me, even with my fiercest resistance, I would not have this moment today. Surrounded by dozens of people that love me for me. That treat me as one of their own. That embraced me from the moment I stepped into their circle.

This. This is family. What it should be. People that love you regardless of what you give them in return. People that love you for what you bring into their lives without expectation. People willing to embrace you during the hard times and rejoice in the best times.

These people are family.

Food forgotten, everyone rises from their seats and takes turns hugging and congratulating us. Each embrace feels more loving than the previous. Each sentiment more heart filled. But it isn't until Cora wraps me in her arms and whispers only loud enough for me to hear that tears sting my eyes.

"Thank you, Devlyn. For loving Shelly and coming into our lives." She tightens her hold, then releases to hold me at arm's length. "This family wouldn't be right without you."

Gavin hooks an arm around her shoulders and meets my gaze. "Damn straight."

I scan the group of smiling faces. Cora and Gavin. Jonas and Autumn. Micah and Peyton. Erin. Trevor and Jasmine. Penny and Jameson. Reznor and Tatyana. Rex and Giana. Iliana and Sage. Jasmine and Anton. Chet. Reese and Trent. Parents and kids. Others from the tattoo family. *My family.*

Shelly sidles up to me and snakes an arm around my waist. I glance down into her eyes and smile as her free hand goes to her belly.

"Love you, Mrs. Reed."

The corner of her mouth kicks up into a soft half smile. "Love you too, Mr. Reed."

two

. . .

Shelly

December 25th—Six months later

My grip on the kitchen counter tightens as I suck in a sharp breath.

Aside from the water bubbling in the teakettle, the house is quiet. Still dark, with the exception of the glowing Christmas tree I plugged in minutes ago in the sitting room. Another two hours will pass before the sun peeks through the windows and brightens the house. And much less will pass before Desirée wakes everyone to see what Santa left under the tree.

I flip the switch on the kettle and add hot water to the awaiting tea bag in my mug. Up and down, up and down, I yank on the bag string and watch the tea bag bob as it steeps in the water. When the liquid is a rich brown, I pluck the bag out and toss it in the garbage.

Two steps toward the fridge for the oat milk and I come to a halt. The muscles and skin around my round belly constrict. One hand goes to my belly while the other reaches for the closest stable surface. I inhale deeply once, twice, then a third time before the sensation fades.

"Is this your way of telling Mommy you want to be the best Christmas present?" I whisper-ask into the dimly lit room. I rub my rotund belly. "Let us get through presents first. That's all I ask."

After I add milk to my tea, I waddle to the small sofa in the sitting room near the tree. Wrapping myself with the throw blanket, I sip my tea and zone out as I stare at the white lights on the tree. And for a little longer, I enjoy the peace of waking early and sitting by myself in silence. Enjoy the simplicity of life in this very moment, because after today, it will be busy once more. But busy in the best way.

My hand traces a continuous loop over my belly as my eyes follow the movement. A small smile on my face. A sense of wholeness filling every part of my life.

"How long have you been up?"

I startle at Mom's hushed tone as she pads into the room from the hallway. "Not long."

"Everything okay?" She tips her head to where I rub my belly.

With a nod, I smile. "Yeah, but today might be a bigger celebration than we prepared for."

Like their big sister, baby two wants to come a little earlier than projected. Not that I mind. I'd rather have a Christmas baby than a New Year's baby. Maybe they heard all the Hallmark Christmas movies I've been watching. Maybe they heard all the fun music and their big sister singing. Or maybe, they just know Christmas is my favorite holiday.

"I'll get started on breakfast. If everyone else isn't up soon, I'll wake them."

"Thanks, Mom."

Mom shuffles off to the kitchen and flips on the soft lights lining the underside of the top cabinets. From my spot on the couch, I follow her with my eyes. She grabs all the ingredients for the breakfast casserole she made every Christmas morning when Micah and I were kids. Potatoes, crumbled maple sausage, cheese, onion, and her special blend of herbs and spices.

On Desirée's second Christmas, Mom insisted on making the casserole every Christmas morning going forward. Usually, we visit Mom and Dad after Desirée has opened all her gifts at home. Casserole had been a brunch meal.

But not this year.

With baby two due any day, Mom suggested she and Dad stay at our house and have Christmas here. Less stress and shuffling all over town. Every aching muscle and tired bone in my body agreed. Although Petal and Vine closed two days ago through New Year's Day, I'd still been working more this pregnancy.

When Elizabeth heard we were pregnant again, she offered to work whenever I needed help. Since her official retirement, one year after Desirée was born, I hired a few part-time employees. With baby two on the way, I'd been gearing them up with what extra tasks they'd take on. Elizabeth said she'd handle most of the financials and paperwork—which has been a major relief.

Maple and herbs float through the air. Mom whips eggs and oat milk in a bowl, then starts layering everything in the casserole dish. As foil crinkles over the edges of the dish, Desirée comes running down the hall with Devlyn on her heels.

Her little legs lock straight, but forward momentum, plus the socks on her feet, keeps her sliding across the wood floor. Once she skids to a stop, her little hands slap over her slack jaw. Eyes wide, she stares at the mountain of gifts under the tree.

"Santa came," she whispers in awe. Before Devlyn or I answer, she dashes to the small plate on the kitchen counter and surveys the cookie crumbs and empty Santa mug. "Mommy, Daddy, Santa ate the cookies I made him. And, and, and he drank the milk."

Devlyn and I stare after our daughter. Each year, her excitement kicks up a notch with the holidays. One day, her love for the holiday season may be stronger than my own. This year, under my and Mom's supervision, she made chocolate chip and sugar cookies. I'd never seen her so careful. Every stir and whisk and measured ingredient had been precise. She refused to mess up Santa's cookies.

"Did he see your letter?" Devlyn asks as he tugs a shirt over his head and ambles toward her.

She nods vigorously. "Oh my gosh! He wrote me back," she squeals.

Devlyn scoops Desirée off her feet and parks her on his hip. Then he picks up the letter and holds it in front of them. "What's it say, little D?" She stares at the paper, her brows pinched at the middle and lips scrunched in concentration. "Sound out the words."

After a few fumbled letters, she reads the words. "Best cookies yet. Merry Christmas, Desirée. Love, Santa."

Wiggling with excitement, Devlyn sets her on her feet. While Desirée flaunts her note from Santa to Mom, Devlyn comes to sit with me on the sofa.

He presses his lips to my forehead, the tip of my nose, then my lips. "Morning." Warmth blankets me as he lays a hand on my belly and kisses me again. "Merry Christmas. You sleep okay?"

I lay my hand over his and tip my head side to side. "Sleep wasn't too bad. But someone woke me early." I glance down at my belly. "We may get another gift today."

Devlyn's eyes go wide. "Do we need to leave?"

I shake my head. "Not yet." A half smile kicks up one corner of my mouth. "I requested they wait until after presents and breakfast," I say on a laugh. "Mom has breakfast in the oven."

"If we need to leave sooner, say the word."

Minutes later, Dad appears and the festivities begin. One by one, Desirée opens her gifts. Devlyn and I are still trying to limit her time on devices and electronics, which becomes more challenging each year, but we managed to find plenty of gifts to spark her creativity without involving electronics. Art supplies, books—coloring and reading—and puzzles. For her big present this year, she got a new bicycle equipped with training wheels. Last night, Devlyn had hidden it in the reading nook near the sliding glass doors. He'd put a note from Santa on it saying it was too big to put under the tree.

The look on Desirée's face as he wheeled it around the corner… priceless.

Halfway through breakfast, the contractions kick into third gear. No matter how much I want to enjoy Christmas morning with our little girl, I can't put off leaving for the hospital any longer. The first contraction had been hours ago. Although they continued during gift unwrapping, I kept my lips sealed and breathed through the pressure.

Now, it is past the point of breathing through it. This baby is coming. Soon.

Mom and Dad help us to the car and promise to keep Desirée occupied until we give the green light for them to come to the hospital.

Buckled up, Devlyn drives us toward the hospital. While he drives, I type out a text in the group chat.

Shelly: Merry Christmas all. FYI… I'm in labor and we're headed to the hospital.

As suspected, my phone and Devlyn's pings with message after message.

Micah: Merry Christmas, little sis. We'll be there soon.
Cora: Oh. My. Gawd! A Christmas baby?! Be there ASAP.
Jonas: Best gift ever! Merry Christmas, Shell!
Erin: Keep us updated! Can't wait to meet them!

Autumn: Be there after we drop the kids at Jonas's parents' house.
Gavin: This is giving me baby fever!
Cora: Gavin, no. Not yet. It's too soon.
Peyton: Auntie Peyton is ready to spoil and squeeze cheeks.

When I look up, Devlyn is turning onto the street leading to the hospital. Before another contraction flares, he parks the car and dashes to my door. The hospital is quieter than expected as we enter the nonemergency entrance. We check in with reception and are soon on the elevator to labor and delivery.

Unlike last time, we are prepared for every worst-case scenario. Since having a cesarian with Desirée, I'd have another with baby two. The procedure had been scheduled months ago for January second.

Should have known the baby didn't like the date.

Nurses guide us to a room and have us change for the procedure. Also unlike last time, Devlyn won't be whooshed from the room. This time, he gets to be on the same side of the curtain as me, holding my hand and welcoming our child into the world.

Dr. Webster comes in and reviews my vitals before discussing the process again and asking if we have any questions. If either of us had more questions after the countless we asked in her office, it'd be a Christmas miracle.

"I'll give you both a few minutes before we start." The door clicks as she leaves and the room falls silent.

Devlyn wraps my hands in his and kisses my knuckles. "Love you so much, Shell."

"Love you, too."

"Boy or girl?"

Over the last couple of months, we have played this game. Boy or girl? Once again, we didn't want to know the sex of the baby ahead of time. We made lists of names—boys, girls, and gender neutral. Each time we played the game, Devlyn would guess opposite of his previous guess the day before. I guessed girl more often than boy, only because I experienced similar body changes. And if you listen to the old wives' tales about your belly position determining the gender, baby two will be another girl.

We shall see.

The next hour flies by faster than expected. Although I experience no pain with the incision, the pressure change when the baby leaves my womb is something I won't soon forget. With each step, Dr. Webster explains what is happening. The entire process is odd and fascinating and unforgettable.

At 12:25 p.m. on December 25th—couldn't have planned that, even if I wanted to—Devlyn and I welcome our second daughter into the world.

"Violet Lily Reed," Devlyn whispers as he lays her on his chest for the first time. "Daddy and Mommy love you so much, baby girl." Devlyn lifts his glassy eyes to mine. He rests his cheek on our daughter's crown. "Best Christmas gift ever."

three

. . .

Shelly & Devlyn's Letters

August 20th—Desirée's shower

How do you start a letter to your unborn child? The task seems daunting, but here we go.

Today, Mommy and I are having a party for you. All of our friends and family are here with food and presents. Can't wait for you to meet them all, and for them to meet you.

I never thought I'd be a dad, but I promise to be the best one ever.

Love you more than words, little one,
Daddy

My little water aerobics instructor… oh, how I love you. I loved you from the moment I knew you were growing in Mommy's tummy. And although we had some disagreements when it came to cheese, we found our way. I can't wait for your birthday. Can't wait to meet the mini-me that fist-pumps when I eat cheesy eggs, bulgogi and consume anything with chocolate.

I love you so much, forever and ever.
Mommy

four

. . .

Shelly

November—Seven years later

Devlyn parks the car as I spin to face the back seat. "Best behavior, girls," I say to Desirée and Violet.

"Duh, Mom," Desirée says with an eye roll she picked up from her newest friend, Kiki.

Gah! If she's this sassy in her preteens, I'll need countless hours of meditation and yoga, and to maybe take up martial arts classes, to survive.

From her booster seat, Violet smiles big and holds up a hand. "Promise to be the bestest, Mommy." Nothing but sweet innocence in her voice.

"Thank you, girls," Devlyn says. "Now, let's go have fun." This garners another eye roll from Desirée.

Heaven help me, if she keeps this up, I will take every damn electronic away from her unless it is for schoolwork. As if he hears my thoughts, Devlyn reaches across the console and gives my hand a quick squeeze.

We exit the car, me helping Violet out while Devlyn

sidles up to Desirée. If anyone can break through Desirée's recent *I know all* attitude, it is Devlyn. She is definitely a daddy's girl. Not that she doesn't love me, they just connect on another level.

Stepping up on the porch, I raise my hand to knock on Jonas and Autumn's front door, but before my knuckles rap the wood, it swings open. Ryker greets us, his dark locks floppy over his right brow as he pushes thick, black-framed glasses up the bridge of his nose.

"Hey, Mr. and Mrs. R." His eyes drift to Desirée, heat pinking his cheeks as he quickly looks away. "Desi." He licks his lips and takes a deep breath before saying, "Miss Violet." Taking a step back, he gestures to the inside of the house. "Come in, please."

We wander toward the kitchen, Violet running ahead of us. "No running inside," I call after her. Devlyn and I set totes on the counter with macaroni salad, baked beans, and homemade rolls while the kids go outside. Soon as they disappear from sight, I take a deep breath and hold it for three long seconds.

Devlyn brushes his knuckles along my jawline. "Everything okay?"

"Yeah." I look toward the back door. "Just wondering how we'll survive Storm Desirée," I say with a hint of humor.

"It's normal for girls her age to be snarky. Promise I'm working on it. But fighting peer pressure is a bitch."

I hold out my pinkie and Devlyn hooks ours together. "Thank you." Stepping into him, I snake my arms around his waist and squeeze. "Let's go join everyone."

Hand in hand, we walk out to the backyard. Halfway through our hellos, a husky with white fur runs up to us. "Siku, heel," Jonas calls in a deep voice. The dog halts in place and looks over its shoulder. Jonas jogs up. "Sit," he commands before looking to us. "Sorry about that. She's still learning."

"Is this the new pup?"

"Yep. This is Siku." Jonas rubs a hand through the dog's coat. "She's well trained, but still a puppy. Can't wait for Clementine to get here."

A few years ago, the summer between Clementine's junior and senior year of high school, Spartan passed. Needless to say, it was a tragic time for all of us, but more so for Clementine. Spartan had been her best friend for ten years. Jonas and Autumn considered getting a new dog the following year, but Clementine was against the idea.

Now that she has had time away at college, has been able to experience life more and emotionally accept what happened, Jonas and Autumn found a new pup to add to the family. Siku will never replace Spartan, but she will add her own flair.

Without a doubt, Clementine will melt when she meets her.

While the kids play or hang out away from the parents, the adults catch up. With most of our children self-sufficient or in school, we have slid back into the regular work routines pre-parenthood. It has also been nice to have the occasional bowling or karaoke night, just us parents. Like old times again, but better.

Just as Jonas announces the burgers and brats are

ready, Clementine walks outside. *God, has she grown.* The sweet, spunky girl who was a mini version of Autumn has grown that much more beautiful. Still a spitting image of her mother, she has taken on a style and fire all her own.

Before she gets a chance to say hello to anyone, Siku charges through the crowd and collides with her legs. Jumping and licking and begging for attention. Aside from the normal rock music playing, the backyard goes silent. All of us waiting with bated breath for Clementine's reaction.

Tears rim her eyes as she looks down at the dog, then up at her parents. Down and up, down and up. And then she drops to her knees and hugs Siku. Dog slobber hits Clementine's cheeks and chin and forehead, and she just laughs.

Devlyn leans in, his breath warm on my ear. "Maybe we should get a dog. Might help with Queen Sassy Pants."

I chuckle. "The idea does hold merit." I shift my gaze to his. "Talk about it later?" He nods.

Once the excitement over Siku meeting Clementine settles, we fall into the same routine we do every Sunday. Food and conversation and great friendship.

Devlyn wraps an arm around my shoulders and inches me closer to his side as he talks with Micah. And for a beat, I sit there and scan the yard. Look at the faces of all the people I love so deeply.

My best friends. My family. Cora and Gavin with Clara and Garrett. Jonas and Autumn with Clementine and Ryker. Micah and Peyton. Erin and her new beau,

Grayson. Trevor and Jillian. Penny and Jameson. Reznor and Tatyana with Ashton and Avery. Rex and Giana, with their five-year-old, Franco. Iliana and Sage. Jasmine and Anton with Lex, the tallest teenager I've laid eyes on. Reese and Trent.

So much love surrounds us, and we wouldn't want it any other way.

It's been an incredible journey so far. Friendships and love. Watching the next generation grow and prosper. This life... it has been surreal. The heartbreak and tears. The laughter and jokes. The hugs and memories. Not a day goes by where I don't appreciate every moment—good and bad.

The best part of it all... we have so many years left together. And I wouldn't want to spend a day of it with anyone else.

up next in the bay area duet series

The Artist Duet wraps up the duet stories in this series, but… two novellas will be available in January 2023. Originally written as short stories for anthologies, ***Reese*** and ***Penny*** will have their own books!

Reese is a MM, billionaire CEO romance with a dash of mystery/suspense.

Never thought I'd settle down.

Not until he walked into my life.

Trent Callahan. One of the most affluent people in the area with a self-built empire. The man with my heart in his hands.

The night he followed me home, I never expected more than a one-night stand. A year later, I still call him mine.

Well, mostly mine.

I want more than just someone to warm my sheets. For once, I want to be put first. But I fear that's not possible. Because he loves his job more than anything.

Including me.

But I sense change in the air. Feel life shifting for us both. All I hope is that it is for the better. Because Trent is someone I don't want to live without.

Penny is a brother's best friend, friends to lovers, workplace romance.

All it takes is four words and my life is forever changed.

When Oscar calls a staff meeting, no one anticipates the news. The sale of the tattoo shop. Our second home, second family, will be broken. Sold to the highest bidder.

But the biggest shock is yet to come.

The bell over the door jingles and I smooth my hands over my shorts, chastising mat attire. Black leather boots step into view. As my eyes drift north, I log each delicious muscle and tattoo.

Our eyes lock and I stop breathing. Jameson Kingsley. My brother's best friend.

The guy I crushed on most of my adolescence.
The guy I fantasized about occasionally in adulthood.
And now… my new boss.

Fuck.

Read the Reese and Penny novellas January 2023!

more by persephone autumn

The Click Duet

High school sweethearts torn apart. When fate gives them a second chance, one doesn't trust they won't be hurt again. Through the Lens (Click Duet #1) and Time Exposure (Click Duet #2) is an angsty, second chance, friends to lovers romance with all the feels.

The Inked Duet

A man with a broken heart and a woman scared to put herself out there. Love is never easy. Sometimes love rips you apart. Fine Line (Inked Duet #1) and Love Buzz (Inked Duet #2) is a second chance at love, single parent romance with a pinch of angst and dash of suspense.

The Insomniac Duet

He was her high school bully. She was the outcast that secretly crushed on him. More than ten years later, he's her boss, completely oblivious to their shared past, and wants no one but her. More importantly, he doesn't understand her animosity toward him.

Transcendental

A musician in search of his muse and a woman grieving the loss of her husband. Two weeks at an exclusive retreat and their connection rivals all others. Until she leaves early without notice. But he refuses to give up until he finds her again.

Distorted Devotion

Swept off her feet by love, life takes a dark, unexpected turn. Now the love of her life may be the cause of her death. Check out this gripping, romantic suspense.

Depths Awakened

A small town romance which captivates you from the start. Two broken souls have sworn off love. Vowed to never lose anyone else. But their undeniable attraction brings them together and refuses to let go.

Broken Metronome

When the music of the heart dies…

Broken Metronome is an angsty poetry collection full of heartache and the possibility of what may have been.

Slipping From Existence

Would it be so bad to slip from existence? Would it be so bad to give in to the darkness?

Slipping From Existence is a dark poetry collection centered around depression and coping while maintaining a brave face.

thank you

Thank you so much for reading **Abstract Passion,** book two in the **Artist Duet**. If you wouldn't mind taking a moment to leave a review on the retailer site where you made your purchase, Goodreads and/or BookBub, it would mean the world to me.

Reviews help other readers find and enjoy the book as well.

Much love,
Persephone

artist duet playlist

Here are some of the songs from the **Artist Duet** playlist. You can listen to the entire playlist on Spotify!

Loveless | PVRIS
Touch | Sleeping At Last
Heart | Sleeping At Last
I'll Be Good | Jaymes Young
Fear | Sleeping At Last
Anger | Sleeping At Last
Big Love, Small Moments | JJ Heller
Hearing | Sleeping At Last
Power | Isak Danielson
The First Glance | Anna Yarbrough
Life | Sleeping At Last

connect with persephone

Connect with Persephone

www.persephoneautumn.com

Subscribe to Persephone's Newsletter

www.persephoneautumn.com/newsletter

Join Persephone's Reader Group

Persephone's Playground

Follow Persephone Online

acknowledgments

First and foremost, I need to acknowledge this series as a whole. I started daydreaming about this series and wrote the first duet before I published my first book. From the beginning, Gavin and Cora were the heart of this circle of friends. Writing the final duet was a challenge—ending the series with such a difficult story and bidding farewell to characters I've been with for years. It's bittersweet, but also a little sad. I hope you loved reading this series as much as I loved writing it.

To my family and friends… Thank you for always being my biggest fans and cheering me on. Your love keeps me going!

To Ellie McLove and Rosa Sharon… Thank you for performing miracles with my punctuation and fixing the typos and boo-boos I miss after reading the manuscript a dozen times. You ladies are superheroes! xoxo

To my author friends… All the constricting hugs! This author gig isn't all rainbows and sunshine, but having you in my circle and corner makes each day better. Love you all!

To the readers and bloggers who read my words... sending you all virtual hugs. Every time I read one of your amazing reviews or see your posts about my books, I cry. Spilling pieces of yourself on paper isn't easy, but your kindness makes it worth it each time I start a new book. A million thank yous to each of you!

And if this is your first Persephone Autumn story... thank you for taking a chance on my words. I hope you loved Shelly and Devlyn.

about the author

Persephone Autumn lives in Florida with her wife, crazy dog, and two lover-boy cats. A proud mom with a cuckoo grandpup. An ethnic food enthusiast who has fun discovering ways to vegan-ize her favorite non-vegan foods. If given the opportunity, she would intentionally get lost in nature.

For years, Persephone did some form of writing; mostly journaling or poetry. After pairing her poetry with images and posting them online, she began the journey of writing her first novel.

She mainly writes romance, but on occasion dips her toes in other works. Look for her poetry publications and a psychological horror under P. Autumn.

www.ingramcontent.com/pod-product-compliance
Lightning Source LLC
Chambersburg PA
CBHW021620030826
48979CB00034B/483

* 9 7 8 1 9 5 1 4 7 7 5 2 3 *